DARK GARDEN

Visit us at www.boldstrokesbooks.com

What Reviewers Say About The Author

"Fulton has rescued the romance from formulaic complacency by asking universal questions about friendship and love, intimacy and lust. The answers reflect both depth and maturity; this is the romance novel grown up a bit. Girl gets girl is always popular; more inspirational is when the girl gets to know herself."—*The Lesbian Review of Books*

"Fulton takes an age old formula for love and plants it in modern surroundings. The writing is smart and quick, and she portrays innocence with loving, irresistible humor. She delivers flesh-warming, flush-inducing seduction and pages of slippery, richly textured sex. Her knack for depicting current social dilemmas also makes her a compelling contemporary author."—*The Lesbian Review of Books*

"Fulton has penned another wonderfully readable, erotically-charged book...fun, and well worth your time."—*Lambda Book Report*

"Fulton tells a dark and disturbing tale of friendship and betrayal, of love lost before it has a chance to begin. That may sound rather hackneyed but her use of these themes is anything but trite. The writing is outstanding...Fulton creates characters that live on in the memory and in the heart...An extraordinary novel. I could not put it down and days later, I'm still thinking about it."—*Bay Area Reporter*

"Perhaps needless to say, the paths the friendships take are fraught with, among other things, lust, unrequited love, infidelity and dishonesty. Good intentions are trampled in the pursuit of passion. Problems, both past and present, shape the relationships the women share...The writing is sharp...a realistic account of contemporary urban lesbian life."—*Melbourne Star Observer*

"The ending left me grinning to myself for hours and wishing for an immediately available sequel...One of the best writers on the roster...Her books are always entertaining and often thought provoking."—*Dimensions*

"I'm not sure why I found the book so completely erotic. The author knows how to tease and how to deliver."—*Lesbiana*

"One of those books that is hard to put down until you finish it... Whether you're in the perfect relationship or still looking for it, you'll enjoy this story."—*MegaScene*

By the Author

ROMANCES as Jennifer Fulton

From BSB:

Dark Vista Series

Dark Dreamer

Dark Valentine

Dark Garden

Standalones

More Than Paradise

Naked Heart

Moon Island Series

Passion Bay

Saving Grace

The Sacred Shore

A Guarded Heart

Other:

Standalones

True Love

Greener Than Grass

CONTEMPORARY FICTION as Grace Lennox

From BSB:

Chance

Not Single Enough

MYSTERIES as Rose Beecham

From BSB:

Jude Devine Series

Grave Silence

Sleep of Reason

Place of Exile

Other:

Amanda Valentine Series

Introducing Amanda Valentine

Second Guess

Fair Play

DARK GARDEN

by

Jennifer Fulton

2009

DARK GARDEN
© 2009 By Jennifer Fulton. All Rights Reserved.

ISBN 10: 1-60282-036-8
ISBN 13: 978-1-60282-036-4

This Trade Paperback Original Is Published By
Bold Strokes Books, Inc.
P.O. Box 249
Valley Falls, NY 12185

First Edition: June 2009

Credits
Editor: Stacia Seaman
Production Design: Stacia Seaman
Cover Design By Sheri (graphicartist2020@hotmail.com)

Acknowledgments

This story, like my earlier Gothic hybrid, *Dark Dreamer*, had its roots in my childhood. Among the novels and poetry I loved most growing up, Gothic works were disproportionately represented and I always wanted to draw some of those themes into my romances. It also helped that I lived for some years in a huge, creaking, isolated house without television and with rather poor electrics. This led to many evenings of solitude in my bedroom, overlooking a dark garden and creepy orchard, reading by candlelight, and listening to the stories of Edgar Allan Poe on a decrepit radio.

You'll find in the pages that follow, a recognizable homage to various authors of the Gothic persuasion: Charlotte and Emily Brontë, Ann Radcliffe, Elizabeth Gaskell, and of course Daphne du Maurier, whose novel *Rebecca* made me want not just to read, but to write something Gothic and creepy. My tip o' the nib to that author can be found in *Dark Garden*, in both the title, and the last scene of Chapter Ten.

My family and friends, as always, gave me love and support. Connie Ward provided helpful encouragement and thoughtful comments for my early chapters, and my patient publisher, Len Barot, kindly allowed me to delay this work when the time to get it written was unavailable. Getting any book published is quite an undertaking when everyone involved cares a great deal about the final product, as the crew at Bold Strokes do. Once this book was finally in their hands, it got a lovely cover—thanks to Sheri, and Stacia Seaman took pains to make the text free of typos and other blunders, under pressure of time, for which I am thankful.

Lastly, I'd like to thank the many readers who've been writing to me over the almost twenty years in which I've been publishing lesbian romances. It's been an honor and a pleasure to write stories for you. I hope this one brings pleasure, too.

Dedication

For JD

CAVENDER FAMILY TREE

Nathaniel
b. 1818 (d) 1869

Fanny Blake
older sister of Benedict

George
b 1824

Hugo
b. 1845

Estelle Gibson
b. 1847 (d) 1870 drowned

Laura Lowell Cavender
b. 1876

Thomas Blake Cavender
b. 1870

Thomas
b. 1893
(d) infancy

Harland *twins* Hope
b. 1895

Thaddeus
*b. 1904, killed
by lover's husband*

Jane
b. 1905

Daniel
b. 1907

Alice
b. 1909

Lucas
b. 1909

Emma
(d) suicide

Joel

Pansy
b. 1964

Anne — Marshall
b. 1902
Governor

Alexander
b. 1900
Presidential candidate
(d) 1962, suicide

Nancy
b. 1920
*(d) 1958
car hit by train*

James
State senator

Ruth
Movie star

Henry
b. 1939
(d) 2005, stroke

Azaria
b. 1947
(d) 1982, cancer

Mason
b. 1973

Lynden
b. 1975
(d) 2008, plane crash

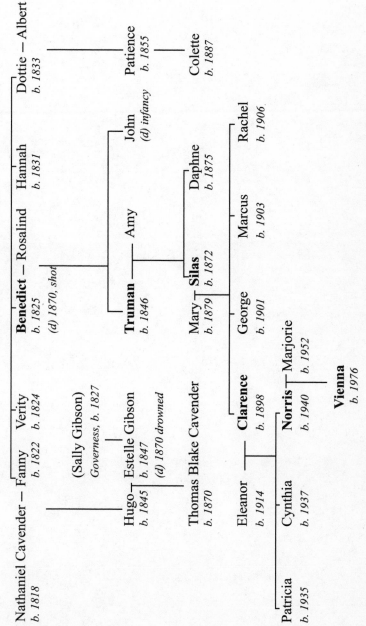

BLAKE FAMILY TREE

CHAPTER ONE

The gun is loaded," said the woman with the rifle aimed from her hip. She was tall and disheveled. Her lank coal-black hair fell heavily around her face. She locked the door behind her. "Move and I swear I'll blow your fucking head off."

Vienna Blake hit the security alarm under her desk. Not that anyone could have missed the fact that a crazy woman had invaded their building. A SWAT team was probably en route already. "What do you want?"

"You know why I'm here."

The intruder was sullen and suspicious, like a wild thing peering out from behind iron bars. Her clothes belonged on the set of a period movie, not in a downtown Boston office. Who wore a three-quarter length velvet coat and a white shirt with some kind of cravat at the throat? Only Mason Cavender. Vienna supposed the coat had provided camouflage so she could smuggle the rifle. But the black breeches and riding boots?

"Can you lower your gun?" she requested. "It's making me nervous."

"A Blake with a sense of humor, whadaya know." Mason strode across the office and halted a few feet from the imposing cherrywood desk. Eyes dark with menace swept over Vienna. "You think this is funny?"

Vienna refused to allow her alarm to show. She'd be damned if a rifle pointed at her gut would turn her into a crybaby. "You're only making things worse for yourself."

"Worse? Your family has destroyed mine. And now you've

murdered my brother. Was that your finest moment? Or did you prefer seeing my father wet himself the day he had his stroke?"

Vienna assessed her chances of extracting the Smith & Wesson she kept in her top drawer before Mason could fire her weapon. Forcing herself to remain calm and think carefully, she said, "I'm truly sorry about your brother."

The long barrel inched toward her chest. "Sorry? My brother isn't cold in his grave and you have the nerve to send me that takeover offer?"

Mason looked like she hadn't slept since the funeral. Vienna recognized that the situation was dangerous, but she refused to allow herself the luxury of panic. People who panicked made mistakes. She belonged to a different ilk—people who made mistakes, survived them, and would never surrender their control again. She forced herself to breathe evenly as she analyzed her options. If she could get the revolver from her drawer, she would only need a single shot. Self-defense. Any competent attorney would ensure no charges were ever laid.

But shooting Mason could only be a last resort. Apart from anything else, Vienna would draw no satisfaction from such an end. She wanted Mason present to witness the final destruction of the Cavender legacy. She wanted her to take that offer because she had no other choice.

"With Lynden gone, there's only one of us left," Mason said hoarsely. "And one of you. The last of the Cavenders takes out the last of the Blakes. Poetic justice, don't you think?"

Vienna sighed. "I had nothing to do with that accident, and if you'd bothered to research your facts you'd know it."

Mason's fist smashed down on the desk. A stack of files toppled sideways, spilling their contents on the floor. "Liar," she chanted tonelessly, as though talking in her sleep. "Murderer."

"The police will be here any minute." Vienna eased the drawer open a few more inches. "For God's sake, you're going to be hurt. They'll shoot you. Do you want to die for nothing?"

Breathing hard, Mason snarled, "Do you think I care? I held my brother in my arms while he took his last breath. I promised him revenge."

"Then at least select the right person for your retribution," Vienna said with disdain. "I suggest you start with the aircraft mechanic."

"Why? Is that who you hired? So it would look like an accident?"

Vienna could almost get her hand into the drawer. She kept her shoulders still to disguise her intentions. Softening her voice, she said, "Mason, I had nothing to do with the crash. I swear it, on my mother's life."

Mason studied her closely for a long while, then lowered the rifle. Her eyelids drooped with exhaustion, but those black, savage eyes still gleamed vengefully from beneath long, dense lashes. "Why is it that when beautiful women lie, it's so easy to believe every poisonous word?"

"Wow, you must knock 'em dead with flattery like that."

The heavy eyelashes swept up and a very different Mason suddenly stared out. Vienna's stomach dived and her pulse climbed sharply. A prickling chill spread its feelers beneath her skin, as though she were being delicately licked all over. Her nipples reacted, pressing against the thin lace of her bra. Vienna bit her lip so she wouldn't gasp, but Mason must have glimpsed the reaction. An insolent heat invaded her gaze and she gave a sensual, cynical smile that bothered Vienna more than the gun.

There was something raw and untamed about Mason that always unsettled her. That hadn't changed since the last time their paths had crossed and, maddeningly, Mason had become even more physically attractive as the years passed. Her coltishness had given way to a long-bodied muscularity unsoftened by feminine curves. The lingering traces of childhood had fled her face, leaving the lean planes and hard jawline more sharply defined. Vienna took in the strange, sinewy beauty of the hand clamped around the rifle stock, the odd combination of elegance and artisan practicality. She knew how those hands felt. Sometimes it seemed she'd spent her whole life trying to stamp out that particular memory. She still couldn't make sense of Mason's effect on her.

Their first disturbing encounter flashed through her mind. The Blakes had held a wedding that day at Penwraithe, their home in the Berkshires. After the formalities the guests were enjoying a tea dance and picnic, hoping an impending summer storm would come to nothing. Everyone fell back in disarray when a huge black horse thundered through the proceedings and halted in front of the picnic blanket where seven-year-old Vienna sat with her dolls. From the frozen faces of her aunts and cousins, Vienna understood she was in danger and slid slowly backward on her butt away from the restless hooves.

Once she was at a safe distance, she scrambled up and brushed off her fancy flower-girl dress. A spatter of rain landed on her top lip as she looked up into the darkest eyes she'd ever seen. Licking the water away, she asked, "Can I have a ride?"

The rider looked surprised. "Do you know who I am?"

When Vienna shook her head, the dark-eyed girl leaned down and offered her hand. Ignoring the protests of those around her, Vienna allowed herself to be pulled up onto the front of the saddle. The strange older child wrapped an arm around her waist, doubled the reins in her free hand, and kicked the horse into a gallop.

As Vienna laughed into the wind, the girl said in her ear, "I'm Mason Cavender. Your family wants me and my brother dead."

Vienna recognized the name instantly and her heart skittered, but even at seven years of age she knew exactly what was expected of her. A Blake never backed down in front of a Cavender. Leaning back to make herself heard, she replied carelessly, "So what?"

Mason's laughter warmed her cheek. "Hold on tight," she warned. And then they were airborne, jumping a stream and racing down a slope toward a pair of towering wrought iron gates.

For a few terrifying seconds Vienna thought they were going to attempt the impossible jump over the obstacle, but Mason slowed to a trot and a man emerged from the gatehouse. As he opened the gates Vienna studied the design on each: a lion, twin crescents, and a serpent.

Mason flourished an arm. "This is where I live. It's called Laudes Absalom."

Huge oaks overshadowed the broad avenue they followed. On the right lay a dark belt of unkempt woods from which drifted the scent of decay and fungus. On the left, beyond the stalwart oaks, a small white temple stood on the brow of a grassy slope just in sight of a lake bordered by pines. Ahead loomed a house unlike any Vienna had ever seen, a baleful fortress rising against the leaden sky. Stone towers loomed, angels propped up archways, demons lurked beneath the eaves. One wing of the monstrous residence was falling down, the roof gutted and the masonry crumbling. Slabs of stone and broken statuary were piled up at the base of a wall jutting from the damaged building. Rambling roses made their way over this barrier like fugitives from the other side, spilling across the rubble in a riot of crimson and pink blooms.

Mason paused on the rise of a bridge halfway along the drive and guided her horse in a semicircle so they could look toward the shadowed lake and the temple. A gust of wind blew the rosebud wreath from Vienna's head and caught at her hair. Mason plucked a long coppery wisp away from her face and smoothed it back behind Vienna's ear. For a few seconds her hand rested on Vienna's cheek.

"You shouldn't be here," she said.

Vienna smiled, thrilled by that wicked truth. She never got to have any fun. Her nanny or some bossy female relative was always tagging along, reminding her of her duty as her parents' only child. "I don't care. Anyway, you shouldn't have crossed the boundary."

"That land where you were having your picnic," Mason said with a note of satisfaction. "It's Cavender land. Your family has to give it back to us next year."

"Why?"

"Because the judge said so."

Vienna had no reply to this unfathomable fact. It came to her in that moment that she was on a dark, fast horse with the very child she'd been warned never to talk to, and they were inside the towering gates she'd been told never to enter. Her father always slowed the car when they drove past Laudes Absalom so he could deliver various lines from a litany of condemnation for their neighbors. *A curse upon their vile hearts and craven souls. One day, we'll see that house reduced to dust. Never trust a Cavender.*

Mason jumped down, telling Vienna to hold the cantle. She took the reins and led the horse the rest of the way toward the house, where she yelled, "Mr. Pettibone," and a man ducked his head to pass through one of several small archways along the front of the house. He lifted Vienna down and led the horse away.

"Don't say anything till we get to my room," Mason instructed as they climbed the steps to the main doors. "That's if you aren't too sissy to come inside."

Vienna paused to stare up at a statue, a sorrowful marble angel with a strange-looking dog at her side. A phantom wind buffeted her, molding her filmy robes to her sleek thighs and firm breasts. One hand clutched at the dog's scruff, the other trailed behind her, the fingers barely brushing the door pillar. She was not so much guarding the entrance as stealing away, looking back as though afraid of being followed.

Mason trailed her fingertips over the statue's hand. "This is my great-great-grandmother, Estelle."

"Was she an angel?"

"No, they gave her wings because she's in heaven. She drowned in the lake."

"Did the dog drown, too?"

Mason gave her an odd look. "You're asking baby questions. Come on."

She took Vienna's hand and escorted her indoors, into a huge wood-paneled hall crisscrossed with fragments of light from rows of high leaded windows on either side. Swords, axes, stag heads, and paintings cluttered the walls, and long, dusty red drapes were tied with fraying golden cords. A gigantic staircase rose in the center, leading to a gallery walkway high above. The floor creaked as they walked and Mason kept tugging at Vienna's hand to make her hurry.

Before they could reach a far-off door, a man's voice ordered them to stop. Vienna heard a cuss from Mason, and they turned around. The man was big and his face seemed to be etched from stone, just like the house. His eyes burned into Vienna.

"What's your name, girl?" he asked.

"Vienna Blake."

"Take her back," he told Mason.

"But I don't have anyone to play with. Why couldn't I go to camp with Lynden?"

He came closer. The smell of alcohol clung to him. The hand at his side formed a fist. "I said get her out of here."

Mason stepped in front of Vienna. "No."

He cuffed her so hard across the face that she staggered and fell. Standing over her, he said, "Take that spawn back where she belongs and don't ever bring her here again."

Vienna shivered at the memory of his rage. She wondered if Laudes Absalom was really as morbid and intimidating as it had seemed that day. Perhaps, with Mason's father gone, it was a just a big old house that needed renovations. Assuming she won the next skirmish in their ongoing battle, she would soon be in a position to decide its fate. Laudes Absalom would finally belong to the Blakes.

She sighed. A hundred and forty years had passed since their families first began tearing at each other's throats, and she was the one who would finally make the Cavenders pay their debt in full. For as long as she could remember, this moment had obsessed her family. Sitting on her father's knee, she had recited the promise every Blake learned along with the first words they could speak: *While Cavenders breathe and prosper, the Blakes cannot rest in their graves.*

The last of the Cavenders was now in front of her, breaking the law, threatening her life, and soon to be led off in handcuffs, or possibly shot by the police. Vienna searched for pleasure in the prospect of her enemy's humiliation and defeat, but she could only find hollow pity and a sense of dismay.

Astounding herself, she said, "Go home, Mason. Just walk out of here. I guarantee you will be unmolested."

"Do I look like a coward? Do you think I would dishonor myself by running away?"

Vienna caught a flash of herself standing at the gates of Laudes Absalom two days after that horse ride, face-to-face with Mason, the heavy bars between them. Mason, with her ten-year-old dignity, had informed her they could never be friends. She kept her head down as if she could hide her bruised face and bloody upper lip.

Vienna had been chastised for their exploit, too. No dessert for a week and her dolls confiscated until she laboriously penned a letter explaining why Blakes did not play with Cavenders. As soon as she'd completed her punishment and apologized to everyone who seemed offended, she'd evaded her nanny and returned to the scene of her disgrace, worried about Mason. The man at the gatehouse had made her promise not to come by again, causing trouble, then he summoned Mason.

Standing on either side of the gate, they'd solemnly shaken hands, forswearing the possibility of friendship and avowing their status as enemies. Vienna could still see Mason's black eye and the grimace of pain as she tried to smile when they said good-bye. She'd stopped once as she walked away, looking back for the longest time. Vienna waved, but Mason didn't respond. It was eight years before they spoke again.

"I think you've suffered a terrible loss," Vienna said coolly. "You're not fully in command of yourself."

"I see. And you think this temporary softness in the head would induce me to accept pity from a Blake?"

"Don't mistake self-interest for pity." Vienna finally opened the drawer far enough to admit her hand. "Do you seriously imagine defeating you in this condition would give me any satisfaction? It's hardly a fair fight."

Mason barked a harsh laugh. "When did that ever stop you or any of your family?"

"Don't judge me by Cavender standards," Vienna said haughtily. She closed her fingers around her revolver. "There are some things I won't stoop to, including cold-blooded murder and taking advantage of a person unhinged by grief."

"How did you come by these newfound scruples? Obviously they're not genetic."

Vienna contemplated the best way to defuse the present threat from her old foe. Liberating the .38 from the drawer, she lifted it into view. As Mason's eyes registered the revolver, Vienna said softly, "Yes, we're both armed. And I could have shot you right then, but I chose not to."

"Proving what? You're a lousy shot and would have missed? Or you don't want a mess on your carpet?"

"For the record, I could take you down at a hundred yards, but I don't have to kill you to destroy you," Vienna replied sweetly. "Let me explain what I have planned. I'm going to buy the last pieces of the Cavender Corporation, and then I'm going to bankrupt you and buy that ramshackle castle of yours and the land that rightfully belongs to the Blakes. Then I'm going to raze your family's edifices to the ground, cut down your trees, and sell every animal on that property for slaughter."

She got no further with her dangerous taunts. Mason lifted the rifle, her knuckles white, and for a split second it seemed that she would pull the trigger. Then she let the weapon fall.

Extending her arms, she invited, "Why waste time plotting and scheming? Just shoot me." When Vienna didn't react, she ripped open the front of her shirt and exposed her naked, heaving chest. "Get it over with. Come on, lay waste to another Cavender heart."

Vienna didn't know when she'd ever seen a body more beautiful.

Mason's breasts were like the rest of her, the muscles sheathed in smooth, pale olive skin. Her small, hard nipples were an unlikely shade of Merlot, a deeper hue than her mouth. Her toned torso flinched visibly beneath Vienna's gaze and her breathing grew more rapid. Vienna fixed her attention on the belt loosely fastened above the rise of her hips. The buckle was silver and ornately carved, a lion and two crescents within the loose coil of a serpent. The Cavender emblem, the same one that decorated the wrought iron gates at Laudes Absalom, supposedly created from an ancient family crest.

There was talk that a Cavender bride had Romany ancestry, accounting for the dark-haired, dark-eyed look of the entire family and for their unruliness, reckless passions, and legendary superstitions. A penchant for gambling, drinking, brawling, and womanizing had ended the lives of a succession of Cavender males over the past two centuries. The women were no strangers to vice, either. Vienna had heard the stories; the Blakes circulated every sordid detail as evidence of their superior gene pool. If Cavender women didn't die in childbirth, they took their own lives or vanished in peculiar circumstances, littering the family tree with motherless children. The men were handsome and charming, and known for their violent rages.

The Blakes were diametric opposites, with their blond or red hair, pale skin, cool nature, and dogged self-discipline. Blakes were conservative, logical, and dispassionate, except for their desire to vanquish the family that had wronged them. But even their quest for revenge was cold and ruthless, tempered by a determination to win by the rules of civilized society. Vienna could not imagine how the two families had ever started out in business together, let alone that their enterprise had thrived and that relations had been so cordial, they'd built their homes on adjoining land. They jointly ran a farm and orchard to provide both households with food. Their children were schooled together. There was even a Blake-Cavender marriage, cementing the alliance.

Taking in the woman breathing hard in front of her, Vienna suffered a pang of deep regret for the divide between them. Neither could cross that treacherous chasm without reaching out to the other, but their mutual mistrust was too great for either to make the first move. For a brief, crazy instant, Vienna wanted to step around her desk and take Mason in her arms. If anyone needed a hug, her sworn enemy did.

She drew a sharp breath and caught a whiff of soap and spice blended with another scent. Mason's. She hated that she recognized it, that it was imprinted in her sense memory just as indelibly as Mason's touch. "What's wrong? Can't stand to besmirch your pretty white hands?" Mason let her arms fall to her sides. Her shirt fell loosely closed. "No, of course not. You're a Blake. You have lawyers and flunkies to do your dirty work."

Lowering her eyes, Vienna tried to distance herself from the physical turmoil she felt. She set her weapon down next to Mason's and almost laughed when she realized she was looking at an antique rifle. Even if Mason had pulled the trigger, the Winchester probably wouldn't have fired. Vienna studied the elaborately engraved silver plate on the walnut rifle butt. Below the Cavender crest, an inscription read, "Presented to Thomas Blake Cavender, 1870."

She frowned. The man who had caused the feud between their families was Thomas's father, Hugo Cavender, who shot Benedict Blake, the family patriarch, in 1870. Was this the murder weapon? Had he bestowed it upon his son, Thomas, to celebrate the crime? Perhaps the same convoluted Cavender logic had made Mason choose this rifle for her vengeance fantasy. Was Vienna supposed to be goaded by this tasteless symbolism?

The phone on her desk started ringing before she could summon a suitable putdown. "That's probably the police," she told Mason. "By now I'm sure they're in the building."

"Then it's time for you to play the poor, helpless victim terrified for her life. They'll buy it."

Vienna picked up the phone.

A man said, "Sergeant Joe Pelli, Boston Police Department. Who am I speaking to?"

"This is Vienna Blake. How may I help you, Sergeant?"

"Just answer my questions yes or no, ma'am. Are you being held against your will?"

"No."

"Is an individual in the room with you?"

"Yes. Ms Cavender and I are having a meeting."

"Are you in any immediate danger?"

Vienna hesitated. "No."

"Is she armed?"

"There are two weapons lying on the desk in front of me, Sergeant. One of them is my revolver, the other is an old collector's firearm that is probably not in working order. Ms. Cavender will be leaving shortly."

"It's not that easy," the sergeant said. "She's broken the law."

Vienna placed her hand over the phone. "He wants to arrest you."

Mason wandered to a club chair in one corner and flopped back into it, arms dangling over the padded rests, legs sprawled in front of her. "Send him up."

"Are you drunk or just absurdly stubborn?"

"I don't drink." Mason took a silver case from an inside pocket and withdrew a corona and a pair of scissors. "There are more pleasurable vices."

"This building has a no-smoking rule." Vienna hated that she sounded like her mother.

Mason severed the cigar cap and indolently lit up. "Bite me."

Her soft taunt awakened Vienna's nipples once more and a dart of awareness jarred her spine. She told the sergeant to stand down his men. Studying the woman filling her office with aromatic smoke, she asked, "Why did you come here?"

"Those vices I mentioned, one of them is pissing off Blakes." Mason kept the cigar in her mouth as she refastened the few shirt buttons that weren't torn off. She took another puff, then perched the corona on the edge of the chair arm. Her expression was one of brooding introspection. "I've just had the worst two weeks of my life, and now I have to leave without killing you. So I guess I'm procrastinating."

"I've heard that's a Cavender trait." Vienna stood. "Look, I have a lunch date. Security will escort you out of the building."

She unloaded the Winchester and the revolver, slid the bullets into her purse, and picked up both weapons so that her unwelcome guest could not take a gun with her. Unable to prevent herself, she glanced at Mason's face. The dark, unearthly eyes flashed at her and Mason's smile, though harder, was as sensuous as ever. In another life, Vienna would have found her impossible to resist. But Mason was the last of the Cavenders. The Blakes would settle for nothing less than her annihilation.

CHAPTER TWO

"Your hands, Ms. Cavender."

Mason unclenched her fists. She couldn't stop thinking about Vienna Blake and her arrogant threats: *I'm going to raze your family's edifices to the ground, cut down your trees, and sell every animal on that property for slaughter.* That stone-cold bitch. Mason could easily believe her capable of such callousness. Yet she'd played right into Vienna's hands with her hotheaded detour to Blake Industries. Her grandfather had ended up in an insane asylum before he killed himself. Was she losing her mind, too, marching into the enemy's camp with her Winchester loaded? She should be thankful that Vienna had let her walk away, but the reprieve grated. Vienna had brushed her off like an annoying insect. As always, her patronizing attitude set Mason's teeth on edge.

"Observe the facial muscles," Stanley Ashworth informed his protégée, Havel Kadlec, a delicate youth with a back deformity that corrupted his walk.

"Yes, master. Very tense." The young man studied Mason's face with the embarrassed fascination of a boy seeing more than he should. In the heavily accented English learned after Ashworth plucked him from a sidewalk in Prague, he noted, "The jaw. The mouth. The eyes. The appearance is…angry."

"A change of music, perhaps," the artist suggested.

Havel replaced the cap on a paint tube and limped over to the CD player. He queried Mason. "Mozart? Shostakovich? Dixie Chicks?"

"Do I look like a give a damn?" She instantly regretted her

churlish reply. There was no need to take out her frustration on someone powerless to respond in kind. Softening her tone, she said, "Classical works for me."

She stared out the tall windows. The afternoon light would change soon and she could escape. She had wanted to cancel this appointment and her next one, with the chief financial officer of the Cavender Corporation. But Ashworth was leaving town shortly to paint a U.S. senator and had insisted on completing their final life sitting first. Mason owed him some consideration. He'd already declined a prestigious commission and changed his travel plans several times to accommodate the Cavenders.

His brush poised, he regarded her dispassionately. "Relax. Smooth brow. Keep your position."

"When can I see it?" Mason asked.

"When it's unveiled."

Havel closed the CD player and the poignant opening strains of Elgar's "Nimrod" plunged the studio into heroic despair. Mason's chest constricted. The famous classic was one of the pieces played at her brother's funeral nine days earlier. Ashworth obviously remembered. He glared at his protégée and slid a finger across his throat.

"Oh, pardon me," Havel stammered. "Please, I am very sorry."

"Don't worry about it." Mason said dryly, "At least it's not 'Agnus Dei.'"

Looking pained, Havel switched to the serenity of Fauré's "Pavane," and painting resumed. Mason worked on keeping her face composed. Her thoughts drifted with the haunting melody. Only a month ago she'd been standing here with her hand resting on Lynden's shoulder as he lolled in the armchair in front of her, posing for their portrait. The photos taken during their sittings were the last she had of him. She was thankful he'd insisted they pose together instead of having separate portraits done for the gallery at Laudes Absalom. He'd also come up with the concept for the painting, a snapshot of a typical Sunday: Lynden slouched in his favorite chair recovering from a hangover and Mason back from a long horse ride, her Winchester under her arm, symbolizing—Ashworth claimed—her protective nature.

She and her brother were opposites in temperament. Mason was a solitary animal, lacking the charm that made Lynden a fixture on the elite party scene, a bachelor profiled in *GQ* as the last in a long line of handsome bad boys, the man destined to reverse the Cavender family fortunes via a glittering marriage and smart investments. From all accounts he'd been well on his way to accomplishing both before the plane crash. According to the *Boston Globe*, the so-called "tragic accident" two weeks earlier signaled "the final throes of the colorful but ill-fated house of Cavender."

Once more, Mason considered Vienna Blake's indignant claims of innocence. The denial was laughable. Maybe she didn't sabotage the plane in person, but the Blakes had been conniving to destroy the Cavenders for well over a century. With talk of Lynden's engagement to a billionaire's daughter, Vienna must have seen their chances of victory slipping away. The marriage would have saved the Cavender Corporation, and the Blakes couldn't allow that to happen. So they'd somehow sabotaged Lynden's plane.

Vienna was too smart to get caught in a murder conspiracy. She must have hired someone who knew how to keep his mouth shut. Fear uncoiled in Mason's gut and she fought off the oily nausea that had bothered her since the crash. She harbored the dark belief that Vienna wouldn't stop until the job was done. The thought frayed her nerves. She could take care of herself, and she could hardly summon the will to care whether she lived or died anyway. But what about the people and animals who depended on her? She couldn't wait to get back to Laudes Absalom and make sure her dog and her horses were safe.

Calming herself, Mason watched a mourning dove bob and weave along the window ledge. It peered into the studio and tapped a glass pane. From the guilty look on Havel's face, Mason guessed he usually left breadcrumbs out but hadn't today. She studied the dove more closely and realized it was missing a foot.

"Excuse me." She dropped her pose and crossed to the window. Unfastening the catch, she asked, "Do you have any food for it?"

Havel hurried over with a bag of sunflower seeds, and Mason scooped a handful and offered her open palm to the dove. It examined her for a few seconds, then took the seeds from her hand.

Havel seemed surprised. "Usually, she does not come to me. I place the seeds and she eats."

"Birds seem to like me," Mason said. "And I guess she's extra hungry today."

Ashworth tapped a jar of brushes against his studio table like a gavel. "When you're both ready…we have thirty minutes of light and I would like to use it."

Havel snapped to and hurried back across the room. Mason spilled the remaining seeds onto the ledge and closed the window. The dove continued snacking. Maimed, it got about the business of survival despite life's crippling blows.

❖

"That's outrageous." Marjorie Blake daintily deconstructed her watercress salad, sidelining the cucumber slices. "Why didn't you have her thrown in jail?"

"Mom, she just lost her brother."

"And she thinks *you* killed him. As if you would risk incarceration over *that* worthless playboy. You should have held your ground."

"It felt too easy," Vienna said. "Like kicking an animal when it's down."

"You're going to have to put her out of her misery sooner or later. The Cavenders are finished and she knows it."

"I'm not so sure she does. You should have seen her."

"They're are all the same." Her mother sniffed contemptuously. "Rash. Unpredictable. Dangerous. Her father was a monster."

"I know. I met him once. Before that day."

Marjorie frowned. "When did you meet him? You never mentioned it."

"What does it matter? He's dead."

"And good riddance. The nerve of him, marching into the house with his paranoid accusations."

Vienna refrained from mentioning that the accusations were well founded. The Blakes had used their political connections to kill a government contract that could have saved the Cavender Corporation.

"As I was saying, she can't run that company without her brother," Marjorie continued. "I heard he was about to get engaged to that girl. What's her name?"

"I can't remember." Vienna cast a look around the restaurant in the vague hopes of spotting a business acquaintance she could greet. A few shell-shocked schmucks were attacking their meals with the same desperation she felt, no doubt roped in for a LouisBoston shopping expedition by pitiless wives. The store's restaurant was a destination for ladies who lunch.

"You were at Winsor with her, weren't you?" her mother persisted.

"We were in different years."

Vienna didn't want to revisit her prep school days, but it was too late. The palm of her right hand was already tingling. Over the years she'd tried to forget the reason for that ghost pain, but the incident was one of her most vivid memories. She was almost fifteen at the time, and Mason was a high school senior. They were hostile opponents in a lacrosse rivalry that was tame compared with their family feud. Vienna, playing center for Winsor in the first game of the season, had expected a competitive matchup when the Dana Hall team took their positions. She'd been stunned to find herself facing off for the draw with none other than Mason Cavender.

Vienna had lost the draw, an omen of things to come. Dana Hall proceeded to outhustle her team in a scrappy game where everything went wrong in the first half. Winsor's passing sucked, their defense was breached constantly, and they gave up three goals out of every four. Dana Hall had built their attack around Mason, who was easily their most aggressive player. And Mason went after Vienna, one-on-one, dismantling her game and making her look like an idiot. Winsor had finally clawed their way back into the game in the second half, chipping away at their opponents' lead after some aggressive ground ball play and a hat trick. Vienna was looking for a fast-break goal when Mason caused a turnover that prevented her from leveling the score. The rest was history, a loss to the school Vienna and her friends viewed as little more than a dating academy for brainless fashion victims.

Afterward, the students were supposed to socialize in a combined picnic but Vienna had decided to walk off her anger instead. Wandering through the unfamiliar Dana Hall campus, she'd ended up at the stables and made her way around the outdoor ring toward the riding center building. There had to be a map somewhere, showing her how to find the parking area. Before too long, she would have to locate the team minivans.

"Lost?" The voice came from a tall figure standing in the shadow of a hunter fence.

"No, just talking a walk."

Mason Cavender strolled toward her. Even then, she'd exuded the blatant self-awareness of a mature woman, not a high school senior. She was so completely unlike the typical Dana Hill student Vienna wondered why on earth she'd put up with being sent there. She couldn't imagine Mason fitting into popular cliques and trolling parties for Belmont Hill jocks. She couldn't be popular, yet five years of preppy hell seemed to have left her unscathed. The other girls were probably afraid of her, Vienna thought, even the bitches.

"It's been a long time," Mason said.

"Miss me?" The flippant response seemed stupid, but what was she supposed to say? It wasn't as if they'd been friends when they were little kids.

Mason studied her. There was an odd warmth in her gaze. "Yes, I've missed you."

Disconcerted, Vienna changed the subject. "Good game." She added mentally, *I hate you, bitch.*

Mason grinned so knowingly Vienna wondered if she'd accidentally spoken her thought aloud. "Your stick-handling needs work. You should play all lefty in some practice games to work on your weak hand. I could give you some pointers."

The nerve of her. Vienna wanted to kick her. "We have a coach, thank you."

"Yeah, looks like that's working out," Mason said dryly.

"It's only the beginning of the season."

"Depressing thought. For you, I mean." Mason looked her up and down with calm insolence. Apparently she couldn't resist rubbing salt in Vienna's wounds. "You'll be off the squad if you can't hang tough out there."

"Oh, please. You don't know what you're talking about." Vienna resented the way Mason's dark stare made her prickle all over. And she knew her face was red. That was the trouble with milky pale skin. Everything showed.

"I get it. You think your daddy's endowment buys you a free pass." Mason's slow smile was infuriating. "Wait till you play Brooks. They're going to maul you."

Stung, Vienna snapped, "Why don't you just go back to whatever rock you crawled out from under and leave me alone."

"It's your funeral. One other thing…your shaft is too short." Something wicked glittered in Mason's eyes. "Mine is longer. I find that helps."

Vienna felt herself blush more deeply. "You're taller than I am."

A dimple formed beside Mason's mouth, in one corner only, drawing attention to the faint scar that made her smile uneven. Vienna caught a flash of that ragged upper lip, bruised and cut the last time they'd seen each other.

Mason looked her up and down. "How old are you?"

Resenting the implication that she was too young to play an aggressive game, Vienna lied, "Sixteen."

"You're small for a center."

"Piss off, Mason."

Vienna had heard enough. She marched off toward one of the bridle paths near the building. Mason wasn't the first person to imply that she owed her place on the squad to her father's hefty donations, but Vienna refused to believe it. Everyone's parents gave money to the school. Still, the comments hurt and she had desperately wanted to prove her critics wrong with a stellar performance. Thanks to Mason, she had done the complete opposite.

"You don't want to walk along there." Mason had the nerve to step in front of her. "The track's really muddy."

Vienna resisted the urge to stamp her foot. "Get out of my way." She stepped to one side.

Mason stepped with her. "I board a horse here," she said in a transparent bid to steer their conversation to neutral ground. "Want to see her?"

"Christ, what's wrong with you?" Vienna exploded. "Why would I want to see your horse? We're not friends. Have you forgotten who I am?"

For a long while Mason stared at her, then she said in a near whisper, "As if I could."

She took a step closer, her expression faraway. To Vienna's shock she extended a hand to touch her hair. Her fingers brushed Vienna's cheek. She immediately looked embarrassed as though realizing she'd done something strange. But instead of withdrawing she stood exactly where she was. Her chest rose and fell sharply and she made an odd, strangled sound as if she'd just forced back some words. Something cleared the dreaminess from her eyes, and she stared at Vienna with an intensity that made her pulse accelerate.

She knew she should back away but her legs refused to move. They felt warm and weak like the rest of her. Blood rushed in her ears, driven by an erratic flurry of heartbeats. Mason's breath fanned her top lip. Her face was so close, Vienna could see the true color of her eyes. They weren't completely black, but obsidian etched with traces of midnight blue. Vienna thought about the irises coming into bloom outside her bedroom window at Penwraithe. Her mother had planted a new hybrid the previous year. The name jumped into her head: *Hello Darkness.*

Unnerved, she stammered, "What do you want?"

Mason smiled and touched a fingertip to Vienna's trembling bottom lip. "What I can't have."

Vienna willed herself to look away but instead she fell into the velvet promise of Mason's eyes. Something in Mason's face made her shiver, and she felt herself sway fractionally, drawn toward the sheltering strength she remembered from long ago, the day Mason stole her from the wedding festivities. She started to shake as Mason's fingers slid past her nape and into her hair. She tried to make herself move but her common sense was no match for the powerful thrall that enveloped her. Something was happening that had never happened. A bubble of enchantment imprisoned her. Everyday life seemed remote.

When Mason's lips finally touched hers, neither of them moved. Her mouth was warm and dry. Later, Vienna convinced herself that the daring act of kissing a girl explained her inertia. It was obvious that Mason had experimented before. She placed one hand firmly in the small of Vienna's back. The other cupped her cheek. And she kissed her like she knew exactly how. Worse, still, Vienna kissed her right back, and what she lacked in experience, she made up for in determination, rushing toward each new sensation when she should have fled.

The warm, slippery glide of Mason's tongue thrilled her. So did the sudden crush of her body as she closed the final inches between them. Her warmth, her strength, the urgency of their embrace addled Vienna's thinking. She couldn't resist. She didn't even try. She was aware of a sense of belonging, the crazy idea that every step she'd taken in her short life had led her here, to a moment destined by forces beyond her control.

She wasn't sure how long that fateful kiss lasted before she heard a shaky groan and realized she was touching Mason's breast. Breathing hard, she stumbled back. Her face was scorching hot. She felt disoriented, as though she'd been blindfolded and set down in a street she didn't recognize. Nothing was the same anymore.

A breeze stirred the branches of the gaunt birch trees beyond them. They were not yet in leaf, but budding with promise. Above them, sunlight filtered through thin mackerel clouds. Spring storms were expected. At this rate, she would be the last one back to the minivans. Coach would be mad at her.

"I have to go," she croaked out.

"No." Mason's hand closed around her wrist. "Please. Talk to me."

"I can't." With a sharp tug, Vienna tried to free herself but Mason lifted the imprisoned hand and planted a kiss on the inside wrist.

"Come with me," she insisted, like the words were dragged from her. "Come back to Laudes Absalom. No one's there. We can have the place to ourselves."

"What are you talking about?" Vienna stammered.

"Don't you see?" Mason's low voice was stretched thin. "We can change things. It's up to us. I've known it all along."

"Don't." Vienna shook her head adamantly, trying to clear the fog that had clouded her judgment. "Don't say another word."

"You feel it, too," Mason insisted. "I can tell."

Vienna could hear a steady chatter echoing in the recesses of her mind. Her parents. Her grandmother, warning her to pull herself together and remember who she was. "You're crazy," she said. "My parents told me everyone in your family has a mental problem but I didn't believe it till now."

"A mental problem?" Mason flung Vienna's hand aside like it was infected with plague.

"Have you told your family that you're a lesbo?" Vienna demanded.

Mason gave her a quizzical look. "Have you told yours?"

"Of course not," Vienna replied scathingly. "Since I'm not one."

"Oh, really? Let's see about that."

Mason grabbed her shoulders and jerked her forward so hard Vienna tripped off balance. Before she could steady herself, Mason's mouth was on hers, silencing her protests. She tried to free her arms, but Mason held them pinned to her sides with the power of someone who spent half her life controlling horses and the other half wielding a lacrosse stick.

"Don't," Vienna gasped, averting her head to end the kiss. "I hate you."

"You hate that you like me," Mason said in her ear. "You hate that you like kissing me. You hate that you want more."

"I do not." Vienna cursed her small build as she struggled to free herself. She hadn't had the growth spurt that changed girls her age into young women. Mason was at least five inches taller. "If you don't let go of me right now, I'm going to report this."

Mason laughed. "Go ahead. Tell them you were kissed by a Dana Hall lesbian. Just wait and see how many friends you have left."

"Bitch."

"Actually, the word you're looking for is butch."

"I'm going to tell my father," Vienna said weakly. Every time she moved, her clothing strained over her breasts, making her horribly aware of her tight nipples.

"No, you're not," Mason said with conviction. "You're going to pretend this never happened. You don't have the guts to tell your family that you got your first kiss from a Cavender."

"That wasn't my first kiss," Vienna lied. "I kissed a boy last summer."

"Sure you did," Mason said sarcastically.

Vienna planted a swift kick to Mason's shin, then realized Mason was wearing tall riding boots and probably hadn't felt a thing. The danger of more kisses seemed to have passed and they stared at each other for several seconds, both breathing fast. Then, abruptly, Mason let go. Her words were acid on Vienna's nerves.

"Come and see me when you've grown up."

Vienna stumbled back a step. Tears stung and she blinked them away, mortified by the weird hurt she felt, the sense that she had been found wanting and Mason had discarded her like a stupid child. She wanted to say something that would hurt Mason and prove which one of them was tougher, but all she could think about was that deep, astounding kiss. That perfect moment, with her eyes closed and her lips pressed to Mason's. She'd never experienced such bliss, but with it came the dread certainty she'd tried to ignore for the past year or more. Mason had obliterated all doubt and confirmed who she was. A lesbian. And worse, a Blake who had kissed a Cavender.

Appalled, she said, "Just wait. One day I'm going to make you sorry you ever touched me."

Mason regarded her calmly. "The only thing I'm sorry about is that you're a virgin. Otherwise we could have had some real fun."

"That's disgusting."

"Can't handle it?" A muscle moved in Mason's neck. "Go home and play with your dolls."

"Go fuck yourself."

"No, I think I'll go fuck a girl who knows how."

Vienna's palm stung almost before she realized how hard she'd slapped Mason's face. She stared at the mark she'd left. Mason licked a fine film of blood from her mouth. She must have bitten her lip.

Shaking, Vienna said, "Don't ever speak to me again."

And six years passed before Mason did.

Chapter Three

Vienna stared down at the palm of her hand, almost expecting to see the ghostly imprint of Mason's flesh. She closed her fingers so tightly her knuckles whitened. Sometimes she thought that first kiss had poisoned her like an enchanted apple, casting her into a slumber no one could awaken her from. None of her lovers had been able to break the spell.

Those failed relationships were a disincentive, Vienna reflected, an excuse she used to avoid dating. Maybe if she were more active, she would improve the odds of finding someone who could make her feel...awakened.

"You're not listening," her mother complained. "I can tell. You're miles away."

"No, I'm listening." She didn't have to be psychic to guess what Marjorie had been saying for the past few minutes. "It's just that I've heard it all before."

"And you'll keep hearing it until you do what has to be done."

"It's in hand, Mom."

"How? I was speaking with Wendell and he says you need to act now. There's an insurance policy, and who knows what she could accomplish with the money."

"A million or two isn't going to save her," Vienna said wearily. "Cavender Steel barely exists and the Cavender Corporation still owes the bank twenty million dollars. With her brother gone, those loans will be called in. All she has are some abandoned factories and that car parts business. Most of the profitable subsidiaries have been sold off. There couldn't be a better time for us to close the deal. That's why I made the new bid."

"Will they go for it this time?"

"Absolutely. They have no choice."

"What about the house? I promised your father—"

"I know, and I told you I would take care of it."

Not quite mollified, Marjorie said, "Your grandmother planted that orchard with her own hands. It killed your father that Cavenders were eating those apples."

Vienna knew better than to argue that it was cancer that had killed her father and the land in question had never belonged to the Blakes in the first place. Her grandfather had attempted to incorporate it into their property, erecting a new boundary fence in the wrong place in the hopes that their useless, hard-drinking neighbors wouldn't notice. For twenty years they didn't. But then, Vienna's father had discovered Mason stealing fruit one day. He'd fired a few shots over her head, just to scare her. To his astonishment, she fired back.

He called the police and had her arrested, but since she was only nine years old and had just lost her mother, the deputies let her go with a warning. But they made the mistake of telling the Cavenders to control her better. A week later Mason's father brought in the surveyors and kicked off another legal battle between the families. This time the Blakes lost and had to return the land. The judge had ordered that the fruit trees be left intact. Vienna's grandfather never stopped talking about it. If he could have staggered off his deathbed and picked up an axe, he would have cut those trees down.

Changing the subject, Vienna said, "Are you going to Bonnieux next spring?"

"I don't know. The thought of rattling around in that old villa by myself doesn't appeal."

Marjorie sounded cranky. She hadn't taken to widowhood as some women did, shedding grief after a few months and enjoying pursuits disdained by their late husbands. She refused to attend social events unaccompanied and had come to depend on her brother, Wendell Farrington, the supposed bachelor uncle of the family, as an escort. In reality, Wendell lived with his gay partner in an elegant Back Bay condo. A snappy dresser with the requisite Ivy League credentials, he charmed mature women and made Marjorie feel special. She saw him as an authority in all matters and constantly spouted his opinions, especially those about the business. Vienna had been groomed since birth to take over from her father, but what was a lifelong internship and an MBA compared to a penis? Bupkis, as far as Marjorie was concerned.

She placed her hand over Vienna's. "Wendell thinks we should take a mother-daughter cruise. He says I need cheering up. I have a brochure from Regent with all their destinations. They're going to have Apollo 14 astronauts on board doing talks."

Vienna couldn't think of anything more appalling, except perhaps taking her mother to *Cats* for the sixth time. "That sounds wonderful. Why don't you and Wendell go?"

"He's terribly busy with his commitments for the opera. Unlike you, he can't just take time off whenever he pleases."

Vienna didn't waste her time pointing out that she was the CEO of a half-billion-dollar company and Wendell was just dabbling in opera fundraising to impress his much younger boyfriend, a B-grade tenor. "Mom, you know I get horribly seasick," she said gently. "What about wintering in Palm Beach? You always tell me how much you miss it."

"I don't think I could bear it," Marjorie said. "Everything's changed. It's virtually *mobsters sans frontières* now, with all those Russian oligarchs and flashy people with bad manners."

"You don't have to mix with them, Mom."

If Vienna's childhood memories were any indication, Marjorie and her B&T Club friends spent most of their time in each other's homes gossiping. They never rubbed elbows with anyone outside their own rarefied circles. Marjorie and Wendell had jointly inherited the Palm Beach home of their childhood, after Grandmother Farrington had a fatal heart attack during a Dead Sea mineral cocoon treatment at the Ritz-Carlton Spa. Marjorie hadn't been down there once during the past three years. Vienna was surprised Wendell hadn't sold the place. He didn't share Marjorie's sentimental attachment to the home they'd grown up in.

"Everyone's selling and moving to Jupiter Island," Marjorie said gloomily. "And who can blame them? These days you can't ride a bicycle on Worth Avenue without being crushed by some ex-stripper in a Bentley."

"I'm planning to spend my next vacation in Bonnieux," Vienna said patiently. "I hope you'll consider coming with me."

Marjorie sighed. "I don't know. France is not what it was. The place is overrun with Muslims. Before long, you won't see people walking through the village with baguettes anymore. They'll be out in the middle of the road bowing to Mecca."

Vienna didn't know whether to laugh or groan. "Mom, I think France will be safe for Christians for a few more years."

"You think I'm exaggerating? I'm not a racist, you know. Perhaps we should sell the villa. All that maintenance..."

The waiter arrived to clear their salads. Vienna had forgotten to eat hers. She dragged the conversation back on course. "We're not selling Villa des Rêves."

"Wendell offered to take it off our hands. Naturally I said he could have it at a reasonable price. He'd be doing us a favor. It needs modernization."

"No, it doesn't. Dad spent a fortune restoring it." Vienna tried to sound patient, but she was hurt that her mother could even suggest palming the Luberon Valley farmhouse off on Wendell. She and her father had made Villa des Rêves their special project, overseeing the restoration during fleeting visits and longer family holidays. She couldn't bear to think about parting with the property.

"We could still take vacations there," her mother said with a sniff of disapproval. "Wendell wouldn't mind."

"It's not happening."

Their entrées arrived and Marjorie inspected her fish as though suspecting the roasted halibut she'd ordered was really horrid bream. Vienna waited for the inevitable complaints, but Marjorie had bigger things on her mind.

"Well, if you're not going to be practical, perhaps we should consider renting it out when we're not using it. Villas in Provence command quite a sum, you know. And then there's the apartment. The taxes are crazy and it's not as if either of us is in New York more than a few weeks every year. Wendell thinks we should let it month to month."

Vienna sliced into her chicken so hard, it went spinning across her plate. "I am not having our homes invaded by strangers. If we needed the income, that would be different. But we don't."

Marjorie was just inches away from a pout, her usual reaction when she didn't get her way. "Wealth is no excuse for extravagance. Blakes don't throw money away on frivolity."

Reading between the lines, Vienna asked, "Do you need an income adjustment, Mom?"

"Income adjustment" was Blake parlance for adding money to the private bank accounts of wives and dependent relatives who'd overspent.

"It's been one of those months," Marjorie confessed. "With the McCain fund-raisers and Wendell's birthday. Then, of course, I had to update my mourning wardrobe for the Cavender boy's funeral." Fretfully, she added, "I can't believe you made me go to that wretched service all alone. Imagine it. Surrounded by Cavenders. Anything could have happened."

"I didn't *make* you do anything of the kind. You're the one who insisted."

"Someone had to represent the family."

Vienna keyed a cash transfer into her BlackBerry. "Fifty thousand okay?"

Marjorie tapped her beige nails. "Round it up, sweetheart. We're going to New York soon, remember."

"Fifty is pretty round." Vienna felt bad quibbling with her mother over money. Still, if Marjorie saw fit to lecture her for extravagance, two could play at that game.

"I still have to find a dress for the Whitney Gala," Marjorie griped.

"You have plenty of time to torture the sales clerks at Barney's." The gala was over a month away, in October. "If you need more cash, that's what your Amex card is for. You know I'll take care of it."

Marjorie huffily sipped her Riesling. "You sound just like your father."

"Perhaps you could remember that similarity when you're telling me how incompetent I am and how I should be getting my business advice from your brother."

"I wish you didn't resent Wendell so much. He could be such a support to you. Especially now, with your cousins chomping at the bit."

"Mom, I'm not afraid of my cousins. They're employees, just like anyone else, and if they get in my face I can always sack them."

"Don't be ridiculous. Your aunts are on the board."

"Not indefinitely," Vienna said. "Anyway, all I'm saying is that I don't need a man to prop me up."

"Don't start on that topic. I don't want to hear about it."

"What *topic*?"

"You know what I'm talking about. I don't mind your lifestyle. I'm not a bigot. But you don't have to prove yourself by emasculating the men around you."

"I'm not even going to respond to that ridiculous statement."

"I blame your father." Marjorie tried to twist her black pearl necklace, but she was wearing one of her Tahitian strands and the pearls were too big. She reverted to cleaning her eyeglasses. "Norris never related to you as a daughter, only a substitute son."

"Please, can we just drop it?" Vienna gave up on her meal. The sooner she got the check, the sooner the homily would end. "I need to get going. I have a lot to do before I leave for Penwraithe this weekend."

The last thing she felt like doing was driving to the Berkshires, but she made the trip at least once a month to ensure the estate was being managed appropriately. She would have been tempted to spend more time there but driving past the gates of Laudes Absalom always unsettled her. Her father's memory was fresh enough without another reminder of the legacy he'd left behind, the task of finishing what her predecessors had started.

"Why do you take everything so personally?" her mother complained.

"Oh, God." To bring their lunch date to an immediate close, Vienna asked the question that invariably made Marjorie run for the hills. "Mom, have you thought about dating again?"

"Dating?" Her mother's small, expertly freshened face went rigid with distaste. She fanned herself with the hand that sported her newest ring, a large canary diamond. The hot flashes had stopped five years ago, but she'd retained the fanning mannerism as a means of showing off her jewelry. "Your father left some very big shoes to fill. And I don't have the slightest desire for a replacement. As if that were possible."

"You're only fifty-seven and you could pass for fortysomething. It's not *infra dig* to look for a companion."

"Norris was the love of my life," Marjorie replied with an air of injured dignity. "I can't expect you to understand what that means, given the parade of so-called girlfriends you waste your time on."

Vienna choked on a sip of water. "Are you talking about the zero dates I've had in the past year? That's one of the great things about running the business, you know. I have no life."

"Just wait. One day you'll meet someone you can't bear to live without. Then you'll understand what I endure on a daily basis having lost your father."

"I miss him, too, Mom," Vienna said stiffly.

Marjorie conceded their shared sorrow with a tight-lipped nod, then rose and smoothed her dress. It was a charcoal shade that hinted at elegant mourning in its high neckline and modest three-quarter sleeves. Black, she was fond of telling everyone, was strictly graveside and no elegant woman wore it as day attire, even one recently widowed. The sober mood of her outfit was lifted by a Hermès scarf in the Axis Mundi design. The blue and gold silk accessory had been a gift from Norris Blake not long before he died.

Hoisting her handbag from the spare chair next to her, Marjorie said, "I must run, sweetheart. They won't stop the auction to wait for me."

Vienna got to her feet. "Good luck. I hope you raise lots of money. What's it for today?"

"Lupus. Such an underrated cause."

They exchanged the usual arm's-length embrace and air kisses.

"Remember," Marjorie could never leave without the last word, "your father's watching from heaven. Don't let him down."

Chapter Four

The sale of the Kirchner painting has brought us some breathing room." Josh Soifer indicated a seven-figure entry on the complex financial report spread out on the desk in his office.

He was his father's son, Mason thought, glancing up at him, a man with an affinity for numbers. Three generations of Soifers had been Cavender accountants, but Josh eschewed the dull conservatism of his forbears in both dress and attitude. Today he wore a sleekly tailored three-piece suit that flattered his sartorial, male-model good looks. His wavy brown hair was cut in a casual style that seemed at odds with his serious expression, but Josh was a man who excelled as naturally at tennis as he did in the boardroom.

Mason had agreed to this meeting, more or less expecting him to tell her they had to accept Vienna Blake's insulting offer. But instead, Josh was talking about a three-year redevelopment plan as if it were feasible.

"If the economy wasn't heading into recession we could probably reduce our debt and trade our way back into the black over the next two years," he summarized after dragging her through various charts and projections. "We're very well positioned because of the way we've diversified. With the Internet companies Lynden set up, we finally have vertical integration for the electronics brands and the auto accessories. Income almost tripled last quarter."

"It's not enough to save us," Mason said. "Although I can see it expands our liquidation options. But it's just too late."

"You're right. Even if we keep trading, all we'd be doing is servicing debt. Which is why," he flipped pages to the balance sheet of a company she'd never heard of, "your brother took a gamble on this."

Mason propped a hand beneath her chin and tried to make sense of what she was seeing. "We own a company called Azaria Technology?"

Josh looked faintly apologetic. "I wanted Lynden to tell you, but he had this fantasy about presenting you with a fait accompli...the family fortunes restored. Azaria is the key."

"Named for our mother?"

"He thought it was appropriate."

Mason stared down at the bottom line and the growth projections. "Are these numbers for real?"

"Actually, they're conservative." Josh's excitement added a higher note to his voice.

"What does Azaria produce? Please tell me we haven't gone into weapons of mass destruction or something."

"Don't think we didn't consider it," Josh said with bland irony. "But you know Lynden. He couldn't handle the ethical vacuum, or the bad press. We're not the Blakes."

Mason laughed and they shared a few seconds of silent grief. Then Josh took a small plastic container from his pocket. He tipped the contents onto a leather binder in front of them.

Mason picked up one of the glittering stones. "Diamonds?" She had a horrible flash of Lynden setting his scruples aside to deal with criminals and terrorists, buying conflict stones as a fast moneymaker.

"Yes and no." Josh handed her a loupe. "They're cultured diamonds."

"Fakes?"

"No, they're as real as a mined diamond. Identical tetrahedral carbon crystal structure. Same optical qualities. Just as hard and brilliant. But the raw crystals are grown in a lab instead of forming naturally underground."

Mason wasn't sure how to react. She didn't know much about diamonds except that big, flawless ones were very rare and mining them was often a shameful enterprise that would make her think twice about buying one to impress a woman. She'd never regretted the sale of most of the heirloom jewelry she should have inherited. Her father had needed the money.

She examined one of the stones under the loupe, not sure what she was looking for. "I think I see a flaw."

"Exactly," Josh said. "There a tiny inclusion in that stone, proof that it's natural, not some artificial compound engineered to look like a diamond."

"And we *made* these stones?"

"Yes, you could say we're diamond farmers. We send most of the rough to Mumbai to be cut, but the premium stones go to Antwerp." Josh picked up a squarish diamond and held it to the light. "That's a two carat Radiant Cut. A mined diamond like that one would normally fetch around eighteen thousand dollars. Our price is less than five thousand."

"Why would anyone want these instead of the real thing?"

"Azarias *are* the real thing," Josh repeated. "And even though fancy colored diamonds are popular, most women still want white. With an Azaria, they get more bling for their buck and a guilt-free diamond. It's the way of the future."

Mason replaced the gem on the binder and studied its companions. "This could be huge."

"De Beers is nervous. They've only had to fight cubic zirconias, Moissanite, and so on. No one has been able to produce cultured white diamonds in quantities that make commercial sense."

Bewildered by the whole idea that her brother had a secret business venture, let alone the process itself, Mason asked, "How do we *farm* them?"

"Your batshit-crazy cousin Pansy made it happen."

"We hired *Pansy*?"

Mason's head was spinning. What else didn't she know about her brother's dealings? After their father died, Lynden had taken over as head of the family business in the oldest son tradition followed by the Cavenders. Mason thought the responsibilities would do him good and they'd made a bargain. She would deal with cleaning up after the past and he would work on building a future. So, while he developed new business opportunities and courted a rich future-wife, she ran Laudes Absalom and handled the nightmare of reorganizing and downsizing various Cavender Corporation enterprises and assets.

She'd purposely kept her distance, trying not to tread on Lynden's toes, but she hadn't anticipated he would cut her out of the loop entirely. The decision to hire their ex-convict cousin should have been made jointly. Pansy wasn't a close relative; the Cavenders applied the term "cousin" loosely to anyone descended from Thomas Blake Cavender. Pansy had been born under a cloud, the only daughter of an illegitimate Cavender. Her mother had fallen into a deep depression after the birth and hanged herself, and the orphaned Pansy was duly cared for by relatives. Brilliantly clever, she'd ended up at MIT, where she fell in love with another science nerd who broke her heart. When he came to a sticky end in suspicious circumstances, Pansy was arrested for his murder. The state only had circumstantial evidence and had cut a deal after the family pulled some strings on her behalf. Pansy had served six years for involuntary manslaughter.

"Lynden felt sorry for her after they let her out of prison," Josh said. "She had nowhere to go, so he put her in the factory. She was sleeping out back and cleaning the place, then she got interested in the process so he let her work as a tech. We were only producing industrial-grade stones at the time. The rest is history."

"She would have had a great career if she'd stayed at MIT," Mason said.

"She's doing okay at Azaria. We made her chief developer. She likes the title."

Mason took a moment to move beyond an odd feeling of hurt that Josh knew all of this because he and Lynden worked together so closely. She wished she'd been the one to share his excitement over the new business. She also felt guilty that she hadn't made more of an effort after Pansy was released. Lynden had brought her to Laudes Absalom for a few days during the breeding season and said he was taking care of her. Mason had been so busy with the horses she had barely exchanged a word with either of them. Perhaps Lynden had intended to tell her about Azaria then.

"I'll give her a call next week," she said sadly. "We didn't get a chance to talk at the funeral service."

"She'd like that." Josh gathered up the diamonds and extracted a hefty document from the binder. "In case you're interested, she prepared this technical report."

"Science isn't my strong suit."

"Mine either. I asked her to write up something for us laymen."

"Hence the title." Mason indicated the contents page. "'Diamonds for Dummies.' Very executive-friendly."

"Pansy thinks you and I should go back to school and get a real education if we can't understand something as rudimentary as this."

"Sayeth the woman with the 170 IQ." Mason grinned as she read the summary.

According to her cousin, the technology Azaria used replicated outer space, where stars burned out and formed crystallized carbon cores like the white dwarf scientists had identified in the Centaurus constellation. By blasting carbon atoms at low pressure and very high temperatures onto a seed crystal inside a special chamber, the deposits formed a rough diamond. The process sounded so easy Mason wondered why everyone wasn't doing it.

"Is this our own patented technology?" she asked.

"We're working on it," Josh said. "There are competitors using similar methods. Chatham and Gemesis have been making colored diamonds for a few years. They're easier to grow and very profitable."

"But colorless stones make more sense for us?"

"Absolutely, if we can produce them in a viable quantity. None of our competitors has figured out how to grow large white diamonds, so we're poised to grab a significant market share."

"What's our business plan?" Mason asked.

"Basically we need a factory that will hold up to five hundred diamond-growing machines built to Pansy's specs."

Mason turned to the section where Pansy had provided details of her invention. She expected to see something NASA would be proud of, but the chambers looked remarkably simple. She examined the technical specs closely and concluded, "We can CAD her prototypes and build these ourselves."

"How? The car accessories plant is at full capacity."

"We still have the Johnstown factory."

"An abandoned shell in a podunk town."

Mason hesitated. "Not exactly."

"Are you telling me Cavender Steel isn't quite as dead as I think it is."

"Let's just say you and Lynden weren't the only ones doing your own thing." With a faint smile, Mason explained, "I had to lay off our last sixty men a year ago and there was no work for them in the town.

I couldn't *give* the damned factory or the plant away. The place hasn't seen maintenance in thirty years and the equipment's old—"

"And was supposedly sold for scrap." Josh tapped his fountain pen on the binder. "What's going on?"

"I let the workers use the factory and the equipment to set up their own small businesses if they wanted to. Some of the men are making steel kitchen sinks in trendy shapes. And there's a team doing patio fire pits. It's great."

"You're not charging any rent?"

Mason shrugged. "The place was only going sit there and rot."

"So, the security guard we're paying to stop vandalism is actually watching a bunch of our former employees make barbecue furniture?" Josh rolled his eyes.

The guard in question was another laid-off Cavender Steel worker. "Things are going pretty well," Mason said. "So I was thinking about partitioning the space and setting up additional small business units."

"Assuming we don't sell."

"No one wants a disused steel mill, not even the Blakes."

The Rust Belt was scarred with vast abandoned factories, the grim ciphers of a prosperous past. A few had been converted to visitor attractions but most presided like ghouls over the industrial decay around them. Mason's father hadn't allowed the Johnstown factory to fall into ruin. He'd never accepted that because China paid its workers peanuts and was willing to let its citizens live under a shroud of toxic emissions, the U.S. would never be able to compete in core industries like steel. Even to the end, he'd believed that the Cavender Corporation would survive and its steel business would somehow become relevant once more, and he had almost proved it by winning a big government contract connected with the Iraq war.

Thanks to the Blakes, the contract didn't pan out and Mason knew her father realized it had been his last chance. If he'd laid off his workforce ten years earlier and moved Cavender's entire manufacturing base to another country, the corporation would have been thriving instead of going broke. He would have been able to lower his bid and not be undercut. But Henry Cavender had been too stubborn to take advantage of the government incentives for large companies to move their jobs offshore.

Mason could understand his dilemma. For all his faults as a family man, her father had been intensely loyal to the people who worked for him. Many had parents and grandfathers who had been Cavender employees and Henry felt responsible for them. In the end, letting them down had literally killed him.

Mason shared his sense of moral obligation, and reading the business plan for Azaria made her almost light-headed with hope. The global rough diamond market was worth about twenty billion dollars and De Beers controlled seventy percent of the supply. Lately their stranglehold had loosened and they were no longer the only game in town. There was room for other players. If Azaria could guarantee supply and consistent quality, they could do exactly what Lynden had envisioned and restore the family fortunes. Mason would be able to re-employ numerous staff she'd had to let go. She was stunned at the potential of the venture. Perhaps the Cavender curse was nothing more than superstition. Her brother, it seemed, had been on the brink of proving that they could put the past behind them.

"The engagement ring market is for white, high-clarity stones." Josh continued to explain their market advantage. "The average guy is trying to put the most bling he can afford on his lady's finger. The big issue will be keeping pace with demand."

"Can we get any help from the bank?"

He shook his head. "The concept would blow their minds, and besides, in this economy, they're only interested in getting their money back. Lynden was working on a venture capital deal when…the accident happened. There's a party coming up in New York City later this month. He was going to firm things up there."

"Who's he talking to?"

"A Russian billionaire, Sergei Ivanov. A gangster trying to launder his cash."

"So, I should go to this party and see if he's serious."

Josh hesitated. "I know it's not your scene, but you're the one with the name."

"As if being a Cavender matters anymore. Times have changed."

"Don't underestimate the power of the Cavender mystique." Josh's tone was pensive. "Lynden knew how to capitalize on it."

"And you think I need to do the same." Mason groaned at the prospect. She loathed schmoozing and the thought of attending parties claw-deep in Manhattan socialites made her ill. Lynden went to all the important ones, making sure he took a prestige date, usually an insipid society girl bewitched by her own reflection. But with him gone, and the need to woo a potential investor, Mason was going to be stuck with the nightmare of the charity season in New York.

"The Ivanovs seem to be shut out of certain events. That's a big disappointment to them," Josh said.

"In other words, two million bucks buys them the right invitations, and Azaria is just a bonus."

Josh smiled, confirming her worst fears. "Think you can be persuasive?"

His doubt was evident, and Mason could understand why. Normally she only went to the most significant social events every few years to quash rumors that she was either dead or locked up. The Whitney Gala next month loomed largest among the bashes she loved to avoid, but it was the ideal gathering to dangle in front of an upwardly mobile investor normally excluded from the invitation list. The Cavenders were long-term donors and automatically had a place at one of the most desirable tables. To procure an invitation for a new-money Russian and a wife who was probably a sable-draped former hooker would be a challenge, but Mason knew the promise of her own seldom-seen presence could tip the scales.

"I can make it happen," she said with a pained grimace.

"The alternative is getting in bed with De Beers." Josh sounded unenthusiastic.

"Instead of waiting for them to crush us?" Mason could see why the diamond giant would want a piece of the action if cultured diamonds were going to make serious inroads on the market.

"Diamond prices are all about supply and demand," Josh said. "The fewer high-grade stones out there, the higher the prices. De Beers controls huge stockpiles and a vast distribution machine. They could kill us in a price war."

"So what we need is a rich partner and a stockpile of our own," she said. "Not a partnership with our worst enemy." Two could play the De Beers game. If Azaria had a virtual monopoly and only released limited numbers of their cultured stones, they could keep the price up.

"Everything we produce for the next six months has already been ordered," Josh said. "We have more orders but we can't increase production without more plant."

"How much capital do we need?"

"We could swing it on two million up front. Pocket change, really."

"But we owe the bank twenty and we're not earning enough to service those loans, let alone fund Azaria."

"In a nutshell, yes." Josh hesitated. "Plus we're out another ten million for the pension fund."

Mason looked up sharply. "What do you mean?"

Josh shuffled through his papers and produced a set of figures. "The numbers you've been seeing…they're bullshit."

Mason scanned the page in bewilderment. "I don't understand. Are you telling me Lynden borrowed money from the *pension* fund?"

"There was no option. He thought if we could make this work you wouldn't need to know."

"You and Lynden hid this from me for the last two years?"

Josh had the grace to look ashamed. "We hid it from everyone. We've filed false returns and sent false statements to employees."

"Oh, my God. Lynden *stole* the money from our employees?"

"No, nothing so simple as that. We created an investment entity that allowed the fund to take a temporary shareholding in Azaria, with buyback provisions for you and Lyndon."

Mason rested her head in her hands. If Azaria failed there would be no way she could buy back that investment. "How many people are depending on us for their retirement?"

"Hundreds."

Mason wiped the perspiration from her forehead. Her damp hair clung to her hand and she realized she was shaking. "What are we going to do?"

"There's an offer on the table," Josh reminded her in a cautious tone. "We could offload the Cavender Corporation to Vienna Blake, pay the bank as much as we can, keep Azaria, and gradually buy back that shareholding."

Mason lifted her head and met his eyes. "Over my dead body. That bitch made a big mistake when she killed my brother. I want her to pay."

"I understand." Josh hesitated. "But please just think about it. We could simplify everything…get lean and mean."

"No." Mason gathered up the paperwork and the bag of diamonds.

"I know she's involved in the accident. I just need some time to prove it. Has that P.I. turned up anything useful?"

"Only what the police already told you. Vienna was out of town when it happened and there's no sign of foul play. The FAA report says engine failure."

Mason snorted in disgust. She'd read the report and it was inconclusive. Something had to have caused the loss of power. For a few minutes, in Vienna's office, she'd almost believed her protestations of innocence, but lying was in the Blake DNA. "There's nothing that family won't sink to, and with Lynden's engagement coming up there was a motive. Tell the P.I. to look harder."

Josh toyed with his pen, his face reflective. "It could be over, Mason. If you both decided to call it a day. You could take the offer and walk away, and she would be the one stuck with the mess. Think about it."

"I will, but I need you to buy me some time." Mason knew from the look Josh gave her that he thought she was only delaying the inevitable, but she had to give the investigator a chance to dig dirt. The Blakes had enemies. If she could get something on Vienna, even some dubious accounting practices that could interest the IRS, she would finally have a lever. And in the meantime she had to obtain the financing for Azaria.

"I'll send the right signals," Josh said. "She'll probably be willing to work with our timetable so long as she thinks she has us on the ropes and you're going to cave."

Smiling bitterly, Mason got to her feet. "I don't think that'll be a problem after today's showdown. She definitely thinks I'm losing it."

"You're lucky you weren't arrested," Josh said.

"Interesting, isn't it, that she didn't want the police involved? She's hiding something. That's obvious."

"I think you're reading too much into it." Josh smoothed his cuffs absently. "Vienna Blake isn't stupid. With an offer on the table, she wouldn't want you in jail, all pissed off."

Mason could see his logic, but she didn't buy it. "No, she's up to something. I can feel it. If anything happens to me, the cops won't have far to look."

Josh met her eyes. "Are you saying you're worried for your safety?"

Mason hesitated, not wanting to sound like she was afraid. "I'm on my guard."

"Chill." Josh adopted a casual, confident tone, transparently trying to reassure her. "She thinks she has this won. Why would she resort to dirty tricks now?"

Mason had asked herself the same question. "I don't know. Maybe because we've been doing this all our lives. Maybe because she needs more than a signature on the bottom line of a contract to feel like she's won."

He was unconvinced. "Have you ever thought that she might want this to be over? And maybe that's why she's made another offer…so you can both move on."

To an outsider, it probably sounded that easy, Mason thought; after all, she and Vienna were two adults. Why not just decide to call it quits? Did either of them even know why their families were still fighting—did it matter anymore? She reminded herself that she'd watched her brother draw his final breath, and but for the grace of God, she would have died with him. Part of her wished she had, but instead she'd walked away with nothing but a concussion and a few cuts and bruises.

She stifled a sob at the memory of Lynden's eyes in the seconds before they glassed over. "The Blakes have ruined us, Josh. They as good as killed my father and now my brother, too. I can't let her get away with it."

"I'm sorry," Josh murmured.

"All I have left is my honor." Mason dragged her knuckles across her eyes. "If I give in to Vienna Blake, I'll lose that, too."

CHAPTER FIVE

Vienna dropped her cell phone onto the passenger seat and slowed down to take in the soothing surroundings. She loved the rugged southern end of the Berkshire Mountains. Her father always used to stop at the general store in Monterey on their trips back and forth when she was a kid. They had also spent time hiking the Benedict Pond loop and Beartown together. Her mother detested outdoor pursuits. All Vienna and her dad had to do was haul out their hiking boots and backpacks and Marjorie would beg off, claiming she was far to busy to waste a day exploring a frigid pine forest.

Vienna sighed. She missed her father all the time, even more since the full burden of running Blake Industries had settled on her. As a child she'd never understood why he spent all day at the office, then came home and worked in his study. Now she wondered how he'd managed to balance his life as well as he did. She struggled to keep lunch dates with her mother, and as for having a personal life, by the time she'd finished each working week, she was so exhausted all she wanted to do was blob on her sofa with a good book.

She tried to remember when she'd last had a hot date. Eighteen months ago? She didn't have real relationships, merely interludes, serial dates with women she never really got to know. She wasn't sure where happy lesbian couples in their thirties found one another. It hadn't seemed so hard in her twenties. She'd had a serious relationship in the final year of her MBA at Harvard, but the pressure of her studies had doomed the romance. After graduation her ex had taken a job offer in Hawaii. Their subsequent attempt at long-distance love had lasted for less than a year.

After that failure, Vienna had settled into casual dating, expecting that one day Ms. Right would come walking into her life, complete with brains, good looks, and an independent nature. But all of a sudden everyone she knew started pairing up and hanging out with other nesters. The few close friends who knew she was a lesbian tried to fix her up with cute single women, but what was once a steady stream of potential partners dwindled to a pathetic trickle soon after she hit thirty. All the good ones seemed to be taken.

It probably didn't help that she was semi-closeted and cautious. Vienna knew she was quite a catch for anyone more interested in the material than the emotional, so she tried to avoid revealing her background. It wasn't easy to get close to someone when she was reluctant to invite the women she dated back home. They started to wonder what she was hiding, and after a few dates, if they seemed genuinely nice, Vienna didn't want to insult them by admitting she hadn't trusted them.

She wished she'd cared deeply enough for someone to make an effort. But the women she liked most were the kind she'd rather be friends with. She didn't want to believe, at only thirty-two, that she was unlucky in love, but it was starting to look that way. Worst of all, whenever she tried to gaze into her romantic future, the face that gazed back through the mists of fantasy was Mason Cavender's. That wretched first kiss haunted her like a bad melody; the more she tried to erase it from her memory, the more tenaciously it stuck.

Aggravated that she'd let her mind wander in that direction, Vienna hit the gas and overtook an idiot driving a huge SUV at about thirty miles an hour. Normally she would stop at Monterey for old time's sake, but she wasn't in the mood, so she took the turnoff to Tyringham. The blue tranquility of Lake Garfield always calmed her, signaling that she was about twenty minutes from home. The trees were rapidly changing color, donning the splendor of autumn. The maples were etched in red and gold, and yellowing willows skirted meadows of pale olive green. Goldenrod and asters lined the roads, and the Japanese hydrangeas were in full bloom in the gardens she passed.

An avalanche of leaves would descend after September, burying the cowpaths around Penwraithe in a rustic mantle that inspired local hobby artists to paint ever more tacky homages to the New England fall. Vienna allowed them access to the grounds of Penwraithe at this time of year and was always stumbling over someone with an easel. To her annoyance, the most popular view they wanted to paint was the one with the absurd Gothic towers of Laudes Absalom in the background. She had switched to a different bedroom years ago so she wouldn't have to see the place every time she opened the drapes. Yet she often gravitated to her old room, watching for a dark figure walking a dog.

With a sigh of annoyance, she fell in behind a line of traffic crawling along Main Street, a stretch of small-town America made famous by Norman Rockwell. Thanks to him, Stockbridge was always packed with tourists posing for the mandatory photo op in front of the Red Lion Inn before heading up the line to Williamstown. Vienna bypassed a minor traffic jam and evaded a group of charm-struck visitors standing in the middle of the road. The famous inn seemed to expand farther around the corner every year, its storybook white façade serving as both a landmark and a fixture on souvenir mugs.

Vienna turned off and drove up past Naumkeag, the mansion that overlooked the village. She was thankful the Blakes had built their own summer "cottage" deeper in the surrounding hills. Penwraithe didn't attract the kind of attention reserved for the mock castles of its era. Occasionally tourists would drift from the imposing iron gates of Laudes Absalom to the more welcoming entrance of the Blake estate, but the house wasn't the stuff of dramatic photographs. Modest by Gilded Age standards, it comprised a mere eighteen rooms. Originally it was supposed to be an Italianate mansion, but after the building began Vienna's ancestor, Benedict Blake, decided he wanted a more American feel and switched to a Georgian style with white shutters and balustrades around the terraces. Not a man who liked to waste money, however, he retained the imposing white marble entrance hall that had already been built. With its black-and-white mosaic floor, high barrel-vaulted ceiling, huge marble urns, and ornate wrought iron stairway, it promised a home of shameless opulence. Guests were subsequently disconcerted to step into rooms that could only be described as underwhelming, both in dimension and décor.

Vienna slowed her car as she passed the gates of Laudes Absalom and approached Penwraithe. Ahead of her, two riders had stopped near the entrance. One of them, her barn manager Rick O'Grady, waved at her and dismounted, leading his horse onto the estate. The other, on a spectacular white mount, continued along the road without looking back. Vienna's pulse accelerated. She was certain, from the noble carriage and Baroque conformation, that she was looking at a Lipizzan. And there was only one in the vicinity.

Trying not to show her irritation, she rolled slowly up alongside the man who took care of her four horses. The chestnut he was exercising was their boss mare and had a suspensory ligament strain. After months of stall rest, they'd brought her through almost a year of rehabilitation. Rick had just started riding her again.

Vienna lowered her window and greeted him with a smile. "How's she doing?"

"Better every day. It'll take a while before we can try a canter, but she has normal flexion so I think we're out of the woods."

"Who were you riding with?" Vienna struggled to sound casual. "That white is spectacular."

"He's immaculate, all right."

"From the Cavender stables, I take it?"

Rick looked slightly abashed. "Yes, that's Dúlcifal."

"Of course." Everyone in the county knew of the stallion after he'd appeared, along with one of Mason's famed Andalusians, in an Animal Planet documentary about so-called horse whispering. "Is he as smart as they say?"

"I don't know if it's strictly intelligence." Rick looked thoughtful. "He's been extensively schooled and he has the most amazing manners. That's partly his gene pool, but they also use special training techniques over there. I've been picking up a few pointers, as a matter of fact."

Listening to him enthuse, Vienna reminded herself that her staff had every right to associate with other grooms in the neighborhood, regardless of what she might think about their employers. In a pleasant tone, she said, "Well, I'm glad you've found someone nearby to work the horses with. Maybe I'll get to meet Dúlcifal sometime."

She felt another rush of shame at her spiteful comment about sending Mason's animals for slaughter. She wished she could take back her vicious words, less for Mason's sake than her own. The very idea was unthinkable and to say such a horrible thing was beneath her. That woman had a knack for bringing out the worst in her.

Rick seemed to miss her hint about meeting the beautiful Lipizzan.

Tightening the wrap around the chestnut mare's hind leg, he asked, "Are you riding tomorrow morning?"

"Yes, no preferences. Whoever needs the work." Vienna avoided disrupting the training regimen on her intermittent visits. She wanted to help out when she was at Penwraithe, not have her staff drop everything to pander to her whims.

Hers were strictly pleasure horses, all of them rescues. She really didn't have the time to be the best of owners, but she could afford to pay for good care. Until recently she'd had six mares, but two were close to thirty and she'd finally let them go before the winter made their arthritis unbearable. Some time soon she would rescue a couple more. She hated to think of unwanted horses neglected and turned out to fend for themselves, and since she could only stable a few personally, she donated to a long list of equine rescue organizations.

"Eight o'clock?" Rick queried.

Vienna normally rose at six but on her days at Penwraithe, she caught up on sleep and appreciated a slower start. "Sounds good. I'll see you then."

She glanced in the side mirror as she drove toward the house and smiled at the sight of Rick patting the mare and feeding her a carrot. He was very calm with the horses and an expert at reading temperament and mood. Her father had employed him on a recommendation from friends in the racing industry after Rick had a serious fall and needed lighter work. He'd been with the Blakes for three years and showed no sign of wanting to return to the race track. Vienna felt fortunate to have him. He was overqualified for his job, having been a head groom with trainer responsibilities, but she gave him a free hand to employ the stable help he needed and he seemed genuinely happy at Penwraithe.

She parked in the garage behind the house and let herself in the back door. A herd of cats immediately laid claim to her, rolling and smooching and coaxing her toward the kitchen.

"You're early." Bridget Hardy dropped a lump of dough on the long butcher block in the center of the room and shook flour off her hands. The Blakes' housekeeper for the past fifteen years, she baked whenever she knew Vienna was coming.

"I got away before the rush hour." Vienna inspected the jars of preserves lined up along the counters. "You've been busy."

"If I see another bucket of zucchinis…" Bridget shaped the bread into two focaccia loaves, placed them on a baking stone, and smothered them in olive oil. "Stick some garlic and rosemary sprigs in one of those, would you, while I make us a pot of tea."

Vienna washed her hands and did as she was told. Working in the kitchen with Bridget was one of her great pleasures while she was at home. The only reason she could cook was that Bridget had taken the time to teach her. She drew a deep breath, inhaling the sweet pungency of the herbs and the yeasty aroma of the dough. "God, it's good to be here."

"You should come more often," Bridget said. "I know it's hard, but you have to pace yourself better. Your father learned that lesson the hard way."

"I know." Vienna set the rosemary aside and poked split garlic cloves into the dough. "Parmesan or kosher salt?"

"How about one of each?" Bridget removed the whistling kettle from the flame and made the tea. In the Blake household coffee was only served with breakfast and dinner.

"How did that new girl from the village work out?" Vienna asked as she slid the focaccia into the oven.

"She managed to show up for about a week, but she spent most of her time texting her friends and living on that bird-watching Web site, whatever it's called."

"Twitter?" Vienna smothered a grin.

"Sounds familiar." Bridget selected the Darjeeling tea canister. "So in the end I suggested she pursue the important things in life at home where paid work wouldn't interfere."

Laughing, Vienna rinsed her hands and sat down at the table near the French doors. The kitchen opened onto a bluestone terrace where Bridget grew her herbs in huge decorative planters. Steps down from the terrace led to the heated pool and a sprawling outdoor patio.

"New outdoor furniture," she noted, fending off the two tortie cats that always vied for her lap.

"Your mom was sick of those green umbrellas."

Marjorie had completely redecorated the house when Vienna was a child, bringing her Palm Beach sensibility to the décor. Dark woods were removed, walls were painted in warm shades of butter yellow and pumpkin, and previously austere furnishings were replaced with more casual, comfortable styles. Marjorie still continued to update the rooms and Vienna was happy to leave her in charge. The latest transformation had brightened their pool area, replacing the dull but serviceable patio furniture with yellow striped umbrellas and deep wicker seats with white cushions. Yellow and turquoise throw pillows were artfully arranged for splashes of extra color.

"It looks very...Caribbean." Vienna wondered where they were going to put the oversize club chairs and loungers when it snowed in a month or two. Their previous furniture, bistro tables and chairs, had been stackable and easy to store in the cabana. Vienna stared at some new yellow planters. "Are those banana palms?"

"Mmm-hmn. And hibiscus. Your mom wants them moved into the conservatory at the end of the month."

"I'll bet she does." Banana palms and tropical shrubs in New England. Only Marjorie would imagine she could make that idea work.

Bridget set traditional bone china cups and saucers on the table along with slices of lemon. As she poured the tea through a strainer, she said, "A gentleman came by and left his cell phone number. You just missed him."

"Another decorator?"

"I doubt it. His suit was crumpled and he smelled like a hot dog." Bridget handed Vienna a slip of paper. "Personally, I wouldn't touch him with a pair of tongs, but he seemed to think you'd be happy to receive him."

Vienna read the name on the note before slipping it into the pocket of her jeans. "Mr. Pantano is an employee of mine."

"Indeed." Bridget lowered a slice of lemon into Vienna's tea before sliding the cup and saucer across the table to her.

"I'm surprised he made it out here today. I should have warned you."

"About his gun or his body odor?"

Vienna sipped her tea. Bridget didn't miss much. Tazio Pantano was New Jersey muscle Vienna hired occasionally. After Mason's unheralded visit to her office a few days earlier, she'd decided to import some protection for her days in the countryside. And while she was at it, she planned to make good use of Pantano.

"He'll be staying in the carriage house while I'm here," she said.

Bridget's neat eyebrows rose above her bright blue eyes. Even in her mid-fifties, she still looked youthful, with her rounded features and rosy cheeks. As a girl she'd probably been the strapping kind, Vienna thought, ruddy and energetic. Time had softened her stocky muscularity, but the distinctive bounce never left her walk. She was the antithesis of their neighbors' housekeeper, the stiff-backed Mrs. Danville. The two knew each other, maintaining a mysterious cordiality that involved exchanges of preserves and smoked meats, chats after church, phone calls after especially bad weather, and modest gifts at Christmas.

Once a year they went out to dinner together, a housekeepers' tradition established long ago, when the households were on friendly terms, and not abandoned when relations soured. On the one occasion when Marjorie had questioned the practice, Bridget had replied that she and her colleague next door were obliged to rely on one another for certain matters of no consequence to their employers but vital to the smooth running of each household. She had invited Marjorie to stock the pantry herself and organize all the household repairs, should she have a problem with that.

"Is there something I should know about Mr. Pantano's visit?" Bridget asked. "Other than his dining preferences."

Vienna saw no reason to create concern. Bridget was at no risk from the Cavender temper. Mason might be angry at Vienna, but she would never menace a household staff member. Such trashy behavior was unthinkable. "He's also here on a business matter for a friend of the family," she said with calm affability.

She could hear her father saying those very words, in that very tone, when no further discussion was welcome. Catching a brief flicker in Bridget's eyes, she knew the housekeeper had recognized the evasion, too. They sipped their tea, then Bridget checked on the focaccia.

"Do you know if our neighbor is at home?" Vienna knew better than to ask Bridget to spy for her, but she couldn't resist making the occasional query about Mason.

"I saw her yesterday." Bridget was still bent over the oven, poking around in the warming drawer. She lifted the lid off a large casserole and inspected the contents. The rich aroma of beef Bourguignon added to the mouth-watering smell of the bread. "Will Mr. Pantano be dining in the house tonight or shall I make a tray for him?"

"We can all eat here in the kitchen," Vienna said, sparing them the formality of a meal in the dining room with a man whose colleagues called him "The Tank."

"While he's in my kitchen, there's no gun," Bridget said. "And that shirt he's wearing, with the ketchup stain and the sweaty-man pheromones, needs to go in the laundry. I'll soak it for him."

"Thank you," Vienna said meekly. "I'll let him know."

Once she was upstairs she called Pantano. He didn't pick up, so she left a voicemail message letting him know he was expected for dinner. As she showered, she pondered her plans. If all went well, she would own Laudes Absalom before she returned to the city.

❖

"Are you lost?" Mason asked the hulk loitering near her barns. With lush dark hair in a sculpted Elvis Presley style and gold rings on most of his fingers, he didn't look like a reporter or a tourist who'd taken a wrong turn trying to find the Norman Rockwell Museum.

A pair of beady brown eyes blinked up at her. In a Jersey accent that was pure cliché, the stranger asked bluntly, "You the owner here?"

Mason felt the horse beneath her twitch, and his heartbeat rose up between her legs. Shamal, her black Andalusian stallion, regarded all men as members of a tribe of vicious horse-eaters. Rolling his eyes, he backed up, ready to spook at the first provocation. Mason dismounted, preferring not to find herself clinging to him as he pigrooted his way up the long drive. She held the reins loosely to signal her confidence and stood between him and the stranger, leaning back a little so her scent dominated those Shamal was taking. She always dabbed her clothing with a mix of frankincense and lavender oils when she rode him. The combination helped him relax.

"What are you doing on my property?" she asked, opening the gate to Shamal's grazing paddock. Mrs. Danville would never just buzz someone in.

Her visitor didn't explain how he'd gotten inside the gates. Maybe he'd followed her earlier when she'd returned with Dúlcifal. He waited until Mason removed Shamal's bit and halter and turned him out, then handed her a business card. A name was printed in a swirling font. She read with disbelief: *Tazio "The Tank" Pantano.* Who included their nickname, especially one straight out of a mobster movie, on a business card?

He got right to the point. "My boss is looking for a country joint like this. You interested in selling?"

From the relative safety of his paddock, Shamal glared and snorted noisily. Mason hushed him. "Laudes Absalom is not for sale."

"The Tank" shook his head slowly. Rolls of neck fat overflowed his straining collar. "Sure, you got an attachment to the place. That's understandable. How's a million sound?"

"*One* million?"

Eighty acres and a Gilded Era "cottage"—even a run-down one— in these parts would fetch at least three, maybe five if the buyer got carried away with the historical aspect. Mason had trouble imagining Pantano's boss as a man of startling contradictions, part Jersey mobster, part country squire, but if he was seeking some kind of legitimacy, surely ownership of a famous house would count for something. The offer was a joke.

Pantano grinned. At some point all his teeth had been knocked out and he had a mouthful of Day-Glo white crowns that seemed to pose a challenge to his lips. These stretched thinly in a smile that was borderline macabre. "I sent photos on my iPhone," he said cheerfully. "Lose the attitude and throw in a few horses and I can maybe talk it up to two."

Mason heard a whinny of enquiry from Dúlcifal's stall. The Lipizzan had his head out over the door.

"Nice animal you got there. Like the one in the movie."

"*Miracle of the White Stallions?*" Mason referenced the Disney film about General Patton's rescue of the Spanish Riding School horses during World War Two.

Pantano wheezed a laugh that was more like a giggle. "No, *The Godfather.*" He wandered over to Dúlcifal and patted his neck. "We already made friends," he informed Mason, as if to hint how easy it would be to repeat the severed horse head scene from the movie.

Appalled, she said, "I'll show you back to the gates, Mr. Pantano. Please thank your employer for the offer. Obviously I'll need some time to think it over."

Pantano waved a chunky hand toward the house. "Place is a dump, right? You're not going to get that kind of money anywhere else."

Mason started walking, knowing if she stood in front of this creep for a moment longer she'd punch him and the outcome probably wouldn't be pretty. Lowering her voice to keep it even, she asked, "What line of work is your employer in?"

"Construction," Pantano said, tugging up his slacks as he kept pace with her.

"And his name?"

"I'm not at liberty to discuss that information. You interested, you got my number."

He'd left his car, a black Chevy Suburban, parked next to the gatehouse. As he climbed into the driver's seat, his jacket caught on the door, exposing a semi-automatic pistol tucked into his belt. Mason shivered. The offer to buy the house was so absurd it could only have been made up on the spur of the moment to account for his presence. Men like Pantano didn't just happen to drive to the Berkshires and stumble by chance on Laudes Absalom. He was here for a reason. Mason felt sick thinking about the possibilities. Her brother had hidden so much from her, she wondered what else she didn't know about. Had Lynden borrowed from loan sharks, or failed to pay gambling debts? Did he owe money to some mobster in New Jersey who thought he could shake her down?

A metallic taste invaded her mouth and she realized she'd drawn blood, biting the inside of her cheek. She didn't wait for Pantano to drive away, but locked the gates and strode back toward the stables. After she'd opened the gates from Shamal's paddock to his barn, she called the private investigator Josh had hired.

"I want you to investigate my brother," she said after a polite greeting. "Maybe Vienna Blake isn't the only person who wanted him dead."

CHAPTER SIX

Wind rattled the windows in Mason's bedroom. The high-pitched howl of a dog left out in the storm carried past the creaking panes. Ralph lifted his head from Mason's thigh and whimpered his concern. She stroked the warm dome of his skull and whispered, "Hush, you're safe."

For a guard dog, one of a long line of finely bred Dobermans, he was a wuss. The noise drew closer and Mason deliberated. Perhaps a dog had wandered into the grounds, lost and seeking shelter. Driving conditions had been lousy in the Berkshires for the past few days. Maybe it had been hit by a car. She pictured an animal in pain, stumbling toward the house or, God forbid, the stables, where canines were not warmly received. Most of her horses tolerated dogs during rides, but Shamal despised them.

Mason tried to sink back into sleep but she had surfaced too fully. After lying with her eyes closed for a few restless minutes, she slipped out of bed and padded across to the windows. The curtains were open and night threw its mantle across the lawn in a silver sheen. She contemplated the moonshadow landscape. Nothing moved. The dark, shimmering lake surface twinkled with the crystalline legacy of far-flung stars. At water's edge the temple cast its own pale glow, standing serenely, marking the passage of time.

Beneath the dome, in a black sepulcher, lay the man who'd built Laudes Absalom. Nathaniel Cavender was entombed next to his wife, grandsire of five generations of Cavenders buried at Laudes Absalom. Other ancestors were interred in a family cemetery at the far end of the walled garden that adjoined the disused south wing, Mason's parents and brother among them. Getting the burial permit for Lynden had been another nightmare in a demoralizing series of events. She leaned her forehead against the cool window frame, flooded with helpless fury. Everything was crumbling around her. She'd lost all she cared about, except the house and her horses, and Vienna Blake was poised to steal them from her in a final coup de grâce.

Needing to clear her head, she stumbled across her room and dragged a coat from her closet. Ralph padded after her as she descended the staircase into the great hall. Moonlight spilled through the leaded windows, shining across the dead marble eyes of countless taxidermied animals. Decapitated stag heads adorned the walls alongside portraits of their killers. Mason shuddered as she passed beneath the shadow of an axe. An image gnawed at her mind like a hyena scavenging for tender morsels: Vienna standing in front of the stables at Laudes Absalom as the horses were led out by rough men who cared nothing for their noble hearts and sensitive souls.

A panicky sweat damped her skin. Fear almost crushed her to the floor. She dragged her bare feet across the smooth wooden boards. Every step she took added a creak to her discordant passage through the hall. Ralph's toenails clicked after her in a metallic staccato that distracted her from the noisy assault of her heart. Mason slowed as she caught an odd scent. The fragrance was floral and didn't belong in the musty gloom. She let her gaze roam. Nothing moved, but she smelled the scent more strongly. Amaryllis.

"Hello?" she called, feeling foolish.

Ralph's ears rose and their hair along his back bristled. Growling, he lowered himself into a defensive crouch at her feet. Mason heard a sound then, a whisper too low to decipher, and the skin on her cheek dampened as though someone had breathed on it. She swung around, sensing a presence behind her. It wasn't the first time. She'd always felt a stifling tension beneath the inertia of the house, a melancholy in certain rooms that made them hard to endure. Mason wasn't sure if the sorrows of former residents had somehow infused the walls and objects, or if the pervasive desolation was her own. The house was so familiar to her, its moods and quirks bothered her no more than its grim décor. But tonight something more palpable had stirred, the watchful entity Mason had glimpsed in the flickers and shadows since she was a child.

"Who's there?" she asked, swatting at thin air.

Her hands encountered nothing. She saw no light, heard no more whispers. When she was younger, she'd convinced herself that the unseen observer was a guardian angel. There was only one possible candidate. Her mother. Before she gave up her fight for life, Azaria had promised she would always be with Mason, watching over her. The thought was comforting, yet in her heart Mason knew the "angel" had been there long before her mother's death. She'd always felt that iciness, that strange silent reverberation in the atmosphere. And so had others.

Visitors to Laudes Absalom were rare, but those who couldn't dismiss their unease as creepy house syndrome would discreetly ask about ghosts, and for their benefit, Mrs. Danville had named the resident phantom The Unhappy Bride. She'd hit upon this evocative soubriquet after a whiskey-soaked houseguest claimed to have seen a woman in a Victorian wedding dress staring out the library window. After he cloddishly made a grab for her, the lady passed through a wall and vanished. On another occasion a visitor had claimed to see the bride standing in the family cemetery.

Mason wasn't sure if Mrs. Danville believed there really was a ghost or if she'd merely chosen to dignify the fantasies of guests out of tact. She soothed Ralph with a pat and resumed walking with her fierce guard dog tucked in close, his body quivering. They passed the padlocked door of what had been her father's office, then ducked beneath the low arch that led to the rear of the house. Pausing in the shadowed recess, she stared back once more, seeking out a shape that didn't belong, listening for a scrape or a footfall.

She heard it again, then, that half-whimpered howl. Moving as quietly as she could, Mason slid her feet into the Blundstone boots she kept next to the back door. Her hand found the doorknob and she turned the long, heavy key and pushed hard with her shoulder. The door scraped across the stone stoop until it couldn't budge any wider. She left it open, sagging on its hinges, and stepped down into the walled garden.

Ralph knew the drill. He romped ahead of her through the dense, wet foliage. In a few minutes he would rejoin her on the brick pathway and they would pass through the wildly overgrown azaleas until they reached the sundial. There, the path branched in three, with the herb garden and summerhouse diagonally to the right. Mason could find her way blindfolded if she had to, so she hadn't bothered to bring a flashlight. The waxing harvest moon drenched the garden in thin light. The damaged south wing towered above her, its charred, crumbling walls etched raggedly against the night sky.

When she was a child, the roses had been left to run wild in that area of the garden, rioting over the walls and trailing down through the smashed windows of the house. Thorny branches roamed through the gutted rooms, draping them in fragrant blooms all summer. Ivy crept across the ruins in a slow-encroaching tide of glossy green that spread farther toward the rest of the house with each year. Ravens nested in what was once a ballroom, and swans occasionally found their way up from the lake to inspect the grand remains, hissing at the peacocks that wandered the grounds.

Mason wasn't sure when the Cavenders had held their last great party. In her time the only guests they had were relatives making a Thanksgiving pilgrimage to pay their respects to the head of the family. Her father Henry was an only child, so she had no first cousins other than those on her mother's side, and they were not made welcome once her mother died. Second and third cousins like Pansy abounded. Traditionally these relatives had found employment within the Cavender empire if they wished. If not, they could count on their famous name to open doors elsewhere in the corridors of power.

The family tree was littered with politicians, Wall Street tycoons, TV producers, and even a governor. Mason's grandfather, Alexander, had been groomed since birth to run for president, but his campaign was eventually scuttled when the Blakes orchestrated a campaign of lies about a bigamous marriage to a former prostitute. A *black* former prostitute. The story had been huge at the time and Mason's father had never forgotten the humiliation, or the price his mother had paid for her role in the sordid debacle. When he drank, he would always insist that his father hadn't *married* the woman, for God's sake. But Mason now managed the trust fund that supported her in her old age, and it was clear from their few conversations that she had really loved Alexander, unlike his wife.

Mason's grandmother, Nancy, seemed to loathe him. She didn't have much interest in their only son either and had returned to her Park Avenue penthouse as soon as Henry started prep school. She used to sweep into Laudes Absalom a few times a year with her city friends, and they would party hard and tear up the countryside. She was killed on one such wild jaunt, when her car stalled on the railway track near Glendale and she was hit by the Sunday morning train. Her death had been the subject of a salacious *Vanity Fair* article titled "Another Doomed Bride—The Cavender Curse Strikes Again."

Nancy's portrait hung in the library next to that of Mason's mother. They both wore the Cavender Diamonds, a famous necklace Henry sold when he was trying to save Cavender Steel by converting his mills into manufacturing plants for auto parts. Unfortunately he'd swapped one dying industry for another, and having invested most of his personal wealth in the new strategy, he was in big trouble when foreign competition started affecting his bottom line. But Henry had refused to believe that Americans would buy cheap imported parts when they could have superior American-made products so he wouldn't move his manufacturing offshore.

And while the Cavender Corporation was crumbling around him, their enemies at Blake Industries were already out of the steel business and had moved into aerospace and high-tech arms manufacturing, buying up patents and investing spare cash in Silicon Valley. Their shareholdings in firms like Intel, IBM, and Apple were reportedly worth a hundred million and Blake Aerospace had just turned down a half-billion-dollar acquisition bid from Boeing. Mason wondered why Vienna was bothering to bid for a relic like Cavender. But, of course, the decision wasn't business, it was personal. Everything between the Blakes and the Cavenders was personal.

Mason cast a desperate look around the garden, struggling with the decision she had to make. If she accepted Vienna's offer, she didn't know how she could keep Laudes Absalom, let alone embark on the restoration she'd always dreamed of. Vienna's offer for the company wouldn't leave her with enough cash to repay both the banks and the pension fund. Laudes Absalom would have to be auctioned to make up the difference. And there would be nothing left to finance Azaria's diamond farming operation if Mason couldn't find an investor. Meanwhile they were falling deeper in debt with every month and the banks were going to pull the plug at any moment. She had two choices. She could accept Vienna's offer, which was higher than the book value of their assets. Or the company could simply file for bankruptcy. Most

Cavender employees would lose most of their pension entitlements, but Mason would be able to keep Laudes Absalom.

The thought turned her stomach. The option was perfectly legal, but she couldn't imagine anything more disgraceful. Robber barons like the men who ran Enron or Countrywide might stoop to stealing money from employees to fund their millionaire lifestyles, but no Cavender would sink so low. Whatever her family's faults, they had always done right by the people who were loyal to them.

"What am I to do?" she asked the garden.

She often found her answers strolling the mossy bricks around the sundial, but tonight all she could hear was the rustle of a breeze through the pines wall and the melodic groans of the bamboo grove that led to the maze. She and Lynden used to hide there when they were kids, waiting for their father to cool off after his rages. Mason would bring icepacks and the first aid kit, and they would treat their respective injuries. When all was quiet, they would creep back indoors and Mrs. Danville would make them sandwiches in the kitchen.

Mason massaged Ralph behind the ears and listened intently as another faint howl carried through the night air. "Damn," she mumbled. If there was an injured dog on her property, she would not be able to go back to bed until she'd found it.

She trudged along the pathway until she came to the family cemetery. Lynden was buried beneath the sycamore tree he used to climb as a boy. Mason paused at the simple black granite crypt. The distinctive citrus fragrance of daphne, a favorite flower of Lynden's, sweetened the woody air. She'd filled the classical urns on either side with freshly cut stems as soon as she'd arrived home after her trip to Boston.

Ralph hunkered down at her side as she paid her respects. She didn't pray. She'd given up doing that when her mother died. Numbly, she stared down at the name etched on the shiny surface. In the moonlight she could pick out the letters that should have been her own. She buried her head in her hands and wept silently. She had no idea how she'd survived that plane crash. A passing motorist had dragged her from the wreckage. Lynden was already dead. All she had was a few scratches and a concussion.

If she'd been at the controls, they would have landed safely.

She was a better pilot than her brother, but she'd indulged his ego and his illusions. Lynden was the bad boy bachelor with the fast cars and the private plane. She'd always boosted his confidence, knowing how important it was for the Cavender heir to become the man the family needed at its head. After three decades of mismanagement, the corporation had to have leadership and Mason would never be a smooth-talking charmer. But now, with Azaria seeking investors, she would be stuck in New York for most of the next two months, pressing the flesh. Then there was the New Jersey mobster.

Mason dreaded to think what that was about. As far as she knew Lynden didn't have a gambling problem, and if he owed money to loan sharks, she was quite sure they would have made their demands before she had time to bury him. Obviously there was something else he'd been afraid to tell her.

"God damn it, Lynden," she choked out. "How could you do this to me?"

She stepped back from the crypt, trembling with barely controlled rage. Of all the emotions suffocating her, the hardest to deal with was her anger. She wanted to claw at something, to throw her head back and howl.

She knew what she had to do, but the thought was unbearable. She almost wished Vienna *had* shot her, although a swift end would have been too merciful; Vienna wanted to watch her squirm. Ralph nuzzled her hand and Mason turned away from her cowardly thoughts and continued along the path with her head down and her shoulders hunched. The gate at the end led onto the lawns. She heaved it open and jogged down the slope toward the lake. Ralph bounded ahead, anticipating their usual foray along the winding path into the pines.

Mason called him back, but fell silent when she glimpsed a pale splash of movement through the trees. It was a dog coming straight for her. Pale, tall, and graceful with a plumed tail. She stood completely still, her body angled slightly away so she didn't spook the nervous animal. When it veered across the lawn toward the temple, she broke into a run, inhaling the smell of wet grass as her feet struck the soft turf. She whistled but the dog didn't look back until it reached the temple steps. Mason slowed, keeping Ralph at her heel as it regarded her. She tried to make out the dog's breed characteristics, but it vanished into the deep shadows of the portico before she could be certain. The face, ears, and tail looked like those of a Saluki. Animals usually responded to her but Salukis were an aloof breed, so this one could be shy.

Signaling Ralph to stay, she walked the final yards to the temple and climbed the moonlit steps. Sidling around the pillars, she listened for the sound of panting. All she could hear was the faint, faraway shush of the north woods alongside the driveway. She made a circuit of the temple and checked the interior chamber. There was no trace of the dog. Puzzled, she stared out at the glassy glow of the lake and the dark mass of the house. The elegant Saluki was nowhere to be seen.

Ralph stood and wagged his stubby tail as she descended the steps. His alert posture and beaming stare had given way to a more relaxed attitude. Mason signaled him and he loped off toward the front of the house. Shivering in the chill September air, she took a last look around, then followed. She was relieved. If the animal had been able to give her the slip so effortlessly, it was uninjured and must have simply strayed into the grounds from a nearby property. By now, it was probably bounding up the driveway at its own home. If the owners were anything like her, they would be outside with flashlights searching for their missing pet.

Smiling at the thought, she went back to the house. Several clocks chimed the hour as she trudged upstairs. It was 3.00 a.m. She was about to face another day without the only person who had ever truly loved her.

Chapter Seven

"What do you want?" Mason asked. Her dark eyes raked Vienna suspiciously. She didn't open the front door any further. In fact, it looked like she was about to slam it.

Vienna stuck her foot in the gap. "May I come in?"

Her neighbor hesitated, then grudgingly swung the door back and feigned a courtly bow. "As my lady wishes."

"Well, this is a promising beginning." Vienna was already regretting her decision to deliver the Winchester in person. She should have used FedEx. She should have known that the minute she entered her enemy's lair she would feel the way she always felt around Mason. Dry-mouthed. Lust-struck. A disgrace to her family name.

Mason wasn't doing anything to cause the change in Vienna's heartbeat. She was simply standing a few feet away, her hands on her hips, those hot eyes flashing resentment. A loose white shirt was shoved into her black jeans. Beneath it she wore no bra and her nipples were distinct shadows beneath the fabric. Vienna couldn't drag her mind off the memory of her breasts and that muscular torso. She wanted to rip the shirt away and touch the flesh Mason had exposed that day in her office. Shocked by the urge, she felt her face flame.

"Ah…my rifle?" Mason prompted.

Vienna presented the weapon to her lying flat across both hands. She couldn't meet Mason's eyes but could feel them burning into her. Yes, this was a bad idea. And she hadn't told Tazio Pantano she was coming here. Wondering when she would ever stop behaving irrationally around her longtime adversary, she said stiffly, "I know you've had a rough couple of weeks. I hope you're feeling better."

"Liar."

Stung, Vienna jerked her head up. "Has it ever occurred to you that this whole situation is no picnic for me either?"

Mason gave a terse little laugh as she took the rifle. "Which part? The part about destroying everything that matters to me? Or the so-called accident? Or trying to snatch my company when we both know there's no financial gain for you? Tell me, is all of this because I turned you down that time?"

"Don't flatter yourself."

"Oh, that's right. How stupid of me to forget. I was supposed to be grateful, wasn't I? A pity fuck from Vienna Blake, the irresistible princess. The woman who could have anyone."

Vienna cringed inwardly. She should have guessed that Mason would throw that embarrassing evening in her face one day. "That was a long time ago and we both know I was drunk."

"Which is precisely the time when people say what they really think. As I recall, you said you were doing me a favor."

"I didn't use those words, and anyway…it wasn't what I meant."

"Like you remember anything about that night."

Mason's contempt blistered across Vienna's conscience, reminding her of events she'd rather forget. She stared out the gap in the door, knowing she should be walking back the way she came, not standing here letting Mason get under her skin again. She wished she *didn't* remember that night, but it was as if the party had only happened weeks ago, not years. The humiliation and rejection were still gut-wrenching.

Mason was the last person she'd expected to see that night. Then there was the date on her arm, a worldly, accomplished woman who made Vienna painfully aware of her own smug sophomore banality. Determined to be noticed, Vienna had tossed back drinks too fast and flirted too obviously, all the while observing Mason with that woman. Leaning over her. Bringing her cocktails. And claiming her with the casual possessiveness of a lover. A touch to the cheek. A lowered head. Constant eye contact. Mason and her girlfriend shared a coded language that excluded her completely. Every hint of intimacy had gouged at Vienna until she was seething with resentment. All she could think about was getting between them, stealing Mason's attention away from the woman who held it.

Looking back, she couldn't believe her immaturity. Or her jealousy. She could still see the incredulous look on Mason's face when Vienna cornered her alone and smoking a cigar in a secluded corner of the back garden. Vienna couldn't remember exactly what she'd said in her clumsy seduction attempt, but the words had come out all wrong. She'd tried to be sophisticated, to sound more experienced than she was. Mason's insolent taunt about her virginity six years earlier had hammered in her mind. *Go play with your dolls.*

She'd alluded to a retinue of lovers she didn't have and flaunted a sexual vocabulary borrowed from girls in her sorority. All the while, as she made a fool of herself, Mason never stopped devouring her with a stare that made every muscle tremble.

When she finally ran out of steam, Mason asked, "What's your point?"

"I'm suggesting we could get out of here and have some fun."

Mason slowly extinguished her cigar. "Why would I want to sleep with a woman who gives herself away so cheaply?"

Vienna cloaked her embarrassment with a phony laugh and a flirtatious pout. "Hey, any lesbian here would kill to be in your shoes, Cavender. They all want me, but I picked *you.*"

"I'm bowled over." Mason's bored response burned its way through the haze of alcohol into Vienna's brain. "But here's the thing. I'm with someone else tonight. She doesn't come from money, but she has real class…I won't even try to explain what that means. You wouldn't understand."

"You bitch."

Mason wasn't done. "Maybe if I was a jerk…and also a moron, I'd dump her so I could fuck you. But shallow narcissists don't do it for me, sorry."

Stunned by the insult, Vienna swung her hand at Mason's face and missed. "I'll make you sorry, all right…sorry you ever said that."

Mason caught hold of her arm before she could take better aim. "You're drunk," she said, frog-marching her toward the front gates. "And you're a menace to yourself and others. I'm taking you back to your room so you can sleep it off."

"Are you kidding me?" Vienna tried to shake herself free. "Who do you think you are?"

Mason had given her an answer, but the words were inaudible and the girlfriend had shown up then. She helped Vienna into the backseat of Mason's car and then assisted her up to her room once they reached the building. She and Mason had stayed for the next hour while Vienna disgraced herself by vomiting and sobbing incoherently about not measuring up to her father's expectations. The girlfriend made coffee and helped Vienna undress, then put her to bed. She seemed genuinely nice, which only made matters worse.

Vienna couldn't remember her name, so days later when she wanted to apologize to her, the only option was to call Mason. But she hadn't picked up the phone. The next time she saw the woman was five years later on a television program about aid workers in Rwanda. She was making a difference, helping genocide survivors start small businesses. Vienna sent a donation.

Running a hand over her stinging eyes, she forced herself present. Mason had just said something else, but she hadn't been listening. "I'm sorry," she mumbled. "Could you repeat that?"

"I said I've never done you harm."

"Perhaps not directly," Vienna conceded. "But your father spent his whole life attacking my family, and your brother was blackmailing one of my cousins, the man who happens to be one of my vice presidents."

"So that's why you arranged the accident. That snake you call a relative likes underage girls, but hey, who cares? You're outraged because my brother called him out! That's mind-bending."

Vienna lifted a hand to her cheek, wiping at something that wasn't there, giving herself time to process what she'd just heard. She felt nauseous. Her cousin's story was completely different. Andy had stood in front of her desk a month ago, begging her to help save his marriage. He'd made a terrible mistake. Somehow Lynden had photos of him with a girl he'd met at a party. It was obviously a set-up. Lynden wanted him to back off a Chinese supplier they'd been pressuring to stop selling products to the Cavender Corporation. He was going to send the photos to Andy's wife.

"My cousin was an idiot, but the Chinese situation is just business. Your brother made it personal. There are children involved."

"Yes, girls kept as sex slaves for men like your cousin to assault."

"That's an outright lie."

"Sure. Go ahead and tell yourself that if it helps you sleep at night." Mason paused, her focus seeming to shift inward. In a curiously absent tone, she murmured, "How ironic."

"What do you mean?" Vienna wished she could dismiss Mason's accusation with absolute certainty, but she kept seeing Andy's face when she picked up the phone to call the police.

He'd begged her to appease Lynden, claiming that if the police got involved his wife would soon know everything. Vienna had seen his point. It ate at her to have to go cap in hand to a Cavender, but Lynden was the perfect gentleman when she phoned him. No crowing. No nastiness. They'd spoken civilly and agreed that if she stayed away from his suppliers, he would destroy the photographs. She'd trusted him to keep his word. That was another Cavender weak spot, their adherence to outdated principles. Lynden, despite his playboy habits, would have gone down with the *Titanic* before he pushed past a woman to get to a lifeboat. His sister was the same, an anachronism.

"Do you ever wonder how things might have been?" Mason asked, as if she'd been brooding on the question while Vienna's mind was elsewhere. "Who we could be to each other, if it wasn't for all…this?"

"*This* is the reality," Vienna replied. "There's no point in what-ifs."

Mason studied her for several long, excruciating seconds, then said in a low, husky tone, "*What if* I told you I want to kiss you. Would that change your reality?"

The air escaped Vienna's lungs in a rush. Disoriented, she repeated Mason's words silently to herself and decided she must have misheard, or worse, unconsciously fantasized. "What?"

"Don't look at me like you don't know what I'm talking about," Mason said bitterly. "We've been dancing around this our whole lives."

"Speak for yourself," Vienna retorted.

"Are you saying you don't think about it?"

"Now who's flattering herself?"

"I take it that's a *no*."

"No. I mean, yes."

"Why, because you get so many better offers?" When Vienna

didn't answer, Mason said softly, "What if I told you I've wanted you since the first time I saw you. I think about taking you…so you can never wash me off."

Knees close to buckling, Vienna said, "Then I'd know you were lying." As soon as she'd snapped the response out, she realized she sounded disappointed.

Mason looked down. The corners of her mouth pulled just enough to hint at satisfaction. "That's what I thought."

Knowing she'd stupidly exposed herself, Vienna reached for the edge of the door but she couldn't escape fast enough. Mason's hand clamped down on hers. Her touch struck Vienna's senses like a sledgehammer, driving a quivering echo through every inch of flesh. She couldn't find words to explain the strange joy of having those fingers sealed to hers and Mason's body aligned against hers. They stood like dancers awaiting a band to strike up.

Unable to help herself, Vienna half turned and stared into Mason's eyes. Something in their depths stirred her unbearably. She knew that look. She'd seen the same wounded craving the day she and Mason stood on either side of the big iron gates of Laudes Absalom when they were children. She felt the same stricken shame now that she'd experienced then, at the sight of Mason's bruises. There were no visible injuries anymore, yet she could sense a pain so deep it tore at her.

Hiding her welling emotion, she looked away. There was nothing she could do. Mason had lost her brother. Vienna was only making a bad situation worse by intruding on her grief. She backed up, but Mason moved with her.

"Vienna. I'm not lying. Don't go."

She was so close each word brushed Vienna's skin like the calling card of a kiss. The thought made her ache. Her eyes fell to Mason's mouth, then to the tug of sinew under the smoothness of her neck. The pulse she saw there matched the relentless throb between Vienna's legs. It was as if she and Mason shared the same ebb and flow, as if their life forces had somehow converged. A rush of warmth rose from Vienna's womb to her chest heralding something deep inside her, a primal creature brought to life and summoned to the surface.

She let go of the door. As her arm fell, Mason's fell with it and she caught Vienna gently around the waist. Bringing her face-to-face, she leaned in until her brow rested against Vienna's. They stood in silent accord, abandoning one language for another, forsaking the thorny tangle of words for the silken subtlety of touch. Mason drew her fingertips over Vienna's eyelids and down her cheeks to her lips. Her mouth followed the same delicate path, sampling the skin, brushing and kissing until Vienna's lips offered the faintest trembling pressure in return.

Mason's body stiffened at the response and her fingers dug into Vienna's hips as though a pawing thing had just unsheathed itself within her. A hand moved to cradle Vienna's head, tilting it back, exposing her to a restless hunger finally given free rein. Mere kisses could never satisfy the devouring need. Vienna could feel the heat emanating from Mason's body and pressed blindly into her, wanting to enfold and be enfolded. Wanting to give herself and hold nothing back.

Mason's taste infused her mouth. Vienna invited her cleaving tongue deeper and dragged the shirt free of Mason's jeans. The flesh she encountered flinched beneath her touch. She slid her hand upward, overlapping the push of breast and nipple, owning every inch her palm and fingers could encompass. A groan filled her mouth. She couldn't tell if the swell of sound was hers or Mason's. The nipple beneath her palm relayed its own tight, hard message.

Wanting more, Vienna stepped back and finished removing Mason's shirt. And there she was, breasts rising and falling with each breath, her desire tangible in the stillness of her face and the fierce intent gleaming from her eyes. One hand dropped to her belt and she flipped the buckle open and dragged the heavy zipper down.

"Touch me," she whispered, drawing Vienna's hand past the open fly.

Damp skin met her fingers and Mason's eyes darkened even more, the pupils voiding all color but for a thin slate-colored rim. Vienna brought her other hand up, trailing it gently over the plane of Mason's cheek. Her thumb brushed across the bottom lip, then they were kissing again and stumbling into the cavernous hall. Their breathing was amplified, bouncing off the paneled walls. Fractured rainbows danced around them as sunlight spilled through the leaded windows. They collided with something solid, the banister of the grand central staircase.

Vienna pushed past the crotch of Mason's jeans, gasping when she encountered moist flesh. For a split second she froze and drew back, blood pounding in her ears. On the walls above, blades gleamed and glassy eyes observed. Painted faces stared down from the upstairs gallery, Cavenders witnessing the unimaginable. Then Mason parted Vienna's lips in a rough, hot kiss that left no room for anything but the slippery urgency of their explorations. With a single sharp tug, she tore open Vienna's silk shirt and slid it down, letting it fall on the floor. The flimsy lace bra followed.

Working her hand back along the seam of Mason's jeans, Vienna didn't hesitate this time. "You're so hard," she said when she found the rigid apex of Mason's clit. Curling her fingers around either side of the shaft, she slowly milked.

Mason breathed, "Oh, God," then her hand stilled Vienna's. "No. It's too soon. I don't want to come yet."

Vienna let her grip relax. "Are you so easy?"

"Where you're concerned, yes." Mason sighed. "You have no idea how much I want you."

"Prove it." Vienna knotted her fingers through Mason's hair and pushed her head down.

Every sensation was exquisite. Mason kissed and bit a hot path to the base of her throat before descending to rest her cheek directly over Vienna's heart. Vienna watched as she took possession of a nipple, circling the pink tip slowly with a wet fingertip before taking the tight, tender flesh into her mouth. At the same time, she cupped Vienna's flushed breasts, squeezing and caressing them until they felt heavy with arousal.

Vienna sagged back against the smooth wood and pushed clumsily at her slacks and panties. Mason paused to drag them down and helped her balance as she kicked them aside. Gasping, Vienna felt the pressure of a hand between her thighs. Mason cupped her almost too gently. A low animal growl rose from her throat, and Vienna's guttural answer came from somewhere deep down, a place she didn't even know existed.

Spellbound, she drew Mason to her once more. Their faces were only inches apart. The air seemed dense, slowing the passage of time, and Vienna recognized something eternal and irresistible between them, a force she'd always known was there. It had been that way from their first look, from the moment Mason had hoisted her onto that horse and carried her off like the spoils of battle.

In the grip of some doomed enchantment, Vienna had belonged to her ever since. She could not imagine belonging to any other. The realization stunned her, and she fought it just as instinctively as she rejoiced in it. Fear pierced her erotic trance, turning up the volume on the frantic voice in the back of her mind that kept urging her to stop. She glanced distractedly around. She couldn't let this happen. She struggled, but Mason pushed her hard against the railing, bearing her weight.

Her lips smothered the beginnings of a protest. The room seemed to recede. "Don't fight it," Mason murmured in pauses between deep kisses. "Wrap your legs around me."

And then she was inside, and Vienna closed her eyes, blocking out everything but the frantic pounding of her heart and the gorgeous thrill of her surrender. Severed from all coherent thought, she dug her nails into Mason's shoulders and bore down, abandoning herself to the rhythmic thrusts. A shudder locked every muscle and compressed her at the core, squeezing Mason's fingers so tightly that they both cried out.

Mason slowed her strokes and Vienna met each upward thrust with a moan of pleasure. When the first faint tremors quivered through her groin, she bit down hard and a metallic rush broke across her tongue. Dazed, she lifted her head and tried to move her swollen lips. *More.* Had the word actually emerged?

Passion cramped Mason's face. Blood stained her mouth. She licked it off, asking hoarsely, "What? Tell me what you need. Anything."

Only seconds from letting go, Vienna couldn't speak. Her eyes were anchored to Mason's. *You.* The answer lay trapped on her swollen lips.

"Come for me," Mason gasped out. "I want to watch you come."

Pressure gathered until Vienna couldn't hold back. Shaking, gasping, she spilled over the fingers buried inside. For a long time they clung together, propped against the side of the staircase, slippery with sweat. Then Mason carefully withdrew and held Vienna while she found her footing. Stroking her hair, she kissed her cheek and murmured Vienna's name.

The naked yearning in her voice rubbed Vienna's soul raw. Her eyes welled. Hardly knowing where to look, she focused on the items of clothing scattered across the floor.

"Are you okay?" Mason asked in a whisper.

"No, not really," Vienna croaked out. She didn't know what she felt. Shock. Desire. Despair. All were eclipsed by a sudden terrible panic that made her wrench away. Choking back sobs, she collected her clothing from the floor.

"Vienna...stop." Mason touched her shoulder gingerly. "Come upstairs with me. I think we should talk."

"There's nothing to discuss." Vienna moved out of reach. Her whole body felt so tender she almost cried out as she dragged on her panties and slacks. Her blouse was unwearable, the buttons torn. Mason picked up her own white shirt and handed it to her.

"Vienna, I—"

"Don't say a word." A clock struck the hour, rattling her nerves. Vienna felt clammy as she buttoned the shirt and rolled up the sleeves.

Mason refastened her jeans with hands that shook. "I'll walk you home."

It took all Vienna's self-control not to scream at her. She couldn't believe she'd allowed this to happen. "No, I'm fine."

"I don't think so."

Somehow Vienna found her boardroom dispassion. "Mason, this was a mistake."

"No," Mason said starkly. "*This* was meant to be."

"I won't deny we have some kind of weird chemistry," Vienna said, refusing to get into verbal sparring. "But whatever just happened... it doesn't change anything."

"It changes *everything*," Mason said, making no attempt to cover her naked breasts. "We just made love."

"We fucked in your hall like a pair of hormonal high schoolers," Vienna corrected her coldly. "Let's not break out the promise rings, okay?"

Mason froze like she'd been slapped. Her face lost its color. In a voice rough with emotion, she said, "I've made a lot of assumptions about you over the years, but I never took you for a coward."

"Well, now you know." Vienna could smell their mixed scents on the borrowed shirt. The tangy residue stabbed at her heart and tore through her senses, undoing her from the inside out. Afraid that Mason would see her turmoil, she headed for the door. "I have to go."

She wrenched the door back and darted down the front steps, cursing under her breath. She heard Mason call after her but didn't slow down. A huge weight seemed to crush her and she felt like a child again, facing her father's wrath after the horse incident. His words rang in her ears. *You let your family down. You let me down. But worst of all, you let yourself down.* The rebellious part of her wanted to yell *Fuck you and fuck the family.* She almost turned around right then and ran back to Mason, but she knew she would be running toward disaster. Everything the Cavenders touched turned to ruin. Mason would destroy her.

Tears flooded over her cheeks and she braced her shoulders against the sobs she couldn't control. The day was overcast. A cool breeze gathered shoals of red and gold leaves and spread them in its wake. The oak trees creaked and the pines rustled. Vienna walked so blindly, she didn't realize she'd veered across the lawn toward the temple until she found herself in its shadow. As though stepping into a dream, her feet carried her up the pale marble steps to the broad portico. She glanced back once from within the colonnade to be certain she hadn't been followed, then slipped into the chamber.

A gleaming tomb stood beneath the high dome at the center, two separate marble coffins side by side. Vienna read the upright Roman letters chiseled into each: NATHANIEL CAVENDER and FANNY BLAKE CAVENDER. They'd married back in the days when the families were allies, so their son Hugo was half Blake. That hadn't stopped him from murdering his own uncle, Benedict Blake. He'd then tried to take over the company their families jointly owned, waging a pitched battle for control with Benedict's son, Truman.

Hugo and Truman had grown up together as inseparable friends, the men on whom the future of their families rested. Hugo's brutal act had made them bitter enemies, and the Blakes and the Cavenders had been fighting ever since. No one really seemed sure why Hugo had murdered Truman's father, but greed was the general consensus. Being two years older than Truman and half-Blake himself, Hugo evidently saw himself as the rightful president of the company. His mother Fanny was the firstborn Blake of her generation, but because of sexism her younger brother Benedict was destined to head the family. All the same, her status and her marriage to the Cavender heir meant that her son had been raised like a prince, the ultimate symbol of their united houses.

But the man who should have personified the best of both worlds, instead betrayed all they stood for. He was never charged with the killing. At the time, the Cavenders' wealth and power made them virtually untouchable. According to Blake legend, the Cavender Curse began that year. Only days earlier Hugo's wife Estelle had drowned in the lake at Laudes Absalom, soon after their son was born. At the time there was speculation that foul play was involved; after all, Hugo had a violent streak and some thought he regretted marrying the daughter of servants. Estelle had always been a problem.

Her mother, Sally Gibson, had been governess to the youngest two of the "Famous Four," the appellation bestowed on Benedict Blake's sisters, legendary society beauties in their time. A woman from a respectable family, Sally had married beneath her, wedding the Blake's head gardener in haste after the couple found they were expecting a child. The Blakes had generously allowed them to remain in their employment despite this impropriety, and had even built a cottage on the property for the pair. After Estelle was born, she was treated like family and allowed to play with Truman, who was only a year older. The two children had their lessons with Hugo Cavender in the schoolroom the families shared.

They were taught by Estelle's mother until the boys were deemed too old to take their lessons from a woman, then a tutor was hired, a scholarly man who educated them before they were sent to prep school. As the years went by, it came as a shock to everyone that by the time they entered college, both Hugo and Truman wanted Estelle's hand in marriage. The girl who'd been like a younger sister to them all their lives suddenly became a cause of tension, with both men competing for her.

The Blakes tried to arrange a more appropriate match for Estelle, but she'd been brought up a lady. She wrote poetry and played the pianoforte. How could she be expected to settle down with a working man? Fortunately, being a Blake, Truman came to his senses in the end and married a suitable debutante. But Hugh Cavender always got what he wanted. Only weeks after his father died, he walked Estelle down the aisle, free of parental disapproval. A year later their son Thomas Blake Cavender was born. He never knew his mother, of course, and was raised by his grandmother Fanny, the woman whose gleaming marble coffin stood before Vienna.

Very few people knew their family histories going back almost two hundred years, she supposed, but the Blakes kept faith with the lessons of the past, handing them down as accumulated wisdom. Vienna had only been twelve years old when she was first permitted to read the diaries kept by Patience Blake, a forebear who had recorded the scandal with fourteen-year-old awe. Patience found the whole episode deeply romantic and had seen herself as a go-between, having at some point carried notes between her cousin Truman and the beautiful Estelle.

Vienna couldn't remember all the colorfully embellished details, but it was clear that Truman's advances were not unwelcome. Naturally Patience had read every letter entrusted to her and faithfully recorded the contents in her diary. Estelle's short missives were models of propriety, offering only circumspect encouragement to the man bent on wooing her. Truman's replies could best be described as the ramblings of a young man besotted. The communications had ceased abruptly in 1869 and Patience's diary recorded the engagement of Estelle to Hugo Cavender, scandalously soon after his father's funeral.

Eventually Patience had traipsed off to Paris where she had a long list of lovers, and gave birth to a daughter, Colette, whose fatherhood was a mystery. Patience's European diaries had found their way back to the Blake library after World War One, carried by a friend of hers who reported that Patience had died of grief after her daughter was killed. Colette had been a battlefield nurse at a casualty clearing station near Saint Omer when German planes bombed the hospital tents.

Several of her letters were tucked inside one of Patience's diaries along with a faded sepia photograph of a soldier who'd been courting Colette. Their contents had always intrigued Vienna because Colette carefully avoided the use of a pronoun when describing her beau and wrote strangely feminine descriptions of him. Vienna had recognized something in those letters that made her question her own sexuality for the first time. She'd always wondered what had happened to the officer in the photograph. Killed, no doubt, in a muddy, rat-infested trench on the Western Front and buried in a common grave.

She sighed and stared out the arched doorway to the lake. Two white swans glided together across the tranquil surface and Vienna recalled that the birds mated for life. Some even formed same-sex couples, like Romeo and Juliet, the famous pair whose return to Boston Public Garden was celebrated with a parade every year. When they were outed not so long ago as two Juliets, the city was in shock for months.

She stepped back outside and sat down on a carved bench

overlooking the water. Her legs had stopped shaking and her mind had cleared, allowing her to reclaim the detachment she'd abandoned earlier. The sky was grim, casting the lofty pines along the lake's eastern shore into deep shadow. Their pungent sweetness hung on the still air, and beneath the gathering rain clouds, the moribund fortress of Laudes Absalom languished in its decay. The deep silence of the surroundings was broken only by the cry of a bird somewhere above.

As Vienna looked up, a raven swooped low over the temple, inspecting her in several passes, then landed on the portico step a few yards away. Carrying something in its beak, the bird pranced fearlessly toward her, its bold eyes fixed on her face. Vienna sat very still and it hopped up onto the bench. Before she could touch its glossy black feathers, it dropped a small, tightly rolled piece of paper in her lap and instantly took flight in the direction of the house.

Disconcerted, Vienna unfurled the note and stared down at two lines of beautiful calligraphy.

When the Gods wish to punish us,
they answer our prayers.

Chapter Eight

"Mason, are you in for lunch?"

Mason turned around, belatedly registering Mrs. Danville's presence in the library doorway. She wasn't sure how long the housekeeper had stood there unobserved. She'd been so preoccupied she hadn't noticed the usual discreet knock or Ralph's arrival. After she watched Ulysses deliver the Oscar Wilde quotation, Mason had thought about going down but she'd vacillated too long. Her infuriated neighbor had fled the temple and was almost at the gatehouse now, her loose red hair billowing as the wind picked up.

"I'll have something in my room," Mason said, checking the button at her collar. She could smell Vienna on her hands, a sensory trigger that rebounded painfully through her body, twisting her nipples and heating her groin.

An appalling thought crossed her mind. What if Mrs. Danville had returned from her weekly expedition to St. Paul's Church in Stockbridge and walked in on them? In her time the redoubtable housekeeper had seen it all, and she knew how to be discreet, but Mason preferred to spare her embarrassment.

"Dinner this evening at the usual time?" Mrs. Danville asked showing no sign that she'd noticed Mason's fluster.

"Yes. Just the household."

Mason stroked Ralph's head so she wouldn't fidget. Mrs. Danville always fed him before she departed for church and he napped near the kitchen fire if she left something cooking. He then stuck to the housekeeper's side for the rest of the day until she slipped him a succulent morsel or two. Mason pretended not to know about these treats. Officially Mrs. Danville frowned on indulging pets or children.

"I'll serve in the kitchen parlor, then?" the housekeeper asked.

No answer was necessary, but Mason adhered to the draconian script that governed their interactions. She was the head of the household and Mrs. Danville expected her to behave accordingly. "Yes, that will be fine, thank you."

"Mr. Pettibone brought in a side of venison," Mrs. Danville said, prompting Ulysses to tilt his head as though captivated by a siren song. He harbored a passion for the housekeeper that was not returned.

Cawing softly, he jumped down from Mason's shoulder to his perch, bobbing and puffing out his lustrous blue-black feathers. When this attracted only doggish wonder from Ralph, he lowered his head and spread his wings, making a gallant bow.

Immune to the display, Mrs. Danville continued, "I'm spit-roasting the haunch in collops."

"Excellent." The thought made Mason queasy. She would only eat the vegetables, but Mrs. Danville took no pleasure in cooking unless she could serve fine meat dishes and good wine, so Mason responded in the manner expected of her. "Have Mr. Pettibone open a Pommard."

Mrs. Danville consulted the notebook that swung from a cord at her waist. "Domaine de la Vougeraie?"

"Yes, by all means." Mason had a huge wine cellar to work through and once a bottle was opened she could offer it to her staff, since she avoided alcohol herself—she didn't want to become her father.

Mrs. Danville's lips thinned a little. "That bird is making a nuisance of himself again, dropping things through the kitchen window."

Poor Ulysses had chosen the wrong woman to try to impress with shiny objects. Mrs. Danville despised sentiment.

Mason offered her usual ineffectual deterrent. "I'll confine him for a few days."

"Thank you." Mrs. Danville flipped a page. As her index finger moved down the contents, Ulysses gazed longingly at the one ring she wore, a plain gold signet. "Miss Blake wishes to meet Dúlcifal."

Mason froze. Had the two seen each other as Vienna was departing? If so, Mrs. Danville would have noticed her wearing Mason's shirt. Very little escaped her. "She asked you herself?"

"Mr. O'Grady informed me."

Surprised that the stable manager hadn't mentioned this unusual request, Mason said, "She can visit the barns tomorrow morning. I won't be taking Dúlcifal out until after nine."

"Very well." Mrs. Danville dropped the notebook and smoothed her hands down her dark gray gabardine skirt. A woman of austere appearance and temperament, she normally wore the skirt with a crisp white cotton blouse and a dove gray cashmere cardigan buttoned all the way up. Today being Sunday, she had exchanged the cotton blouse for one in silk crepe with a dainty crocheted border of ivory lace. Her face was framed on either side with the soft reverse roll hairstyle she adopted for outings that warranted a hat. For dinner the hair would be drawn back up into the usual tight silver-white topknot and speared with the art deco comb her mother, also a Cavender housekeeper, had handed down to her.

"There was a man hanging about the stables yesterday, by the way," Mason said. "I have no idea how he found his way into the grounds, but he's not to be let in again."

"Ah, the ruffian in the brothel creepers?"

"I didn't notice his shoes. Pantano is the name."

With a disdainful sniff, Mrs. Danville recorded this information in her notebook. "I can't image the fellow is acquainted with an honest day's work," she tonelessly observed, "yet it appears he is employed by our neighbor."

Shocked, Mason said, "By Vienna? Are you sure?"

"According to Mrs. Hardy he consumed half a beef Wellington last night, virtually single handed. And without a green vegetable."

Mason stilled her hands by clasping them behind her back. "In what capacity is Mr. Pantano employed, do you know?"

"One can only speculate. He has some business here on behalf of a family friend in New Jersey, or that's the story, for what it's worth."

Mrs. Danville was always miserly with information acquired from her contacts in the village, or directly from Bridget Hardy. The two housekeepers always gossiped after church and Mason knew exactly what must have changed hands that morning, apart from mutual dismay over Pantano's gluttony. If the Cavenders had venison, it would also be served at the Blake household this week, along with some vague explanation of its origins. Everyone knew the widowed Mr. Pettibone was enamored of Mrs. Danville and brought offerings of pheasant and venison whenever he and his son went hunting, and that Mrs. Danville shared this largesse. But the Blakes always acted as if dressed game fell from the sky. God forbid anyone acknowledge that the staff pooled resources between the two households.

Mason thanked Mrs. Danville and returned to her post at the window. She didn't buy the "family friend" bullshit for a minute. *That bitch.* She'd hired a Mafia thug to do her bidding. The veiled threat to Dúlcifal now made sense, as did the lowball offer. Well, if Vienna thought she could trick Mason into selling Laudes Absalom for peanuts, she had another thing coming. Was that why she'd arrived on the doorstep earlier—Plan B: weaken the enemy's defenses by seducing her?

Aggravated, Mason put Ulysses in his aviary, dropped the stopper in her inkwell, and strode out of the library. Once she was upstairs in her room, she stripped off her clothes and turned the shower on. How she could have fallen for that blushing damsel act she had no idea. Those nervous looks, that quivering mouth. Disgusted with herself, she stood under the hot jets and scrubbed all trace of Vienna off her body. But she couldn't erase the memory of her. The soft cries of pleasure. The irresistible wetness and writhing pleas for more. Those eyes, as beguiling as the ocean, and just as treacherous. Mason should have known better than to believe what she saw in them, the craving that matched her own.

When would this enchantment end?

She sagged against the tile wall, every nerve end quivering. She never felt like this, she never pined and mooned over any woman. Only Vienna. Wanting her was like a sickness. At times she thought she was cured. Months would pass. A year. Life would draw her in. The symptoms would fade. But then she would wake from another of those dreams, fully aroused, desperate for release and capable only of seeing *her*. That face, that throat, that walk. And she would have to deal with the throbbing pressure between her legs, seeking release just as she was now.

Delaying the moment, Mason let herself drift into a favorite fantasy. Soft focus. A field of wildflowers. Vienna in a long clinging dress like a medieval virgin, her red hair rippling past her waist. Mason would kneel in front of her and pledge her loyalty. Vienna would bestow a token, her girdle. Mason would wear it off to war, all the while imagining her beloved sitting at a window, chastely awaiting her return. Finally they would marry and on their wedding night, Mason would be afraid to touch her bride in case she was rejected—that in seeing who she really was, stripped of her armor and sword, Vienna would not love her.

In her fantasies, Vienna always took over then, and Mason would find herself on the edge of exploding, afraid to move an inch. Vienna would barely touch her. Their lips would meet and Mason would know everything, see it all with such clarity. They were meant to be joined like this. She knew no other way to feel complete.

Gasping, she closed her eyes tightly against the hot spray of the shower and drove her fingers down hard, calling up the image that always pushed her over the brink. Vienna with her legs spread and her hands on Mason's shoulders, drawing her deeper, demanding, "Come. Come now."

And Mason did.

❖

The face was handsome, the hair and eyes dark, as far as Vienna could tell from the degraded sepia image. She tucked the photograph back inside Colette's letter, disturbed that everywhere she looked she saw Mason Cavender. She'd just spent the past two hours trying to shake herself free of Mason's touch, but her body refused to be soothed into denial. She had bruises along the inside of one thigh where Mason's belt had dug in. Her throat wore the purple evidence of teeth. And the flesh Mason had invaded was exquisitely tender.

Vienna wasn't used to roughness. Her lovers, not exactly a legion, were too considerate to leave her sore. She never felt their impression inside her body afterward. Her stomach hollowed at the thought and she was instantly, infuriatingly wet again. Her nipples hurt. She couldn't swallow properly. Her thoughts were chaotic. She even entertained the idea of going back to Laudes Absalom and dragging Mason upstairs. Maybe, if they spent all night getting their fill of each other, they could get this inconvenient physical attraction out of their systems.

The thought was tempting, but not because she could convince herself that a night of limitless sex would end her infatuation. The real reason was less palatable by far. She felt cheated. That frantic coupling in the great hall hadn't been nearly enough. Vienna wanted more. She yearned to explore every smooth, firm contour and hidden recess of Mason's body, to feel every quiver of arousal. Mason was so responsive. So passionate. Vienna was both unnerved and fascinated by the dormant self Mason had awakened in her, a sexual being unfettered by common sense or duty, driven only by desire. Even now it strained restlessly within, like a wild thing wanting to return to its mate.

She'd seen the same compulsion blazing darkly from Mason's eyes and it had thrilled her. She recognized that need, she'd glimpsed it in veiled flashes since the first time they'd met. But this time was different. This time Mason didn't hide it, or couldn't fight it. Vienna loved that she had the power to inflame her, to make her betray her better judgment and ignore her reservations. And she had plenty of those; after all, she still blamed Vienna for her brother's death. Part of Vienna found that hard to endure and wanted to prove Mason wrong in her assessment. But the Blake in her cold-bloodedly assessed this new turn of events. She now had an extra weapon in her arsenal; the question was whether to use it. Imagine how completely she could defeat the last of the Cavenders if she also struck a blow to her heart.

Vienna cradled her head in her hands, repelled by the thought. A realization struck her then, a certainty she could not escape. If she did such a thing, if she seduced Mason into an affair and then discarded her, the heart more deeply wounded would be her own. Vienna stopped breathing. For several seconds she thought she was about to faint. Disbelief crowded her reasoning. No, it wasn't possible. She could accept that she was physically drawn to Mason. There'd always been a heightened awareness between them. But she refused to believe that the attraction was also emotional.

She decided she must be experiencing some kind of post-orgasmic elation. Brain chemistry was notoriously susceptible to hormones. Given the way hers were raging, she couldn't trust a single impulse she had, let alone an epiphany about her feelings for her enemy. Next thing she would be seeing the image of Christ in a can of beans.

Besides, Vienna didn't have to sink so low as to take her fight to the bedroom. Everything she'd worked for was coming to fruition. She could beat Mason cleanly, and that was the way she wanted to end this nightmare. The feud between the Blakes and the Cavenders had been personal for decades, but Vienna had never felt personally attached to their destruction. For her, the task was a business matter. She had a huge, complex corporation to run and couldn't afford to waste time on the family obsession. The Cavender issue was a distraction, one other family members were not above using as a lever. She was sick of hearing about the Cavenders, and in the end her father had been fed up, too. In his final days he'd offered her a piece of advice. *Finish it and move on. Don't let it eat you alive.*

The words weighed on her, for all they said about the choices he'd made and the regrets he seemed to have. Since childhood he'd been single-minded in his determination to live up to his father's expectations. Vienna knew how much it had pained him to "fail." He never stopped talking about Blake senior's deathbed wishes. Even dying of pneumonia in his eighties, the old man had the Cavenders in his sights. He blamed them for his illness. Cavender dogs kept coming over to Penwraithe, chasing the Blake cats. He was chasing an offender one day and had gone after it with his rifle. That was when he fell and broke his hip. He'd caught pneumonia in the hospital.

Vienna had only vague memories of that stressful period. She was six years old and sometimes sat at her grandfather's bedside holding his hand. She remembered the funeral because it was the only time she'd ever seen her father cry. Looking back, she realized that the wedding incident, when Mason disrupted the celebrations on her horse, must have rubbed salt in her father's fresh wounds. The episode had occurred less than a year after his father's death. Norris was still grieving and had shouldered the entire responsibility for running the family business. Vienna knew now how alone he must have felt.

His two sisters, in the Blake tradition, had received cash settlements from the family trust and shareholdings that would revert back to the company when they died. In exchange, the company would pay cash to their beneficiaries. For six generations, the Blakes had used this system to avoid boardroom battles. Ownership was not diluted across numerous descendents. Instead, eldest sons made out like bandits and everyone else had to content themselves with adequate wealth and very little influence. That was her father's other failure, Vienna reflected. No son. He never mentioned his disappointment to her or to Marjorie, but he didn't have to.

Henry Cavender had never missed a chance to rub his face in it. For that reason, as much as the wrongs of the past, Norris had been consumed with hatred for their neighbor. Desperate to ensure that there was nothing for his rival's son to inherit, he'd all but wiped the Cavenders out. There was little left for Vienna to do to complete his life's work but nail the lid on the coffin. She owed him that, and the day couldn't come soon enough. She wanted the deal done and was willing to pay a premium just to get the Cavenders out of her hair.

Under normal circumstances, she wouldn't have gone after the company at all; it was worthless. And the house was an even worse proposition, given the repairs it would need if she didn't demolish it. But Laudes Absalom symbolized victory even more than the Cavender Corporation. Once the Blakes owned the property, her ancestors could sleep easy in their graves, knowing justice was finally done.

Vienna wasn't planning to rip Mason off. She didn't care if she had to pay twice what the place was worth, so long as she could present a fait accompli at the next family gathering. Her two aunts, whose lifetime shareholdings gave them votes on the Blake board of directors, would hold her feet to the fire until she delivered, and her cousin Andy saw his VP position as nothing less than president-in-waiting. He constantly overreached and ran his own loyal clique of staff, who did their best to make Vienna feel irrelevant in her own company.

Vienna hadn't expected to find herself fighting battles on two fronts the day she took over Blake Industries, but her aunts thought Norris had made a huge mistake vesting his ownership entirely in her. They didn't want their shares repurchased by Blake Industries, and instead had plans afoot to transfer the holdings to their sons. Vienna knew an internal power struggle was inevitable, and to win it she needed to be free of the Cavender problem. Only Mason stood in her way.

Hence Pantano.

The move was clumsy, but it was a means to an end. Mason needed cash, and five million for that property was a good offer. Vienna had wanted to make it easy for her to accept by starting the bidding high. Unfortunately Pantano had taken it upon himself to try for a better deal. That was the trouble with enforcers of his ilk, it never crossed their minds that some people wouldn't just grab the money and run. One lousy million—Vienna was surprised that Mason hadn't set her dog on him. She only hoped he'd been convincing about buying the place for a boss back in Jersey who needed to lie low for a while. If Mason thought Vienna was the real buyer, she'd never sell.

She got up and made herself another espresso. Having a machine in the study meant she could work without interruption when she needed to. As she sipped the coffee she pondered her options once more. She had just instructed Pantano to go back tomorrow and put the real offer on the table. She was willing to go to eight million if Mason continued to hold out.

But what if Mason sent Pantano packing again? Vienna would be a fool not to use all means at her disposal to get what she wanted. She had no doubt that Mason desired her. Hopefully she hadn't blown her chances of closing the deal by running out on her after their encounter. She smothered the memory of Mason's words: *Do you ever wonder how things might have been?* Her drawn face and hurt stare still stabbed at Vienna. Mason hadn't even tried to hide her emotions. She'd exposed herself, just as she had that day in Vienna's office, only this time Vienna had taken a shot.

She knew her callous remark about the promise rings had hit home. That was her intention. She'd set out to trivialize the intimacy they'd just shared and had expected retaliation in kind, not that pained stare of betrayal. Not the jarring accusation of cowardice. And certainly not a message delivered by a raven. *When the Gods wish to punish us, they answer our prayers.*

Her prayer, for as long as she could remember, was to ruin Mason Cavender. She'd always known there would be a price to pay. But she never realized that money would be the least of it.

CHAPTER NINE

W ould you like to ride him?"
The low voice behind Vienna made her start. Heat flooded her cheeks. Willing herself not to sound unnerved, she said, "I'd love to, if a stranger won't bother him."

"Dúlcifal is beautifully mannered. Treat him with respect and he'll refrain from throwing you."

Vienna summoned the strength to turn around. Her power of speech deserted her at the sight of Mason in a black riding coat and breeches, looking as darkly etched and muscular as the stallion in the barn next door. She was carrying a saddle. Her expression was so impassive that Vienna had trouble reconciling her with the fiery, sweating lover whose mark she still bore. Memory immediately pummeled her senses. Her lungs seemed to collapse inward, ejecting the breath she was holding in an audible gasp, as if the wind had just been knocked out of her.

"English okay for you?" Mason asked, holding up the all-purpose saddle.

"Yes, fine," Vienna answered, and fifteen pounds of leather was dropped into her arms.

"If you want breeches, you'll find spares in the tack room. Help yourself."

Vienna glanced down at her jeans. They would suffice for a short turn on horseback. Besides, she was already self-conscious enough without wearing skintight pants. "It's okay. I'm fine, thanks."

Mason slipped a halter over the Lipizzan's head, crooning, "Hello, handsome. Want to earn some carrots?"

The pale stallion pricked his ears and arched his neck. He stared deeply into Mason's eyes, then laid his cheek against hers and they seemed to be whispering together. Mason looked up after a moment, as if she'd suddenly remembered Vienna was present. Awkwardly, she checked the fastening at her throat, then let her hand slide down to rest over her heart, pressing inward as though to still it. For the briefest second, Vienna glimpsed the passionate Mason then, staring mutely through the haze of all they couldn't say to each other. Their eyes met, and she tried to remember the scheme that had brought her here, the bargain she'd made with herself to do whatever it took. But her concentration had lapsed. She had come here to see the Lipizzan, then she planned to knock on Mason's door, apologize, and soften her up for Pantano's next move. Yet at the first sight of Mason, her resolve was breaking down.

Torn between emotions she could not quite fathom, she couldn't marshal her thoughts around her goal. Instead her mind wandered through a mishmash of fragments, trying to assemble an orderly whole that could explain her confusion. This moment. That impression. Bright, clear memories. Muddled recollections. In the center, eluding definition, was a dream she'd once had.

At the time, immediately after waking, she'd rushed for a pen and paper, wanting to record the details because the dream seemed important. But as soon as she started writing, her memory blanked. The only sentence that made it to the page was: *I'm in Mason's bedroom.* Vienna could add nothing more, probably because she'd never been in that room and couldn't draw on real experience to embellish a fast-fading figment of her imagination.

"Go ahead." Mason indicated a saddling area. Then she folded the stall guard back and led Dúlcifal out, murmuring to him and caressing his cheeks.

Excluded from their private world, Vienna felt the same writhing envy she'd experienced at that party long ago. Mason loved that horse. Their effortless accord was fascinating, but almost unbearable to watch. Vienna moved a few yards toward the entrance and directed her attention deeper into the barn. Hanging over every stall, a head was angled their way. Like teens with a crush, Mason's horses were transfixed by her every move. Irrationally, Vienna wished she could stare just as insatiably without being caught. She wasn't at high school anymore, but one look at Mason made her feel like that smitten kid.

"He can be quirky, but he's just messing with you," Mason said as she saddled the Lipizzan. "Sedate walks aren't his cup of tea."

"He wants a challenge?"

"Exactly." Mason looked up as if seeing her fully for the first time. "He's a dressage horse. It's in his blood."

Vienna glanced toward a large arena beyond the barns. She could imagine Mason putting him through his paces in full dressage turnout, that magical energy flowing between them. They were obviously bound by the perfect intuition that allowed horse and rider to work as one.

"You seem to have a way with animals," she said inadequately.

"In general I find them a better class of company than people."

Disconcerted, Vienna tried again to reach out, not because of her agenda but because she yearned to close the strained distance between them. "Mason, there's something I need to say."

"If it's about yesterday, consider it said." The tone was even, but a warning note vibrated at a lower frequency.

Dúlcifal reacted immediately, turning his head to inspect Mason, ears flicking back and forth in a semaphore of concern. She stroked his neck and he seemed to become more beautiful with each caress, his eyes soft with love. The tenderness was mutual and none of it spilled over to Vienna. Mason's touch was nothing more than an impersonal courtesy when she helped her onto Dúlcifal's back, but her sexual energy was hard to ignore. In her presence, Vienna couldn't trust her body. Every cell reacted. Tiny explosions went off as Mason checked the girth and adjusted the stirrups.

"Relax," Mason said and imparted the helpful information that the Lipizzan liked to get airborne if he saw a swan wandering across the lawn toward him. Opening the gate, she instructed, "Head for the lake and I'll join you shortly."

Mason followed the fluid motion of Dúlcifal's hindquarters as horse and rider departed. He was a muscular horse, long of shoulder and taller than most of his breed at over sixteen hands, but proportionately ideal. His bearing was that of a war horse, proud and gallant, his neck wide and finely arched and his stance powerful. He had eyes so dark and expressive, only a person dull of soul could not be lost in them and wonder what he was thinking. His temperament seemed to match her own. They were both strong-willed and loyal, but where Mason could be rapid in her emotional reactions, the stallion was slower to anger. Still, like her, he felt things deeply.

Mason hadn't planned to own a Lipizzan. The Cavenders had bred Andalusians since World War One, after a family member brought the first of their black stallions back from Spain, a gift from King Alfonso. With him came a gray mare, and over time, they had added several more mares and successfully bred other black colts, a rare color among Andalusians. The horses were registered in Spain, since there was no registry in the U.S. until the 1970s, after the breed become better known. Even now Andalusians were far from common and the black color was so rare that Mason had acquired Dúlcifal and two Lipizzan mares in exchange for one Shamal's colts.

She wished she could expand her breeding operation and work with her horses full time, but she lacked the capital, and dealing with the ailing Cavender Corporation had consumed most of her energy for the past two years. It would be a relief when she'd finally off-loaded most of the company's assets and could think about what she really wanted to do with her life. For that reason alone, she was tempted by Vienna's offer. If she could clear the debts and repay the money owing to the pension fund, Mason wouldn't care if she was left with nothing. So long as she had Laudes Absalom and her horses, she could make a living as an owner and trainer. Animal Planet had invited her to propose a TV series about her supposed training "secrets." Lynden had loved the idea. They'd planned that after they were back on their feet financially, she would follow up on that opportunity.

Mason let herself daydream as she saddled Shamal and set off after Vienna. Maybe she could make a DVD and sell it to horse owners. She wouldn't get rich, but she would be doing something she believed in, teaching gentle schooling methods for dressage and eventing.

"Nice serpentine," she said as she came alongside Dúlcifal.

Vienna glanced at her sideways. "It was entirely deliberate, a real art form."

Her deadpan humor made Mason laugh. Apparently she knew she had too much tension on the inside rein. As a consequence, Dúlcifal was veering this way and that, following every cue with the patient forbearance of a horse feigning obedience for the sake of appearances.

"You're just limbering him up," Mason said generously.

"Oh, please. I'm sadly overhorsed and he knows it."

"You're welcome to take him out again," Mason offered. "If I'm not here, just ask Mr. Pettibone and he'll have one of the grooms take care of you."

"Thank you," Vienna said stiffly. "I didn't realize you had so many horses."

"Fourteen." Mason had increased numbers since her father died, trying to arrest the total decline of the operation. Henry had preferred dogs. "There were nearly thirty each breeding season back in my grandfather's time, but we were involved in horse racing then."

"You don't breed for the track anymore." Vienna sounded pleased.

"No. I get asked to train a few Thoroughbreds, but I'll only do that for owners I like." Attempting to hold up her end of their bland conversation, she changed to another neutral topic. "I guess you don't get much time at Penwraithe these days,"

"I'm there every month." Vienna sounded mildly defensive, perhaps bothered that her comings and goings were noticed. No doubt she thought Mason was spying on her.

"I usually hack past the house every morning," Mason explained, trying to place her observation in context. "That's how I know whether you're home or not. It's a pity about…how things are, or I'd come by and invite you to ride with me. Those horses of yours could do with the work."

Predictably, Vienna was a little stung. "That's why I hire a groom."

Mason nodded and didn't say a word. She hung out frequently at the Penwraithe barn, talking horsemanship with Rick and helping him out with problems.

"Are you telling me Rick isn't doing his job?"

"Not at all. He loves those mares to death. But let's face it. There are four of them and only one of him."

"How do you know so much about my horses?"

"I help out when there's a problem. I delivered one of your foals last year."

"No one tells me anything," Vienna muttered.

"On that subject, I guess you wouldn't know if anyone on your staff owns a Saluki." Mason realized the question probably sounded pretty odd. In case Vienna had no idea what she was talking about, she explained, "That's a dog."

Vienna nodded absently. "Yes…like the one in the statue."

It took Mason a few seconds to grasp what she was referring to—the statue of Estelle on the front steps at Laudes Absalom. She felt foolish to have forgotten it, and intrigued by Vienna's recollection. She didn't know what had happened to her great-great-grandmother's Salukis after she drowned. Estelle was devoted to the breed. Salukis appeared in every portrait ever painted of her. Perhaps no one could bear to be reminded of her and the dogs had been given away. Estelle's son, Thomas Blake Cavender, had started the Doberman tradition, importing a champion breeding pair from Germany in the early 1900s. Ralph was descended from those dogs and Mason planned to keep a puppy from the next litter he sired.

Struck by the coincidence that one of the rare breed had wandered onto the property, she said, "I saw one in the grounds a couple of nights ago, that's all. I wondered if it was lost."

Her thoughts shifted to yesterday. Had it made the same indelible impression on Vienna as it did on her? The possibility made her pulse accelerate so hard that Shamal reacted, briefly breaking his gait.

Vienna shook her head. "It's not one of ours. My mother has Yorkies and she doesn't visit very often. The gardener adopted some kind of bulldog mix after his sheepdog died last year. But he's the token dog, really. We have nine cats."

"Yes, of course." The precious felines supposedly chased by Cavender dogs.

Mason could remember Blake senior and her father ranting on the subject. They'd virtually come to blows after the old man wounded one of the Dobermans. It had to be put down. He was always climbing a ladder at the boundary fence, taking pot shots, and the dog had been wandering in the orchard between Laudes Absalom and Penwraithe, the strip of land at the center of a legal battle between the families. Henry thought nothing of thrashing his kids, Mason especially, but he adored his dogs and the incident had made him crazy. By way of revenge, he'd obtained several huge buckets of offal from a local butcher and spread the contents over the Blake's front steps. He then shot out every decorative window along the front of the house while

Mrs. Blake and the housekeeper looked on in horror. The police came to Laudes Absalom later that day and told him he would have to pay for the damage. When the bill arrived, he had the bank make the sum up in thousands of pennies. He transported these to Penwraithe in his car, throwing them from the windows as he swerved all over the Blake's manicured lawns. Over the next month a team of workers had been there with magnets every day, trying to pick them all up. The Blakes were still finding coins years later, according to local gossip.

Not long after the pennies vandalism, Blake senior returned to his anti-Doberman campaign and was firing across the fence one day when he fell off the ladder and broke something. He then caught pneumonia and died. Smote, Mason's father said. In fact, he'd expressed that sentiment in the sympathy card he sent along with the vet's bill for the euthanization.

"I don't know of anyone around here who owns a Saluki, but I'll mention it to Bridget." Vienna glanced nervously toward Shamal, who had drifted within biting range.

Mason tugged down slightly on one rein, letting him know she was paying attention, and he tracked left, but not before tossing his head and flashing his teeth at his perceived rival. Dúlcifal ignored the unsubtle alpha display. Mason had trained the two stallions to coexist with good manners. They could even feed together without incident. When she bought the Lipizzan home, she hadn't expected them to become such good friends, but Dúlcifal tolerated Shamal's bouts of intimidation, and his optimistic nature seemed to boost Shamal when he got into one of his moody spells.

"He seems quite…compliant," Vienna said, eyeing Shamal.

"I bribe him." Mason grinned.

"So this is his best behavior?"

"Absolutely, but as far as stallions go, he's not mean, just high maintenance."

"You've built trust in him."

"He's never been mishandled and I don't isolate him. He gets his privacy, but he's not treated as a pariah. Outside of the breeding season, I stable him with his mother and his favorite mares." Mason added, "You rode his father once. When we were kids."

She half expected a blank stare or a dismissive shrug, but a sweet smile flitted across Vienna's face. "Yes, I remember. Such a fast mover...so powerful...just breathtaking." With an air of innocence, Vienna added, "The horse, too."

Mason fumbled with her reins like a beginner. "Very funny."

Vienna wasn't just teasing, she was flirting. Her kissable mouth was slightly parted and her cheeks were infused with pink. She looked carefree in her jeans and sweater, her red hair coming loose from its careless ponytail, her eyes bright with daring.

Did she know how desirable she was? Mason doubted it. Vienna's sophistication was effortless, yet she seemed strangely unawakened. Mason decided she probably only had sex between clean, white sheets with a partner she could control. No doubt she'd already reinvented their encounter the day before as an aberration, sex foisted on her by a woman who led innocents astray.

"This is nice," Vienna said.

Holding Mason's gaze, she smiled, not the calculating, sharp-edged smile Mason was used to, but something more honest and spontaneous that pierced her defenses and made her stomach roll. Unable to look away, she smiled back. She wasn't capable of an intelligent comment.

A tiny frown settled on Vienna's brow and she blinked as if she'd just awakened from a long dream. Emotion clouded her eyes before she could shutter them. "I can see why you love it here."

Mason searched for an agenda in the quietly spoken words but could only see that beautiful child from her past, now grown-up and riding at her side. She had a crazy urge to reach across and take Vienna's hand. Halt and dismount. Walk her to the temple and stand on the steps, looking out over the lake and the house, then lay Laudes Absalom at her feet as a gift.

Shocked, she turned her gaze straight ahead and summoned to mind Vienna's vow to kill all the livestock on the property. A hollow threat, surely. Vienna wasn't made of the same stuff as her crazy dog-hating grandfather. Still, if the worst happened, Mason wasn't going to take any chances. She would move every living soul off the property before Vienna set foot inside the gates. *Give* Laudes Absalom to her? Hell would freeze over first.

She glanced sideways again and noticed Vienna had finally relaxed in the saddle. Dúlcifal detected the change and lifted his tail a notch. Mason loosened her reins and tapped her heels, moving into a sitting trot. Vienna followed suit, providing Dúlcifal with the cue he was transparently hoping for. At any moment she would surely transition to the passage, the piaffe, and finally the pesade, accompanied by the usual lavish praise. Admittedly, they weren't in the dressage arena where he usually performed his ballet and there was always the possibility of those hated swans, but he had his head down and ears pricked regardless, his whole body poised in anticipation.

"If you have any moves, now's your chance," Mason invited dryly. "He's desperate to show off."

Laughing, Vienna said, "Trust me, the only airs above the ground you're likely to see will be me flying over his head, and it won't be pretty."

Mason took the lead as they reached the pine forest, skirting the edge of the lake. The buckshot snap of twigs corrupted the quiet air and the soft thud of hooves made the dry leaves vibrate. They followed a serpentine up the slope toward the fork at the farthest boundary. There, on the hill, the trail divided, skirting Penwraithe on one side and Laudes Absalom on the other. Mason dismounted in the clearing, looped Shamal's reins over a shrub, and looked back down toward the lake. A fine mist clung to the surface and swirled around the pines and the temple. The dome glowed whitely, and with its edges shimmering in the morning sun the temple looked like a mirage resting on the water.

"It's beautiful." Vienna tied Dúlcifal to a branch several feet away.

"My brother and I had a tree house up here." Mason pointed to a few rotting planks in a huge pine. "We could see everything."

Vienna stared out toward Penwraithe. "You watched us, too?"

"I watched *you*."

"It's strange. Sometimes I felt that." Vienna paused, lowering her gaze. "For a while, I tried to send signals."

"The dolls?" Mason queried.

"You knew?"

Vienna looked up again with startled delight. Her eyes were not the glassy emerald sometimes seen with her coloring, but a drown-in-me deep chrysoprase as dark as a winter sea. A shadow floated beneath the surface of her stare, as though cast by some inner cloud. Mason had always been intrigued by that dreamy stare, even as a child. The first time she'd looked into Vienna's eyes, from the back of her horse, she'd wanted never to look away. She felt just as powerless now, twenty-five years later.

"Did you ever notice the flags I tied in these trees?" Mason asked. "I was signaling you back."

"I didn't realize. I thought it was a game you and Lynden played. I used to wish I could sneak away and play, too."

"You should have."

"I wasn't brave like you."

Mason shook her head. "You were brave. I know you came over here when you weren't meant to. Mrs. Danville told me."

"Why wouldn't you see me? I knew you were at home." Vienna touched Mason's hand. "Was it because of your father?"

"Our fathers were both…"

"Irrational," Vienna completed softly. Her hand remained in Mason's.

Lifting it, Mason held it to her cheek. The fingers were cool and smooth. Vienna didn't withdraw from her clasp. Mason pressed her lips into the soft palm. "I was afraid for you. See…not so brave after all."

"My father would never have raised a hand to me," Vienna said.

"I know."

Comprehension brightened Vienna's stare. "Ah…you mean *your* father." Her fingers drifted over Mason's cheek in a tender caress. "I was frightened for you, too."

She moved in, letting Mason's arms close around her as if it was the most natural thing in the world. And it seemed that time stopped and spread out like a blank scroll on which the future was not yet written. Mason could almost believe they were free of the past, if only they chose to be. That they could stake a claim on a different tomorrow, starting right here on the boundary that divided their land, their lives, their destiny. Vienna felt so warm and contented in her arms, she couldn't let this moment pass without trying.

Crushing her close, and with a desperation she couldn't hide, she whispered, "Can we stop fighting?"

For the longest time Vienna didn't speak. Her breath fanned Mason's cheek and Mason could sense she was struggling with something. A film of sweat broke, making her shirt cling to her. Mason felt her own, damply glued to her back. Gentle fingertips traced her hairline, followed by the soft brush of lips on her cheeks. The corner of her mouth. Vienna's tongue teased her lips open. Silken heat invaded her mouth. Their kiss was slow and hot and slippery. Throbbing, aching, she could feel Vienna's breasts brushing hers, her heart pounding against the flesh and bone that confined her own.

"What are you asking me, Mason?" she murmured.

Another kiss followed. This time more urgent. Their warm, mingled breath damped Mason's face. Their thighs glided together. Pressure built. Her clit strained for contact. She looked past the auburn sweep of Vienna's hair toward a bed of pine needles. Not what she had in mind at all. Her voice emerged, thick with passion.

"Come back to the house."

"I can't."

"Yes, you can." Mason licked the taste of coffee from Vienna's lips. Between more intense kisses, she said, "I know you want me inside you again."

A tiny moan escaped Vienna. Their faces were just inches apart. Mason could see petals of dark blue in Vienna's dreamy irises, like a tiny lobelia had flowered in each.

"Yes."

"Say it again," Mason demanded.

"I want you inside me."

Mason groaned. Vienna's tongue was on her neck. Her teeth traced the tendon to its base and sank in just enough to confuse her senses. Pain or pleasure? Mason didn't know and didn't care. Desire weakened her legs and soaked her groin. Sleek muscles moved beneath her hands as she caressed Vienna's back and hips. Vienna undid a couple of shirt buttons and slid a hand inside. Mason's nipples were so tense, she jumped at the first glancing flick of a fingertip.

"When?" she gasped out.

"Not yet," Vienna whispered. She pushed Mason's shirt open and delivered one hot little kiss after the next. Then she lifted her head and slid the tip of her tongue just beneath Mason's upper lip. Sucking, biting, she murmured, "Let's have dinner."

Mason had been teased enough. "Will you spend the night?"

Vienna nodded.

"In my bed?"

"Yes."

The soft reply scorched Mason's skin like a brand. Her body heaved as she released a strangled breath. "I can't wait that long. I have to have you."

"Hold that thought," Vienna said, and Mason caught the ripe promise of her scent.

Closing her eyes, she let its musky pungency flow through her. Only when she was drenched, and there was room for nothing else but the smell and feel and taste of the woman she belonged to, did she back away.

Chapter Ten

W hat do you mean, she's gone?"

Mrs. Danville swept Vienna with a frosty stare. "She left a few hours ago."

"Just like that?" Shock thinned her voice. "Did she leave a message for me?" She felt like an idiot for asking but held her ground, refusing to be intimidated. "It's just that we'd talked earlier about having dinner together."

Mrs. Danville bestowed one of her superior smiles, little more than a reluctant flare of the lips. "There was no mention of entertaining a guest for the evening, Miss Blake. But you're welcome to wait in the parlor while I telephone her. Perhaps I misunderstood."

"That won't be necessary."

Vienna glanced despondently past the housekeeper into the great hall. She could see the staircase and could almost feel Mason's body against her own. How could Mason have gone, after all they'd just said to each other? Vienna felt as though they'd finally built a bridge to stand on, safe from the floodwaters of the past. For once she'd allowed herself to listen to her heart, not her head. But things had happened so fast, she needed to stop. She found Mason impossible to resist. It would have been all too easy to go home with her and make love, but Vienna wanted to make that decision when her judgment wasn't clouded by physical desire. She had to find out if she would still choose to be with Mason, because if she did that would change everything.

Mrs. Danville elected to stop torturing her. "Something urgent arose in the city. She said if anyone was looking for her, I was to extend her apologies."

"I see." Vienna recognized her cue to leave but she couldn't bear to walk away, having come this far. "Is she planning to return late?"

If Mason had something urgent to deal with, perhaps she would drive back afterward. Vienna could be here when she arrived home, keeping that promise to spend the night in her bed.

"I had the impression she would be away for several days," Mrs. Danville said.

Vienna couldn't believe what she was hearing. It made no sense after what she'd seen in Mason's face only hours earlier. "Why?" she whispered.

Mrs. Danville looked at her oddly. "I suggest you ask her yourself, Miss Blake."

Through a film of tears, Vienna studied the marble statue near the door, trying to compose herself. She shivered as a gust of wind sent dry leaves flurrying over the broad front steps. "Yes, of course."

Go, she thought, but she couldn't bring herself to begin the journey back knowing what she would be leaving behind. She had the irrational thought that she might never see Mason again. The possibility struck her like a blow.

"Are you quite well, Miss Blake?"

Vienna couldn't speak. Her whole body shook. She made a sound that surprised her, a thin little scream not quite stifled as it emerged. The noise seemed to startle Mrs. Danville as well.

"I think it might be wise for you to sit down," the housekeeper said. "You've gone pale."

She led Vienna indoors and ushered her into a small parlor close by. Vienna sat down on a chaise lounge, thoroughly embarrassed. "I'll be perfectly fine in a moment. I forgot to eat today, so I guess the walk made me light-headed."

Mrs. Danville allowed her to get to the end of her burbled excuses, then said, "If you'll excuse me, Miss Blake, I'll make you a cup of tea."

Vienna didn't waste her time arguing. Mrs. Danville was already walking away. "That very nice of you."

She received an unsmiling nod and Mrs. Danville vanished out a door at the other end of the room. Vienna surveyed her surroundings bleakly. There were no windows, a deficit for which those who liked to sit here had compensated by means of landscape paintings on several walls. The largest of these drew Vienna's gaze. The bucolic country scene it depicted was strangely familiar. A Clydesdale horse pulling a cart, several stone cottages that could only be British, some sheep. Jarred, Vienna looked away. The painting wasn't the only familiar item in the room. A large Chinese vase was displayed on a dark Victorian stand. Staring at it intently, Vienna had a flash of herself lying here on the chaise lounge transfixed by the elaborate brushwork of the flowers and tiny figures. She'd been here before. But when?

"Lemon?" Mrs. Danville's voice made her jump.

"Yes, thank you," Vienna replied automatically, then heard herself blurt out the very question she knew better than to ask. "Mrs. Danville, do you remember the night of the ball?"

The housekeeper started as if a pair of invisible hands had clamped down on her shoulders. She set the teapot down with a clatter and her thin fingers closed over the key ring dangling at her side. "That was a long time ago."

"Yes. Ten years." Vienna hesitated. "I guess the trees made me think about it. The colors. As I was walking here. I used to go for walks after I got out of the hospital, and it was fall by then."

Nothing could have been further from her mind when she knocked on Mason's door than this uncomfortable topic, but the woman in front of her knew more than she admitted, Vienna was certain of it.

Mrs. Danville handed her a cup and saucer. "I was out that evening."

"But you know what I'm talking about, don't you?" Aware that she was craning forward, Vienna forced herself to relax and take a sip of her tea. "The police spent a lot of time here, didn't they?"

"Under the circumstances, that's not surprising."

"What did they find?"

"Your mother is the person to ask about that. Or the detective in charge."

"As you know, he's retired, and I always get the same answer from my mother. I find that strange after so many years. Nothing ever changes. Not a word." Vienna wrapped her arms around herself. "It's not like a memory. It's like…lines in a play."

"Mrs. Blake's choice of language is not my concern."

The dismissal was delivered with such cold courtesy, Vienna felt like a child again, the same child who had knocked on the door several times after she and Mason had agreed that they couldn't be friends. She'd been turned away by the woman in front of her. This time she wasn't so easily deterred.

"Why won't anyone talk about it?"

"What is there to say?" Mrs. Danville snapped like a crack had opened in her stalwart composure. "Take my advice and let sleeping dogs lie."

"Sleeping dogs…" A phrase one didn't use for trifling matters. Determined to uncover the truth, Vienna said, "For heaven's sake, it's been ten years. Henry Cavender is dead. So is Lynden."

Mrs. Danville looked nonplussed, then seemed to collect herself. "I made my statement to the police at the time. I have nothing to add."

Vienna lost her temper. "Whatever he did, he can't be arrested now. Don't you see?"

"Who are you talking about?"

"Your boss, of course. Who else!" Was she imagining it, or did she detect faint signs of relief in Mrs. Danville's face? She set her cup and saucer aside and made herself speak more calmly. "Look, I just want to know what happened."

"You don't remember anything at all?"

"They say I probably won't, after all this time," Vienna replied. "All I remember is walking in the garden."

In her mind, she retraced her steps, through the gap in the fence and down into the pines, past the lake, and toward the house. She'd found a gate in the high stone wall near the ruins and entered a dark garden. The air was heavy with the scent of lilies and the sappy pungency of the daffodils crushed beneath her feet. It was the violet hour, shadows closing on the anvil where night reshaped day. Around her blooms hung big and pendulous from climbing roses and the last of the rhododendrons. She collected a handful of petals and buried her face in them, lost in the heady essence of a perfumed world, where beauty reined and time stood still.

She remained on that fairy threshold for too long, held prisoner by her senses, heedless of the encroaching dark. When she finally realized the stars were out, she stumbled into the garden, but she was suddenly filled with unease, imagining that she was being followed or watched. She looked over her shoulder, then shrugged off her fears as the jabs of a guilty conscience. Anxious to escape the deep shadows and threatening shrubbery, she hurried along the path and found herself in a cemetery. The boy hadn't mentioned that. He'd told her about a small summerhouse. That was where she was supposed to go, although she'd forgotten why.

Her parents had been angry about that, the affront of her sneaking away from their ball on some dubious assignation at Laudes Absalom. They didn't believe her story about the boy. There was no child at the ball who matched his description and the police couldn't find the child when they began their investigation.

"What happened?" she asked Mrs. Danville. "Please tell me the truth."

The housekeeper was silent. She seemed to become her real age then, as if a waxen cloak had fallen from her, the one that normally smoothed every surface, concealing the toll of time. Even her hands looked more wrinkled.

"You know!" Vienna accused. Hot tears filled her eyes. "You know and you're not saying. Who are you protecting—the dead? It's a bit late for that, isn't it?"

"Miss…" An old man emerged from the gloom of the hall and stood in the doorway. After a moment's hesitation, he stepped in behind Mrs. Danville and placed a hand at her elbow. "You'd best be going. We're not free to speak on these matters and you do wrong to ask."

The quiet dignity of his reproach struck home and Vienna was filled with shame. She had crossed that line and compromised a principle held dear by her family—staff should not be coerced by those in a more powerful position. Wiping her tears, she stood and said, "Forgive me, Mrs. Danville. It won't happen again. Thank you for the tea."

Without waiting for a reply, she left the room and crossed the great hall.

"Miss Blake?" There was a rare emotional timbre to the voice that arrested her.

Vienna turned and met Mrs. Danville's eyes. "Yes?"

"Your father was here that night."

"When?"

"Much later. He and Mr. Cavender had Scotch in the study."

"They drank together?" Vienna couldn't imagine why her father would have sat down with the man he blamed for the attack. No one had ever mentioned that meeting to her. "I don't understand. What did they talk about?"

"Perhaps your mother knows," Mrs. Danville suggested, moving to open the door. Her tone was back to normal and it was clear that Vienna had overstayed her welcome.

She offered a polite farewell and, with a despondent glance at the statue, descended the broad front steps. Like the marble woman fleeing with her dog, she could not resist a backward glance. But Vienna wasn't sure what compelled her more. Sorrow over Mason, or fear that a knife was about to land between her shoulder blades.

❖

Mason slammed the door of her office and rested her shoulder against it. She wanted to punch her fist through the timber veneer. Something had to break and it couldn't be her. She slid down the door until she was sitting propped against it, then drew her legs up to her, slouching over her bent knees. Perhaps this was her version of the Cavender Curse—she had to suffer. She'd outlasted her father's beatings, walked away from a fatal plane crash, and had just made it through a high-speed drive only someone who had sold her soul to the devil could expect to survive.

Was that the Faustian bargain she'd made ten years ago? Was she condemned to pay for her actions that night until she felt true remorse? If so, she was doomed. Even knowing all she knew now, she still wouldn't change a thing. Yet she felt mortally wounded, her hopes slowly draining from her. She'd lost her family. She was going to lose the only place she could feel truly at home in. And once the corporation was sold, she would be severed from the past that defined her.

Yet she'd been willing to let go of everything. She would have traded it all to have Vienna. Like a fool, she'd believed that was possible. Mason's stomach churned with the bitter gall of the truth. She'd believed what she wanted to believe, that Vienna also felt incomplete without *her*. That they could work this out because they both wanted the same thing. Each other. Vienna's promise to spend the night with her felt like proof.

She didn't care if Vienna wanted to make her wait for

consummation, but she was restless with fear and anticipation as soon as their ride was over. The minutes ticked by too slowly. Doubt set in. She'd waited so long to be at Vienna's side, it was unbearable to be stuck at Laudes Absalom marking time. Mason wanted to trust the evidence of those incredible kisses, but she had to know that Vienna meant what she said. She couldn't bear to contemplate the alternative.

Torn between fear and hope, and driven by the yearning to hold Vienna in her arms again, she'd set off on foot for Penwraithe. Mason heard her voice first, as she approached the rear of the house through the tree line. Vienna was talking on her cell phone, sitting at a table beside the swimming pool. Mason crept closer, wanting to look at her unobserved, knowing that beautiful body would soon be hers to touch. Fragments of conversation filtered through the noisy rush of blood to her ears.

"Mom, I told you I will do whatever it takes." Vienna cradled her head in one hand. She sounded frustrated. "I refuse to be sidelined over *this*. Blake *males* have been trying put the Cavenders out of business for the past hundred and forty years, and *I'm* expected to pull this off in a few months or I'm considered too weak to run the company? They can kiss my ass."

Each word landed like a blow. Mason couldn't stop herself from shaking. A silence stretched out as Vienna listened to her mother. She was facing the other way so Mason couldn't see her expression, but tension in her body was unmistakable. When she spoke again her tone was hard and devoid of emotion.

"When I'm done out here, you can tell my aunts I'm going to bring a countersuit and force a buyback of their shares now. Then I'm going to sack their precious sons and call the IRS down on their heads. They want to play hardball? They haven't seen a thing yet."

Mason covered her mouth to stifle the rising bile. Vienna would never be hers. Everything that had just passed between them was a farce. Vienna's kisses. Her tenderness. All phony. Vienna's arousal was real, but entirely sexual. The only passion driving her was the desire to conquer. The deep emotional bond that had endured in Mason all these years did not exist for Vienna. Mason had blinded herself to the clues. Vienna's rejections. Her careful evasions. The mixed signals Mason always picked up were not a reflection of some internal struggle between duty and passion. Vienna was simply a predator outmaneuvering her prey. She was opportunistic, looking for weaknesses she could exploit, and Mason had exposed herself.

She should have guessed the situation wasn't as simple as it seemed. The Blakes would eat their young and it sounded like Vienna was in the middle of a battle to keep control of her company. Mason was in her way. Nothing more. Raw emotion choked her. Rage. Frustration. Abject misery. She buried her face in the tree bark, unable to move.

"Mason is exactly where I want her to be," she heard. "Now, stop worrying. I know what I'm doing."

Steeling herself, Mason turned back the way she came. She'd heard all she needed to hear, and there was nothing to be gained from a confrontation. The magnitude of her loss almost defeated her. She didn't know how she would ever claw her way back to a semblance of happiness. She'd spent her entire adult life trying to extinguish her hopeless yearning to be Vienna's lover. She'd taken refuge in the arms of women who gave her pleasure and lessened her loneliness. She'd done all she could to build a connection with those she liked and admired most, but nothing ever penetrated the cocoon that imprisoned her. She was irrevocably bound by an invisible silk that only seemed to tighten the more she struggled against it. There was no escape, no tearing her way out, no rescue to be had at the hands of other lovers.

Mason knew what she had to do. If she wanted to end this enchantment, she had to cast a stronger spell of her own. She had to find a way to strike back with the only weapons she had.

❖

Vienna jerked up on her elbows, roused by a sound she couldn't identify. She listened in the darkness, her mind fogged with sleep. She'd been dreaming, a strange dream that almost suffocated her.

She was standing at the gates of Laudes Absalom, calling for someone to open them. On the other side, nature had run wild, reclaiming the once rolling lawns and all but concealing the house from sight. The woods were dark and twisted, crowding the driveway with huge overhanging branches and rising roots. Moss and weeds clogged every crack, forming a confluence of green rivulets that would one day flow in a single stream and wash the house away.

Pale saplings struggled up through the snarled confusion, their tender limbs grotesquely misshapen. Competing for sunlight, they sandwiched themselves between monstrous tree trunks and clumsy shrubs. Every plant fought its neighbors for the few inches of space as yet unspoken for. Vines bound them together in their struggles, creeping from the depths of the forest to strangle their unsuspecting hosts.

No one had tended the grounds in years, and from what Vienna could see of the house, it was similarly abandoned. Helplessly, she rattled the gates and shouted for help. Grass grew out the broken windows of the gatehouse. No one was coming and the way was barred.

She heard something then, a low soft whine, and a dog emerged from the dense undergrowth. It stood a few feet away, tall and elegant, its wheaten hair shimmering. A woman materialized next to it. She was dressed like a bride and her face was strangely familiar. Vienna could have been looking in a mirror that magically transformed her irregular features into finely wrought perfection. The eyes were a velvety dark blue that defied description. If rose petals came in such a color, their exquisite softness might compete. The woman's expression was that of a nymph who'd stumbled into a strange new world. She wore her hair in a loose braid. Its color was hard to describe, somewhere between auburn and gold.

She came toward Vienna and, with a beseeching look, stretched out a cupped hand. She was holding something. Vienna craned to see it but the dog was in her way. "Open the gates," she said, but the lovely stranger didn't hear her.

The dog tugged at the bridal gown, drawing his mistress back toward the hideous tangle of vine and branches. She seemed to take root then, right in front of a willow, becoming one with the tree's twisted form. The dog kept pawing at her gown, which was now a pale tree trunk. Finally the wooden folds parted to admit his slender body, then, from within the tree, he howled.

Vienna opened her eyes and stumbled out of bed. The Saluki. The lost dog Mason had mentioned. Apparently it had stuck in her mind, along with pangs of conscience over her former plans to drive the last of the Cavenders away from her ancestral home. It wasn't rocket science to interpret the dream; her mixed feelings were not exactly buried in her unconscious.

She turned on a lamp and padded into the bathroom. As she splashed water on her face, a dark suspicion crawled out from the fringes of her dream, a latent knowledge inaccessible when she was fully awake.

Her destiny was inextricably linked to Mason Cavender.

CHAPTER ELEVEN

N ow," Vienna said, sucking in her stomach.
        Her makeup artist, Pimento, forced the zipper closed and
leapt back as though expecting her to explode. "Okay, princess, breathe.
Very slowly."

"Have I put on weight or was this dress a bitch to get into when I
bought it?"

Pimento twiddled absently with one of the heavy gold rings in his
earlobes. "Both."

"You bastard." Vienna turned slowly in front of the mirrors in her
dressing room.

The John Galliano evening gown was languidly form fitting, in
Hollywood-siren style. No one could possibly imagine how hard it was
to squeeze in and out of the carefully structured gray satin. The color
made her auburn waves seem even redder and her skin absurdly pale.

Pimento regarded her intently. "The lips are too dark." He held
up a tube of pale beige-pink and read the label, sarcastically intoning,
"Voluptuous Virgin. What could be more appropriate?"

"I don't know. I'm not eighteen anymore. The ingénue look seems
rather…desperate."

"For you, the look is far from ingénue," Pimento assured her. "It's
natural. Confident. Effortless." He steered her to a high stool, fastened
a nylon cape around her neck.

"Whatever, so long as you're not turning me into one of those
pinky-dink Tinsley Mortimer clones."

"As if." He carefully removed the burgundy shade from her lips.

When he'd finished applying the dewy nude tone, he stepped back and examined her. "Divine."

Vienna gazed at the results, pleasantly surprised. She hadn't expected the understated look to work so well. "Nice. Pity we have to spoil the effect."

"Ah, yes." Pimento removed the cape and lifted an oblong jeweler's attaché case onto the dressing table. "What have we dragged out of the bank vault today?"

"Something you haven't seen before." Vienna entered the combination and lifted the lid.

"Oh, dear God." Pimento clutched his throat. "Are those the real thing?"

"What do you think?"

Vienna lifted the diamond necklace uneasily from its velvet tray. Her father had given it to her for her twenty-first birthday and she'd only worn it a few times since. She felt embarrassed to be seen in opulent jewelry, normally preferring to be discreet about her wealth. The necklace also brought back some unhappy memories, but Vienna was fed up with running from a past she had no power to change. Buffy Morgan de Rochester's party was one of the most important on the calendar, and this year De Beers was offering a prize for the most beautiful diamond necklace. A hundred thousand dollars would be donated to the charity of the winner's choice. The least Vienna could do was try to win the money for a good cause.

She fastened the glittering gems around her neck and positioned the pear-shaped center stone just above her modest cleavage. It beamed white light like a large, icy teardrop.

"Does it have a name?" Pimento hadn't stopped drooling over the rock. "Like the Hope Diamond?"

"Not that I know of."

Her mother had suggested various silly-sounding names for the stone, but Vienna flatly refused. It was one thing to acquire a famous diamond with a history, quite another to dignify a gem of shady origins with a pretentious sobriquet. Her father had been cagey about how he came by the necklace, merely referring to "a private sale years ago." He assured her that he'd verified the gem's provenance, but Vienna didn't care to dwell on Norris Blake's idea of an acceptable past.

Looking pleased with himself, Pimento said, "Violà. The lips are a perfect match." He indicated the three round peach-pink diamonds set on the platinum bail above the suspended pear. "You look disgustingly elite, my darling. Don't forget to mention my name to that Russian gangster's wife."

"You can't seriously want her as a client." Vienna slid on the ring that went with the necklace, a five carat solitaire in the same pear cut. "She's so…"

"Blatant? Appallingly sable-clad? Fantastically Botoxed. Preposterously big-haired and *generous* with her tips."

"Let's just say she makes a dramatic entrance." Vienna groaned. "God, I sound like such a snob."

"Duh." Pimento brushed some lint off his jacket, a Vivienne Westwood design in purple silk velvet. This was teamed with paisley pants, a yellow shirt, and a floppy crimson bow-tie.

"Get out of here," Vienna told him. "You're a bad influence."

"And you, my angel, are a vision. Those Park Avenue vipers will be baring their fangs in envy." The buzzer chimed and he picked up the intercom. "Your car's here. Sure you don't want me to be your exquisite guest?"

Vienna shook her head. "I think Buffy's fixed me up with one of her über-tan walkers."

"Nice work if you can get it."

Vienna gathered up her evening purse and coat. "Come on. It's early. I can drop you off downtown before I head to the party."

As they rode the elevator to the lobby, she sampled the new fragrance Pimento had dabbed on her wrists, Sarrasins by Serge Lutens. The initial jasmine-and-leather rush had faded, making room for the scent of honeyed almonds.

"How do you like it?" Pimento asked.

"Delicious. Not quite as sweet as A la Nuit."

"It's a non-import," he divulged with satisfaction. "Available only in Europe."

"Did you leave the bottle?"

"Heavens, no. I don't like you *that* much."

"I thought you were supposed to suck up to your clients."

"Only the ones who really need it." He held the door for Vienna to move ahead of him and they strolled to the limo. As they settled into the backseat, he said, "Promise you'll kiss someone gorgeous for me."

Vienna laughed. "Don't hold your breath."

❖

Thickets of pillar candles poured saffron light in pools across a gleaming dark maroon floor. The walls were hung with sensuous art. Black bamboo grew in huge glazed tubs that sectioned the vast space into schmoozing zones furnished with soft couches and armchairs, all upholstered in ivory. Several chic modern chandeliers dripped from the high ceiling in mesmerizing crystal cascades. Enormous floral arrangements created lush focal points, each a mass of blooms in shades of cream and pale green. Handsome waiters ferried platters of faux-rustic finger food from one clique to the next. Atop a two-level dais at the far end of the room, a well-known performer played a Steinway grand piano.

"Darling." Buffy Morgan de Rochester kissed the air somewhere near Vienna's cheek. "Do come and meet Stefan. The poor fellow has only been in town for a month and doesn't know a soul. I thought you two would hit it off. His sister married a Winthrop."

They arrived in front of a handsome guest with silver streaking his temples, and Buffy rattled off a string of names that identified him as minor European aristocracy. Stefan's handshake was brief and genteel, his accent vaguely Italian, and he smelled of costly cologne and fine cigars. After Buffy left them to get acquainted, they sipped Dom Perignon, remarked on the sweeping views from the floor-to-ceiling windows, and watched various haute society regulars drift in.

Predictably, when Oxana Ivanova arrived, she noticed Vienna immediately, or at least she noticed the rope of diamonds around her throat. Abandoning her husband at the bar, she charged through the gathering like a Versace-clad rhinoceros.

"Exquisite." She elbowed Stefan aside and fluttered her stumpy fingers over the necklace. "Magnificent."

Vienna fought the urge to back out of reach, instead halting a waiter and selecting a creamy lobster canapé dusted with shaved truffle. She wasn't hungry but eating the elegant morsel would allow her to keep a polite distance. Between nibbles, she said, "Nice to see you again, Oxana. It's a lovely party, don't you think?"

"Yes, very high class. We can fortunately count on Buffy to invite the right people. Such beautiful fashions. And the diamonds..." Back on message, Oxana plucked the pear-shaped stone from between Vienna's breasts and tilted it so the light radiated from its facets. "Over thirty carats?"

"You have a good eye." Pretending to be riveted by the idea of comparing baubles, Vienna said, "Are you wearing something special yourself tonight?"

Oxana shoved a hand triumphantly in front of her. A large octagonal-cut pink diamond weighed down her ring finger. "Want to swap? My ring for your necklace?"

She laughed at her own joke, but Vienna recognized the unsubtle hint. Oxana and her husband Sergei were avid art and jewelry collectors. Unlike many of Russia's newly minted billionaires, Sergei had never been part of the governing oligarchy. He came from humble beginnings and compensated for his miserable childhood with lavish purchases. Oxana helped him in this cause by squandering large sums of money at every antique auction she attended. Between times, they indulged their many pets and traveled between several glamorous houses around the world.

They'd purchased their Upper East Side duplex six years earlier, and it had taken them a while to realize that their 10021 zip code did not confer the automatic social success they'd expected. Being rich and flaunting it was not enough to get them invited to A-list gatherings like Buffy's. There was no underling they could bribe or threaten, and no "somebody" who owed them a favor and would pull strings. The best they could hope for from their publicist was the occasional picture in *New York* magazine. Social climbers were common currency in the city that drew them from all over the world. The Ivanovs had realized that if they wanted an entrée to the highest tiers of Manhattan society, they would have to exchange self-indulgence for self-promotion.

To that end they'd hired a team of social consultants and endured a complete makeover. They had their duplex redecorated by a celebrity designer and their walls hung with the right art. They cadged invitations to upscale store openings and trolled the benefit circuit, trying to strike up conversations with the right people. Oxana signed on to New Yorkers for Children, a charity known to put up with anyone if they had enough money.

However, despite several years of perseverance, their diligent efforts had only landed them in the same boat as every other preening poseur trying to make a splash. Worse still, the Ivanovs lacked the advantages of youth and beauty. They were in their late forties and Oxana was no swan. Even after starving off a hundred pounds, she couldn't follow the path carved out by pretty young things who wore the right dresses and married into the Park Avenue peerage. Oxana already had a husband, and no one who mattered was playing golf with him.

Yes, it seemed the Ivanovs would never make it onto the short lists of the party wranglers who determined which of the ever-swelling tide of arrivistes had actually arrived. For while anyone could attend the Met's Costume Institute Benefit Gala, a personal invitation from a Memorial Sloan-Kettering matron was a rare and coveted commodity, and so far the gatekeepers had deemed the Ivanovs unworthy. If they wanted success, they would have to get Oxana accepted by the ladies who lunch. The trouble was, nothing devalued an exclusive brunch or soirée more than the presence of outsiders who corrupted the rarefied atmosphere with the "wrong vibe" and scared off the real elite.

So, Sergei and Oxana remained out in the cold, languishing at boring charity circuit bashes where publicists shoved their clients in front of the cameras and organizers paid alleged celebrities like Paris Hilton to show up. They plumbed a depressing low at the annual Dressed to Kilt fashion extravaganza, when they were snubbed by Donald Trump, himself only resentfully tolerated by the old guard. The incident was then mocked on Socialite Rank, the since defunct Web site run by those nobodies, the Rei step-siblings.

Most people would have lost patience and joined the migration to the more democratic social order downtown, no longer cutting hefty checks to the Smithsonian. But the Ivanovs were nothing if not determined. They ratcheted up the scale of their donations and hoped someone would eventually notice. And to their surprise, they discovered a certain enthusiasm for giving away chunks of their fortune. They began to worry less about making it to an important table at the

Whitney Gala and more about the people they could help. Philanthropy was an art, however, and when giving ceased to be a mere expedience, benefactors needed expert advice. Unsure who to ask about a couple of hefty endowments, Oxana had finally sought help from the head of one of the charities she'd adopted.

A day later, after a series of phone calls, one of Buffy Morgan de Rochester's cronies called her to plead Oxana's case, claiming the Ivanovs seemed "genuinely good, underneath it all." Buffy, a woman who liked to make her own decisions, had decided to inspect the couple firsthand. Her party provided the ideal opportunity, she'd confided in Vienna, formal but also small and private, so people could be themselves.

Vienna had met Oxana at a few events over recent years and found her overwhelming, but she and her husband were refreshing characters in a social milieu that often felt stifling. Vienna supposed it was easy for her to grumble about the insularity of these circles. As a Blake, she was automatically a member of the tribe. Various scions had made Manhattan their first or second home over the generations, intermarrying with families listed among Mrs. Astor's Four Hundred, and the Blakes were fixtures at every event that mattered.

When Vienna's family wasn't at their Upper East Side apartment, as she grew up, they were on Beacon Hill, in the original family townhouse built in 1820 by Benedict Blake's father. Benedict and his Famous Four sisters had grown up there and that was where he was murdered by Hugo Cavender. The townhouse subsequently became the Boston base from which generations of Blake patriarchs ran the family's ever-expanding empire. Marjorie lived there now and Vienna had her city apartment in the top floor of the Blake Industries building.

"If you ever wish to sell…" Oxana's croaky whisper startled her from her thoughts. "Think of me."

"Of course. I would only want to sell to a true connoisseur."

Oxana flushed with pleasure. "What a sweet girl you are. May I ask you a personal question?"

"Certainly." Vienna adopted a warm playful tone. "Although I can't promise to answer."

Chuckling, Oxana leaned in close and asked in a loud whisper, "Why aren't you married? Are these men fools?"

"Let me tell you a secret." Vienna produced a shy pause that had Oxana eating from her hand. "I've promised myself to my childhood sweetheart."

Oxana gasped with delight over this fiction. "Are you engaged?"

"Alas, there are obstacles."

"Obstacles? Surely not...a wife?"

"No, nothing like that."

The ample bosom heaved. "I'm very relieved. But if there is no other woman, what is the obstacle?"

With a tragic sigh, Vienna confessed, "The past divides us."

Clearly a woman of the romantic persuasion, Oxana squeaked a dismayed, "No." She clasped Vienna's hand, her fingers milking it like a goat udder. "You must not let anything stand in your way. If you're meant to be together, don't let your true love slip through your fingers."

Vienna freed her hand gently and managed to keep a straight face. The people closest to her knew she was lesbian, but as the Blake heiress, she'd learned a long time ago that she was media fodder, so she tried to stay out of the headlines. She'd been deflecting questions about her single status for years, using the childhood sweetheart story as her cover. Until now, the irony hadn't struck her.

"By the way, I have a name for you, Oxana," she said, changing the subject. "My makeup artist...he's a genius. It's probably of no interest. You always look striking, but..."

"No, no. I love new ideas."

Vienna extracted Pimento's business card from her purse. "He has a wonderful feel for the woman beneath the face. If you ever want to try someone different, you might like him."

As Oxana slid the card into her evening bag, Vienna glanced around, seeking an escape route. Stefan had drifted into conversation with a couple a few yards away. They were speaking in French. She was about to excuse herself and join them when Buffy's arm hooked hers.

"May I steal you for a moment?" After complimenting Oxana on her gown, she steered Vienna into a quiet corner. "My dear, you won't believe this. Look toward the piano."

"What am I looking for?"

As soon as she'd spoken, Vienna knew the answer. Near the wall, next to one of the planters, was the very last person she'd expected to see here. Vienna knew she was blushing. She couldn't help herself. Her pulse had careened out of control. Somehow Mason managed to make black tie look wanton. Her dinner jacket was cut longer than the norm. Her white dress shirt was tucked into black pants worn with a cummerbund that seemed carelessly pleated, as though thrown on in haste after a back-room assignation. The black bowtie around her wing collar was not quite centered and she'd opened the button at her throat. She had one thumb hooked loosely in her waistband, the other hand cupped a rocks glass. As usual, her hair looked like someone's fingers had just tangled in it. She was staring past the pianist, out the windows, looking like she'd rather be anywhere else on earth than Manhattan.

"What's she doing here?" Vienna asked in dismay.

"Her brother was supposed to come with Tory Delacorte and her parents," Buffy said. "Dreadful business. But I've always said private airplanes are a menace."

Vienna conjured up an image of Tory in her Winsor days, with her flat-ironed blond mane, heiress-chic fashions, and limitless devotion to her appearance. She wondered what Lynden Cavender could possibly have seen in her. Money, obviously. Everyone knew he was trawling for a wife with deep pockets. Vienna forced her gaze elsewhere. Her nipples had visibly hardened beneath the thin fabric of her gown. She felt like swatting them back where they belonged.

"Whatever was I supposed to say?" Buffy lamented. "I could hardly refuse when she phoned. And now I'm one short, since she came alone."

Vienna considered making an early departure so that she didn't have to confront Mason over their broken date and the two weeks that had passed without so much as a phone call. So much for *I can't wait…I have to have you.* But the Morgan de Rochesters were old family friends and she didn't want to insult Buffy.

"If you're concerned about a scene, don't be. I'll simply avoid her."

"That shouldn't be difficult," Buffy said with dry humor. "She doesn't exactly work the room."

They were silenced by a tap on the microphone. The emcee welcomed the guests and introduced Kahlil Pederson, a diamond buyer from De Beers who was going to judge the jewelry award. He summoned the candidates to the dais and the pianist struck up a medley of tunes like "Diamonds Are a Girl's Best Friend."

Vienna could feel Mason's eyes on her as she slipped into the line next to Oxana. Her skin prickled and heat blasted between her legs. She could feel herself opening like a wet bloom. Memory took her prisoner once more, tormenting her with certain undeniable facts. She hadn't just consented to sex with Mason that morning in the great hall, she'd initiated it. And that kiss on the hillside. In the two weeks since, she'd hardly been able to think of anything else. But the more time that went by without hearing from Mason, the more confused she felt.

At first, she'd invented various explanations for being stood up. Then she concluded that Mason had backed off, needing to get some distance to think through the sudden change between them. Vienna had felt that way herself, so she'd left the ball in Mason's court instead of phoning her. But maybe she'd sent the wrong signal. Was this some kind of test—was Mason waiting for her to make the next move? Or had she decided to put their personal relationship on hold until she could see how the business situation played out? If so, a phone call would have been in order.

Vienna had no idea where she stood, but she didn't want to blow the delicate truce they seemed to have forged, so she'd instructed her chief attorney, Darryl Kent, to play a waiting game with the negotiations. There hadn't been a word from the Cavender people and Vienna couldn't keep things on hold forever. Her family expected results. But she could no longer treat Mason as her enemy. Too much had passed between them and, as an extra complication, she still desperately wanted the woman whose head her family expected to see on a platter.

She forced a smile as her turn approached for the mandatory photographs. Each diamond-dripping woman offered the usual hand-on-hip pose while they all waited for the judge to make his decision. The photographer took extra pictures of Vienna, making her even more self-conscious. The whole time, as she angled her head and positioned her hands, she was aware of Mason's scathing regard.

Third and second prize were announced and then Vienna's name was called and Stefan materialized to escort her up to receive her prize. Telling herself it was worth behaving like a giddy nitwit to net a contribution to a worthwhile cause, she burbled something inane about the blight of child exploitation.

The De Beers front man heaped congratulations on her, then asked, "Would you care to tell us about your beautiful necklace?"

"It was a birthday gift from my late father, Norris Blake. I miss him very much, and I'm wearing it in his honor tonight."

A ripple of empathetic applause ensued.

The buyer remarked on Norris's reputation as a lion of industry and a patron of the arts sorely missed, then reverently asserted, "I recognize the necklace."

"You do?"

"May I?" Kahlil Pederson whipped out his loupe. Vienna lifted the glittering center stone and after examining it for several seconds, the buyer referred to his BlackBerry, then confirmed, "Indeed, it appears the Cavender Diamonds have resurfaced."

Chapter Twelve

Audible gasps rippled through the gathering as those in the know registered the ramifications and darted uneasy glances toward Mason. A film of perspiration made Vienna's dress cling. She felt nauseous. Apparently mistaking the horrified tenterhooks of his audience for delighted thrall, Pederson embarked on a potted history of the stone.

"As many of you know, the diamond necklace you see tonight was made famous by Nancy Cavender, who had it created by Cartier. She was a glittering figure in her time, a true icon. The necklace was, of course, her signature look at all the big events and she was wearing it the night she was tragically killed."

An elderly woman a few feet away murmured, "Decapitated, you know. They found the necklace hanging in a tree."

Vienna felt close to fainting. She stepped back and leaned against one of the pillars decorating the dais. It was made of cardboard and wobbled more than her legs did. In her worst nightmare the necklace was Nazi loot. She hadn't even considered the possibility that its grim past was one her family had a role in.

"The necklace came from a huge diamond discovered in South Africa in 1867." Pederson's narrative was in full swing. "Mr. Isaac Asscher of Amsterdam cleaved the rough into two pieces from which he cut the Aphrodite, a round now owned by Sheikh Ahmed Fitaihi, and the magnificent flawless pear you see before you, which Mr. Hugo Cavender purchased for his bride. As the story goes, Mr. Cavender wanted the larger round, but had to settle for a mere thirty-six carats, plus, of course, several hundred carats of smaller stones eventually used to create the necklace."

A tinkle of laughter greeted this final comment.

"Are you saying that diamond is Le Fantôme de l'Amour?" Mason's question ricocheted across the room like a stray bullet. She stared accusingly at Vienna.

"Yes, that's the name originally given to the pear. The Ghost of Love," the buyer translated from the French. "But the spelling was doubtless too much for our esteemed friends in the press and when Nancy Cavender allowed it to go on display, the necklace simply became known as the Cavender Diamonds."

"How did the Blakes get hold of it?" Mason asked bluntly.

The buyer looked nonplussed. "Unfortunately, we cannot disclose details of client transactions, so I really can't say, Ms. er…"

"Cavender."

Every head in the room swiveled. Buffy, anticipating trouble, rushed to the fore. "What a fascinating story. Don't we all adore the idea of a diamond with a past, especially one that connects two of the most prominent families among us."

The guests clapped and craned to see Vienna's reaction. Buffy signaled the pianist and he began to play softly. She thanked Pederson, reminded everyone about the Whitney benefit in two weeks' time, and steered Mason away. Vienna decided to make her apologies and leave the party early, but before she could excuse herself, the De Beers representative cornered her.

"Ms. Blake, I was just speaking with our North American vice president. He wonders if your family would be willing to allow us to exhibit the necklace."

Agitated, Vienna glanced toward the door again. Her father had never said a word about the necklace once belonging to their neighbors. Vienna was surprised by that, she would have expected him to gloat.

"I don't see any problem with that," she told Pederson quickly, wanting to make her getaway before any more awkward questions from Mason. "Assuming we can agree on security arrangements."

"And with the authentic Le Fantôme, of course, rather than the replica."

"The replica?" Vienna kept her tone very even, screening her confusion.

"Don't worry." Pederson adopted a conspiratorial air. "Naturally I didn't want to mention it. We encourage all our clients to keep their important diamonds secured and wear replicas." He studied his BlackBerry again and announced with a triumphant smile, "I thought so. The CZ is one of our own custom stones. Made to order for your father, in fact."

"My father?" Vienna felt like a simpleton, echoing every pronouncement. It had never occurred to her that the center stone in her ostentatious necklace was not the real thing. And since Marjorie had been bothering her to sell it, offended that she never wore the costly gift, it seemed she had no idea either.

"Yes, I gather the previous copy was damaged in the car accident." Pederson ran a finger across his throat. "Ghastly neck injuries."

Embarrassed to be asking questions to which she should probably know the answers, Vienna said, "There was another fake?"

"Yes, the one provided when we first auctioned Le Fantôme in the nineteenth century."

"Well, I'm afraid I have bad news," Vienna said without expression. "As far as I know, we don't own Le Fantôme."

"Are you saying it's been sold?" Pederson looked dismayed.

"Not that I know of."

"Oh, good God. It's *missing*?"

"I have no idea. Don't you keep records of stones like this?"

"If they pass through our hands or are sold through the usual channels, we can trace the provenance." He lifted his BlackBerry to his ear. "Let me make a call, Ms. Blake."

Vienna accepted a glass of champagne from a passing waiter and sipped it as she tried to eavesdrop. The Blakes were methodical about their record-keeping. She could easily find out much the household had spent on butter a hundred years ago and which mantua maker had created the party dresses for the Famous Four. If a priceless diamond was locked away in a bank box in Boston, her father would have mentioned it in his will. And there would be a receipt.

Pederson turned back toward her wearing a frown. "Our records date back to the 1869 auction when Mr. Truman Blake sold Le Fantôme. He would have been your…"

"Great-great grandfather," Vienna said in bewilderment. "I don't understand. I thought you said the Cavenders bought the stone."

"Yes, Hugo Cavender purchased it at the auction."

"From Truman?" Nothing in this tale made any sense at all.

The buyer consulted his BlackBerry. "According to the provenance, Mr. Blake was the first owner of both the round Aphrodite and Le Fantôme. It was actually he who named the stones. Quite the Victorian romantic, it would seem."

Ghost of Love. It was hard to imagine a Blake male so giddy with passion he would throw a fortune away on a couple of huge diamonds, let alone bestow a name that would forever brand him a soppy sentimentalist. But Vienna had read the letters between Truman and Estelle. He was obviously infatuated and seemed to expect that he and Estelle would be married. He must have bought the diamonds in anticipation, then auctioned them when Estelle became engaged to Hugo.

"Le Fantôme remained in the possession of the Cavender family until it was sold privately to your father in 1985. Our records include the valuation made at the time for insurance purposes."

Vienna tried to comprehend what she was hearing. Her father had bought the necklace when she was just a little girl, then held on to it for years, waiting for her to grow up? Even more astonishing was the fact that Henry Cavender had sold it to him—turning over a prized heirloom to the Blakes. It was unbelievable.

"Well, Mr. Pederson, I regret to say, I can only assume my father decided not to leave his capital tied up in Le Fantôme. He must have resold the stone but retained the necklace to give to me."

The theory had something going for it. Vienna could imagine her father impressing everyone with his extravagant gift, then selling the single pear to reimburse himself for the cost of the whole necklace. She recalled the startled envy of her aunts and their speculation over the price he must have paid for the gems. Millions. Such was his devotion to his only child. She laughed inwardly. Norris must have been very pleased with himself to create all that buzz over a gift that ended up costing him next to nothing.

Pederson's expression was politely skeptical. "May I ask a great favor?" he inquired. "If you have any family papers, would you mind checking them just in case there's a record of your father selling Le Fantôme? It would be marvelous if we could trace the new owner and arrange to borrow the genuine stone."

"I'll do what I can," Vienna promised, taking the business card he offered.

They shook hands and she wandered toward the windows, her mind sifting through memory and fact. Truman Blake was the ancestor who had declared war on the Cavenders. In his shoes, Vienna would have done the same thing. His father, Benedict, was murdered in cold blood, and knowing justice would never be done in the courts, Truman had set out to avenge the crime. He'd devoted himself to severing the business ties that bound the two families and to bringing down the Cavenders.

Back then, the Cavender name was more powerful than the Blakes', and even now, despite their declining fortunes, the mystique remained. Wealth, glamour, and tragedy were a heady combination, and the Cavenders had always served up gratifying doses of each. Their women were gorgeous and their men were dangerous. There was even a movie based on the most public tragedy that had plagued the dynasty, the sordid tale of Alexander Cavender's failed presidential bid and his wife's dreadful accident. The story could have been written by F. Scott Fitzgerald. Like Daisy Buchanan, the shallow beauty in *The Great Gatsby*, Nancy Cavender was a pampered socialite who seemed to have little interest in being a mother or even a supportive wife. How her car had ended up on the railway tracks, with her unconscious at the wheel conveniently waiting to be hit by a train, was a mystery.

Most men didn't want their infidelities, or those of their wives, to be common knowledge, and men running for president had even more reason to shrink from scrutiny. But Nancy hadn't concerned herself with her husband's political ambitions. Heiress to a fortune, reckless and beautiful, she appeared to live under the spell of her own charm, certain of her invulnerability. If there was a line not to be crossed, she only noticed after the fact and *if* there were consequences. For Nancy, there seldom were. Until that night.

Intense speculation had swirled around the accident at the time, but the Cavenders had so much influence that they controlled both the police investigation and the newspaper coverage. The story was hushed up, only to find new life when Alexander Cavender blew his brains out four years later. His suicide would normally have been big news, but as if he was trying to fly beneath the radar, he'd picked his moment. In the same year that Martin Luther King Jr. and Robert F. Kennedy were assassinated, a dead Cavender would only make the inside section and the society pages.

The Blakes considered Alexander's demise an almighty coup and believed the rumor that had circulated ever since, that the police had finally assembled enough evidence to arrest him for Nancy's murder. Rather than have his family's name dragged through the mud, he'd ended the matter like a gentleman. The story might have died down, but Hollywood moviemakers, always adept at picking the low-hanging fruit, had decided to capitalize on public fascination with the Cavender name. But instead of making a cheesy starlet vehicle, they produced a dark meditation on the American Dream, posing disturbing questions about ambition and greed, and inviting the audience to weigh moral ambiguities.

To the chagrin of the Blakes, the movie was an Oscar-winning box office hit, and their family wasn't presented in a particularly positive light. One of the main characters in the film was Vienna's grandfather, Clarence Blake. According to the plot, he'd had a fling with Nancy early in her marriage, after she discovered that her husband had a mistress with whom he'd fathered a child. The encounter with her husband's archenemy was Nancy's version of revenge, and in pillow talk she'd admitted her reasons, telling Clarence that she even suspected Alexander had made a bigamous marriage. Worse yet, the mistress was a mixed-race woman.

Once the presidential primaries began heating up, Clarence had leaked the information to the press, ending Alexander's bid for the Oval Office. The film implied that Nancy's death was an act of revenge on her husband's part. Alexander had never told anyone except her about his indiscretion, and even though their marriage had been on the rocks for years, he thought her self-interest and desire to be first lady would guarantee her silence. He knew nothing about the one-night stand with Clarence and had concluded that Nancy must have told the press herself, a betrayal he couldn't forgive. The rest was history, adding another sordid chapter to the Cavender myth.

Vienna slid her fingers over Nancy's necklace. She felt strangled by the weight of its past as much as the platinum setting. She liberated a martini from a passing platter and edged her way through the crowd, heading for the door. She wanted to escape before the guests were summoned to dinner. The thought of having to sit through a five-course meal made her stomach turn. All she could think about was getting to Penwraithe so she could dismantle the library and find out how her father had obtained the Cavender Diamonds and who had Le Fantôme de l'Amour.

She began moving toward the door, but it wasn't easy to remain unobtrusive when she was constantly stopped by acquaintances who wanted a closer look at the famous necklace. She was going to have it broken up and sold, she decided angrily, as yet another guest bemoaned the ironic twist of fate that saw Nancy Cavender's diamonds worn by the granddaughter of Clarence Blake, the man whose actions had almost certainly led to her death. One thing jumped out at Vienna. If Pederson's account of the damaged paste replica was correct, Nancy had not been wearing Le Fantôme the night she was killed. Vienna found that puzzling. Why would a woman who seemed so careless in every aspect of her life, but who was incredibly vain about her image, wear the fake when she could flaunt the real thing? Nancy didn't seem like the type who would worry about possible theft. And why would she take pains to safeguard an heirloom that belonged to her husband's family, when she despised him?

There was one person who might be able to answer those questions, but Vienna didn't feel confident approaching her. For some reason Mason's attitude toward her had hardened, and Vienna didn't know why. She spotted her deep in conversation with Sergei Ivanov and couldn't help staring with helpless fascination. The Russian's beady gaze was equally intent. Mason placed something in his pudgy hand and he reacted by patting his face with a white handkerchief, a mannerism he seemed self-conscious of, because he immediately stuffed the handkerchief back in his pocket.

Vienna took a step toward them, then stopped as if she'd slammed into an invisible wall. Mason's eyes blazed at her and she pushed a dark unruly strand back off her forehead. Vienna's mouth watered with the sense memory of their last kiss, and her body instantly followed suit, reminding her that it was desperate to be rejoined with Mason's. No one had ever looked at her the way Mason did. No one had ever laid claim to her with such resolve, leaving her no place to hide, no safe retreat into passivity. Her nipples refused to settle. The dull, wet throb grew stronger between her legs. Her heart thudded so loudly in her ears she could hardly hear the conversation around her.

Off balance, she averted her eyes and joined the nearest discussion, only to realize the topic was the late, lamented Lynden Cavender.

"So personable," gushed a middle-aged matron wearing classic Chanel. "Not at all what one is accustomed to these days."

"Humble," someone noted. "A throwback, really."

"Oh, yes. The complete gentleman. An aristocrat."

Lynden had never had to make his way by paying attention to mature women, but he'd made an effort to woo every one of them regardless. As a result he had a devoted following among the society queens of New York and Boston. No one had left his name off her party lists. Even Buffy, a staunch Blake ally, had been so smitten with him she'd intimated more than once that it was time for bygones to be bygones. Vienna supposed it was some consolation that Mason had no hope of taking his place. While her brother had used the Cavender mystique to full advantage, she could never do so. She made everyone too uncomfortable.

The Chanel devotee touched Vienna's arm, "My dear, you must have known him quite well."

"Not really."

"Even with that…atmosphere between your families, aren't your country estates adjoining?"

Vienna smiled vaguely. "We spent very little time there when I was growing up, so I never really got to know him."

"That's not what I've been told." A woman with pearls weighing down her neck coyly added, "We'd positively kill to hear your side of the story, wouldn't we, girls?"

An eager hush descended on the small clique. Obviously no one could believe that Vienna was immune to Lynden's metrosexual charm, and the tired old story about a romance between them was still circulating.

"I thought that particular rumor had died a natural death a long time ago," Vienna said.

The woman in the pearls sighed archly. "Your discretion is admirable, darling, but you're among friends here."

This sentiment was echoed by the Chanel-wearer, who also offered a few consoling words. "It can't have been easy, the situation being what it was. No one was really surprised when you called it off."

"There was never an engagement," Vienna issued her customary denial. "We never even dated."

She knew how the ludicrous story had begun. Guests at her parents' anniversary ball had invented explanations for her disappearance from the celebration and the subsequent drama when she was found unconscious in the grounds of Laudes Absalom. When Vienna couldn't explain what she was doing there in the first place, some people had added two and two and decided she was concealing the truth—she and Lynden were starcrossed lovers trying to hide their romance from parents who hated each other.

Even the police found the story credible. It made no difference that both she and Lynden denied any involvement; the events of that night became another installment in the Cavender's never-ending soap opera. Even Vienna's parents drew the wrong conclusions, overlooking the fact that she was a lesbian, which they both viewed as an unfortunate phase. They almost seemed happy to persuade themselves that she'd crept away for an assignation with their neighbor's handsome son. Lynden was not the true villain of the piece, in their eyes. Their theory was that Vienna had been waylaid by Henry Cavender, who forced an admission of the affair, then turned his fury on her, beating her unconscious.

The Blakes wanted him arrested, but the trouble was he had an alibi, one the detectives weren't willing to discount. The witness who stood between him and a prison cell was none other than his loyal housekeeper, Mrs. Danville. Her story had never wavered over the years. She was out that evening playing bridge and had a car breakdown on her way home. She'd walked back to the village to telephone her employer, who picked her up, then spent at least an hour trying to fix the problem. In the end, Henry had towed her car back to Laudes Absalom.

Remarkably, the motor fired up without a problem the next morning when the police checked. They'd verified Mrs. Danville's story, interviewing the ladies who played bridge with her and someone who claimed to have seen her at a public phone. But even if that part of the story was true, no one but Mrs. Danville could swear that the man who came to her rescue was Henry Cavender. The Blakes thought it was actually Mr. Pettibone and that Henry had never left Laudes Absalom. Yet again, a Cavender had gotten away with murder, or an attempt at it. They were outraged.

Apart from Mrs. Danville, there was only one other person who knew the truth. Mason wasn't there that night, but Vienna had a hard time believing she was as ignorant of the circumstances as she'd always claimed. The Cavenders had simply closed ranks. The case was left open with Vienna's assault ascribed to an "unknown assailant who may have been interrupted in the course of a separate crime." As if any self-respecting burglar would break into the Cavender's run-down old mansion. What was there to steal?

After her conversation with Mrs. Danville, Vienna had asked her mother about that evening once again, this time mentioning the meeting between her father and Henry. After a stony silence and some crocodile tears, the conversation hit the usual dead end, and Vienna was so frustrated she went to the police and demanded to see the files for herself. She was fobbed off there as well, sent on a wild goose chase to the DA's office where some twelve-year-old told her the cold case files were housed elsewhere and she would have to wait until a detective had time to look into the matter.

Irritated, Vienna let her gaze roam. Maybe it was time she confronted Mason directly about that evening. She was owed the truth, and no one could be hurt by it now. Buffy caught her eye and made some kind of gesture, probably a signal that she should reattach herself to Stefan in time for the impending meal. The party organizers were folding back the screens that separated the cocktail area from the dining tables. Mason was nowhere to be seen.

Vienna moved through the crowd looking for her. There were only a hundred guests. A hefty man with a shock of platinum hair and a woman in black tie couldn't be hard to single out. She looked around again, but couldn't even spot Oxana. There wasn't a chance that the Ivanovs would leave before the meal, so they had to be holed up in the restrooms, fixing their hair and refreshing their fragrances. But Mason? Had she gone?

The thought made her spirits sink, a response that appalled her. Disgusted with herself, she drained the rest of her martini, turned around sharply, and almost smacked into a white shirt-front. "Oh, I'm sorry. I…"

Mason didn't apologize or step back politely. Her nightshade eyes swept Vienna slowly up and down before settling on her mouth.

"Looking for me?" she asked.

CHAPTER THIRTEEN

God, she was beautiful, Mason thought, as addictive as a drug. There was something delicious about watching Vienna blush. Her skin was so alabaster pale everything showed. A rosy hue spread beneath her cheeks, driven by an emotion Mason could only guess at. Anger? Guilt? Arousal? Her expression gave nothing away. She wore the mask of cool serenity women of her class hid behind. And apart from the faintest stiffening at their near collision, her body sent no signals. She was the worst kind of Siren, resolutely distant. Blindingly irresistible.

"Well?" Vienna queried tightly.

Mason raised her eyebrows. She was being asked to explain herself. Vienna wasn't used to being stood up, especially by those who were supposed to be grateful for the crumbs she threw.

"I guess I should have phoned," Mason said with mock contrition. "My bad."

"Is that all you have to say to me?"

"Er...you look ravishing tonight." Lowering her gaze to the diamonds, Mason added, "But you should get that necklace cleaned by an expert. I can still see specks of my grandmother's blood."

Vienna's jaws clenched just enough to reveal a struggle for self-control. "If you're trying to upset me, I should warn you, I'm not as a susceptible as I once was."

"That's a pity. You were very fetching when you were... unschooled. I once had quite a crush on you."

"I see you got over it," Vienna snapped. "What are you doing here?"

"I decided I need to get out more," Mason said flippantly.

She wondered why Vienna still bothered to try and pass herself off as straight at this type of gathering. Her "date" was obviously a stranger, one of those solo males hostesses like Buffy kept on ice for women who failed to bring a guest. Mason had just been offered one of the breed, an English poet Buffy could call upon at short notice. She'd offered a better suggestion.

"By the way," she said pleasantly. "I told Buffy you won't be needing what's-his-name...the Italian count. I said she can seat us together for dinner."

"You did what?" Vienna's voice rose slightly in pitch.

"It's only a meal, and we've had more intimate encounters." Mason watched the color wash down Vienna's throat to her breasts. "I told her I've been thinking it's time the Blakes and the Cavenders made up. She agreed. I think she wants to be instrumental."

Mason enjoyed the soft intake of breath that greeted this disclosure.

"And you expect me to participate in that fiction?" Vienna fidgeted with her hair.

"It shouldn't be difficult. You and your family are masters of hypocrisy."

"If you think I'm going to force the issue and make people take sides, you're mistaken. I refuse to be painted as the villain to my friends."

"No, you wouldn't want to appear mean-spirited," Mason said softly. "To shun a woman after her brother's tragic death...then set out to ruin her. Quite unbecoming."

"If I cared what people really thought of me, I would never get a minute's sleep."

"Well, I wouldn't want you tossing and turning at night on my account." Mason smiled. Oh, yes. She was getting under Vienna's skin. Mason glanced down at the idle hand resting on the gray satin. The slim fingers shook slightly.

Vienna cast a distracted glance toward the dining area. People were drifting in and taking their seats. Her fingers jerked to life, plucking at the slippery fabric. "I don't know what game you're playing," she snapped in a terse undertone, "but you're not backing me into a corner. I am not partnering with you for dinner."

"Why not? You have to admit we look good together, and we're the only lesbians here."

No instant rejection was forthcoming. Mason's pulse increased. It had occurred to her that there was more than one way to lay siege to this particular Blake. If they had to wage a war consisting entirely of financial power and legal strategies, Vienna would win: she had more weapons. Mason's opportunity lay in the other battlefield she'd established. When it came to sex, Vienna had definite vulnerabilities. So far Mason had failed to exploit these. She'd been too obvious and revealed far to much of herself.

She let her gaze travel over the beautiful, arrogant face upturned to hers and knew she'd struck the jackpot. Vienna's pupils dilated as their eyes met. She immediately evaded Mason's stare, looking straight through her. But the telltale flicker of awareness told Mason all she needed to know. Nothing had changed. In fact, Vienna seemed even more susceptible to her.

Up until now, Mason had been afflicted by some misguided notion of chivalry, and hadn't forced the issue. She'd allowed Vienna to slip through her hands unscathed, but she would not make the same mistake again. This time she would do whatever it took to teach her a lesson. Vienna's smug words repeated in her mind: *Mason is exactly where I want her to be.* She was in for an unpleasant surprise.

Mason already had a verbal agreement from Sergei Ivanov. He'd virtually salivated when he examined the diamonds she'd brought to the party. A man whose wife loved jewelry as much as his did was keenly aware of the market for Azaria's product. He wanted a piece of the action and Mason had arranged for him to see the factory tomorrow. Once he watched a real diamond growing inside a machine, he would be throwing money at her; he'd almost written a check tonight. Instead Mason had him sign the nondisclosure agreement Josh had given her.

As soon as she'd secured the investment, she would dispatch Josh to their bankers and beg for an extension to the loans about to fall due. In the meantime she had to hold Vienna at bay and keep their negotiations alive. So long as the bankers thought the Blake deal was still in play, they would feel secure about getting their money in the end. A takeover process was usually punctuated with drawn-out discussions and legal wrangles before the final deal was closed. Mason would drag that process out for as long as she could, but Vienna Blake was no fool.

If she suspected she was being toyed with to buy time, she would go straight for the jugular.

Mason knew it was time for the unexpected. Lust was a powerful urge. In its thrall, Vienna had already shown she would abandon her good judgment. And she'd been ready for a repeat encounter. Mason smiled. It would be hell finding out just how far Vienna was willing to go to, and this time there would be no backing out.

"I was about to leave." Vienna's mouth tightened, only narrowly avoided a pout.

"How inconsiderate of you. After all, you're the main attraction."

"They'll get over it." Vienna's chest rose and fell with a short, sharp breath. "And Buffy can find someone else to sit with you."

From the corner of her eye, Mason could see their hostess introducing Stefan to an elderly lady with pink-bronze hair and an insipid young girl. They looked thrilled. Throwing down her next challenge, she said, "Why didn't you bring a real date, by the way?"

"Why didn't you?" Vienna retorted.

"Because they always want me to fuck them and I'm not in the mood tonight." Mason added gallantly, "I'd make an exception for you, naturally."

There was no mistaking the effect of her uncouth compliment. Vienna's nipples rebelled against the confines of her designer gown, forming two small puckers against the shimmering fabric. Sounding breathless, she said, "Don't do me any favors."

"Oh, it would be my pleasure." Mason subjected her to a lengthy appraisal. "And I must say, you look like you need some…relief. You're very tense."

"If that's a pick-up line, you really do need to get out more." Vienna was signaling someone to come to her rescue.

Concealing a grin, Mason followed the direction of her gaze. Oxana Ivanov hadn't noticed the frantic eyebrow lift, and was smiling benevolently on both of them. Mason hoped her husband had kept silent about their agreement. She didn't want the details leaking to Vienna.

Buffy's party planner dispatched his minions to wrangle the remaining guests to their tables. Stefan had the pink-haired old lady on his arm. A beardless youth trailed behind with the mousy girl. Vienna was seething, having been abandoned to Mason's tender mercies. Mason could almost smell her perturbation.

Buffy came toward them, her diamond chandelier earrings swinging. "You two are at my table," she said brightly. "I must say, I'm so happy that you're putting an end to this silly quarrel at last. This is what happens when women finally take charge."

Mason offered Vienna her arm. With a hissed "Christ" Vienna accepted the courtesy and Buffy led them into the dining room, where a wave of applause rippled through the crowd. Mason wasn't sure whether the approbation was for Buffy, or if guests were reacting to the startling evidence of a truce between the Blakes and the Cavenders. She recognized various faces as they made their way to the front of the room. Buffy had assembled the remnants of old New York society, many of whom had long-standing ties to the Cavenders. There were elderly widows who had spent weekends at Laudes Absalom. Younger men who'd played polo with Lynden. Mason had seen the same faces at her brother's funeral.

She could feel Vienna's tension, although no one would have guessed from her graceful nods and genteel smiles. It had always amused Mason that the Blakes were supposed to be so coolheaded and measured, traits that didn't seem to come naturally to Vienna. On the few occasions they'd encountered each other in previous years, Mason was the one in control of herself. Vienna usually seemed to have trouble keeping her temper in check. Right now Mason knew she was ready to throw something.

She slid a chair out for Vienna, sparking a few curious second looks, but no one at the table would dream of showing disapproval. Mason had a free pass. She'd never pretended to be anything but the lesbian she was, and anyone who invited her to a party knew exactly what they could expect. She'd never worn a dress in her life and most of the people in this room had probably heard at least one of the rumors about her love life. Her brief affair with a U.S. senator had led to a very public divorce, an outcome Mason had never intended. She'd declined to comment to the press, but that didn't stop the salacious speculation. Not long after the fuss died down over that scandal a set of photos was published in *People* magazine, showing Mason with actress Kinsey Wade.

They'd met at college and had a short-lived fling before Kinsey landed her first speaking role. She'd been pretending to be straight ever since. After her Oscar loss several years ago and a lead role in a movie that bombed, she hit a rocky patch and contacted Mason for support. Someone had photographed them at a party where Kinsey was baked on substances. The public clinch they'd shared became a headliner on a slow news week. Mason was described as "the lesbian sister of *GQ* Man of the Year finalist, Lynden Cavender" and the article went on to state that sources close to the actress confirmed the steamy affair.

Kinsey had hired a new publicist to make the most of the exposure and reinvented herself as a hip veteran on the indie circuit, meaning she was over thirty and could act. She'd even appeared on *Larry King Live*, talking about Mason as if she were some kind of lesbian Howard Hughes. In the weeks that followed, Mason had virtually become a prisoner at Laudes Absalom, with journalists and paparazzi staking the place out in the hopes of seeing Kinsey or some other famous woman visiting "the infamous Cavender love nest in the Berkshires." They'd even pestered her with inappropriate questions at Lynden's funeral.

Mason hoped someone would photograph her with an arm around Vienna. She could imagine how that would turn up the heat at Blake Industries. That vile creep Andy Rossiter was already starting to bypass Vienna. He'd called Josh a few days ago, asking for a status update.

"Where are you staying?" Vienna asked, after indicating her wine preferences to a waiter.

"At Lynden's condo on Bond Street."

"Noisy?"

Mason shrugged. "It could be worse."

"Be thankful you're not in Tribeca. I was down there yesterday and my ears are still ringing. I have friends in the Dietz Lantern Building. The pile drivers never stop."

Mason nodded politely. Noise pollution was always a safe conversation topic in New York. She lowered her gaze to the Cavender Diamonds and pondered the strange twist of fate that saw the necklace around the bitable neck of her enemy. She knew the diamonds had been sold out of financial necessity, but Mason couldn't imagine her father humbling himself by selling the most important family heirloom to his worst enemy. Even at his drunkest and meanest, Henry had his pride. The idea that he would allow his mother's necklace to grace a Blake throat was unimaginable. Mason assumed the necklace must have passed through the hands of a third party.

Vienna didn't seem to know anything about its history and was obviously embarrassed by it. But perhaps she knew how her father had acquired it.

"The necklace," Mason asked. "Did your father buy it from a private collector?"

Vienna looked uncomfortable. "Actually, he bought it directly from your father."

Mason was silent for a long moment, searching Vienna's face for some sign of deception. Finally she managed a comment. "How gratifying for Norris."

"Mason, I had no idea." Vienna smoothed her auburn hair unnecessarily. "Maybe Dad thought I wouldn't wear it if he told me."

"Because it's tainted by generations of Cavenders?"

"No, that's not what I meant." Vienna's long eyelashes descended, veiling her gaze. The chandelier over their table lent a coppery sheen to them. She didn't wear mascara, just some soft brown eye pencil and subtle shadow. Her skin was spectacular close up, its smooth, pale luster virtually unchanged in ten years.

Mason tried not to let her mind slip back to that night, but it was the only time she'd ever been able to look at her for as long as she wanted. There was so much blood, she'd been panic-stricken, certain that Vienna was dying. Mason had cradled her, stroking her face and talking to her until the ambulance came. The EMT responders took over then and Mason had kept her distance, knowing she couldn't remain at the scene. She hadn't spoken about that night for a long while, but Mrs. Danville had brought up the topic recently.

Apparently Vienna had been at Laudes Absalom asking awkward questions. She still remembered almost nothing about that night, but Mrs. Danville was worried. Mason hoped Vienna would let it drop once she found herself faced with a wall of silence. There was a still a reward on offer for any information concerning the "hippy-type guy" EMTs described seeing at the scene, but the case had gone cold long ago.

Over the years Mason had considered turning herself in, but the consequences would have been intolerable. She wasn't willing to go to prison because she'd done something rash in the heat of the moment. The Blakes had cooked up an explanation for Vienna's assault, a love affair between her and Lynden that provoked Henry into a drunken attack. The Cavenders had made no real effort to prove otherwise. The story had served as a useful smokescreen.

Mason glanced around the table, dragging herself present. Ten years had passed since that night and she'd sometimes thought about telling Vienna the truth, but the opportunity never seemed to present itself. Besides, she was reluctant to place another potential weapon in her enemy's hands. Some people might feel honor bound to maintain silence over such a disclosure, under the circumstances, but a Blake?

"I was thinking about the Cavender Curse," Vienna conceded in a strained voice. "Isn't it supposed to be connected to the necklace?"

"The media likes to think so," Mason said.

The Cavender name had been selling newspapers for over a century and reporters had stumbled onto a winning formula with the Curse—supernatural forces destroying the lives of rich people within a powerful dynasty. The only thing missing in their saga was an assassinated president, and they'd tried to make up for that in their recent hype over Lynden's death. One article had claimed he was seen as a future candidate. His lack of qualifications didn't seem to strike commentators as a drawback, and perhaps they were right. Now that the presidential race had turned into something like *American Idol—the POTUS edition* maybe Lynden could have made the jump into politics. His prospective father-in-law had certainly thought so.

"A necklace didn't cause my grandmother's death," Mason said. "The explanation is much more banal. Your grandfather was a dirtbag, and mine was a murderer."

Ignoring Vienna's nervous cough, she got to her feet and lifted her sparkling water as the guests toasted Buffy. She wasn't drinking champagne, she wanted to be sharp tonight. As soon as the crowd had settled back into their seats, the waiters rolled out the food and the noisy conversation became a polite hum. Mason thought Vienna would take the opportunity to change the subject, but she seemed reluctant to let it go.

"Do you think your father kept a record of the sale?"

Mason frowned. "What does it matter?"

"I was just…curious." Vienna's tone became reflective. "My great-aunt Rachel knew something about the necklace. I remember her at my birthday party, when she saw it."

"Are you talking about Rachel Blake, the aviator?"

"Yes, she's over ninety now, but she still thinks she should be allowed to fly." Vienna sampled a morsel of Kobe beef carpaccio and remarked on its exquisite tenderness before continuing. "She was angry with my father. At the time, I assumed she was having one of her sulks. She'd just had her hip replaced and was feeling sorry for herself."

"I met her once," Mason said. "At Great Barrington Airport. I was taking flying lessons and she showed me how to get out of my plane fast if I crashed." The advice had helped save her life. With faint irony, she added, "I'm sure she didn't know who she was talking to."

"She knew," Vienna said with certainty. "Rachel wouldn't have cared. She thought the feud was ridiculous."

"Ah, a Blake with an independent spirit? What a shock."

"She was friends with your grandmother...Nancy."

Intrigued despite herself, Mason asked, "What did she say about the diamonds?"

"I didn't realize they were talking about the necklace. She asked if Dad knew what he was playing with. He told her she was being silly and superstitious. I remember she said, 'How many has it cursed?' Then they saw me in the doorway and stopped talking."

"You never asked her what she meant?" Mason drizzled vinaigrette on a slice of Mozzarella di bufala. She'd foresworn the Coromandel oysters. Her vegetarian habits weren't confined to four-legged creatures.

"No, I thought it was probably more Cavender angst and I was sick of the whole subject."

Mason understood the sentiment. A week had seldom passed at Laudes Absalom in which the Blakes weren't vilified. She'd learned to tune out before she finished elementary school. As for asking questions about the Curse, why invite another rant?

"I suppose it's strange to see me wearing it." The color deepened around Vienna's throat in stark contrast to the icy glitter of the diamonds. "Really, it should have been passed down to you."

Mason met her troubled gaze. Surprised by the show of sensitivity, she said, "Seriously, do I look like the kind of woman who'd wear a fancy necklace? I'm sure Dad knew it would just sit in a drawer gathering dust if I had it."

She'd inherited most of her mother's jewelry, at least the pieces Henry didn't think were worth selling. The only item she wore constantly was an old-fashioned bloodstone pinky ring etched inside with her mother's initials. She kept Lynden's family crest ring in a trinket box in the library.

Vienna eyed her quizzically. "You don't seem angry."

"What would be the point? What's done is done. Besides, it looks good on you."

Mason studied the heavy Titian ripples drawn back from Vienna's temples. Her face was strong. Even in the soft golden lighting, her cheekbones were high and her nose a little too long to be girlish. It went with her Blake chin, stubborn and solidly formed. Her mouth laid claim to a sensuous femininity she could have enhanced with dark red lipstick, but she'd chosen a modest shade. The same understatement was evident in her elegant gray satin dress. The gown was form-fitting but not revealing, seductive but not overtly sexy. It spelled out the woman Vienna had become—sleekly untouchable.

Mason pictured her naked and abandoned, pinned beneath her. Begging. Moaning. The tantalizing image faded fast as she found herself wondering if she could persuade Vienna to let herself go again, or if their kisses, and that pent-up moment in the great hall, were nothing more than a concession to curiosity, after years wondering how it would feel. Maybe she'd blown her chances by backing off and leaving Vienna in the wind for the past two weeks. And maybe the child who'd rebelled against her family and reached for Mason's hand so long ago was truly lost.

The thought stabbed her. With one look, Vienna had owned her. Savage providence…it had gnawed at her all these years, the belief that Vienna was meant for her. That somehow the joyous innocent she'd stolen from the Blakes that day would be hers. She'd never been able to shake that conviction. Over time she'd crushed the senseless adoration she harbored for the girl next door, only to face a darker enemy. Her desire for Vienna had packed on muscle in its lonely prison, sucking strength from her connections with other women and afflicting her with a sense of helplessness.

Mason stared down at her food. If there *was* a Curse, she lived it, the Cavender who wanted a Blake. She resented her condition bitterly and resented the woman at its core. Even now, wearing the guise of civilization, she was aware of the pawing, insistent creature within, the predatory self wrestling its chains. If she had a pelt it would be standing on end in Vienna's presence, at the merest possibility of her touch. She wondered if Vienna sensed that hungry presence. Was that why she kept looking away?

What was she afraid of—that she would succumb once again and allow Mason to kiss her, to force her open? Mason's mouth trembled. She took a sharp breath, inhaling the mix of scents around her. Jasmine. Grape. Tannin. Honey. Juniper. Her own musk and sandalwood were also detectable, because she was perspiring. Her body tingled, as it did when Vienna ruled her mind. She was never free of her fierce yearnings and a pounding sorrow over what might have been.

She should have risked everything and told Vienna the truth a long time ago, back when there was a chance that they could write different rules. When they were too young to have hardened themselves. They could have thrown off the swaddling of their birth and drawn strength from each other. But too much had happened since those callow days. Even if they tried, Mason doubted they could be anything but foes now. She no longer trusted that fate would contrive in their favor and deliver happiness as if by entitlement. Reality had intervened.

The only question now was how to make her new game plan work. She needed Vienna to believe that she was going to do the deal, but she didn't want to lie outright. The sexual tension between them made a chink in Vienna's armor, but it wouldn't be enough to blind her. She was naturally suspicious and also forearmed, having allowed herself to explore the forbidden two weeks ago. Her ambivalence had been apparent even then, and still Mason wondered if that night in her bed would have happened, even if they'd had dinner together. She suspected not. By then, Vienna would have changed her mind and suppressed the impulse.

If Mason wanted to manipulate her, she would have to dismantle that formidable self-control. Luckily, rocket science would not be required. Jerks through the ages had fallen back on the same reliable seduction method.

Intoxication.

CHAPTER FOURTEEN

Mason eyed Vienna's wineglasses and knew she faced a challenge. Vienna had taken perhaps three sips of her Krug and the red Montefalco Rosso sat untouched. She was drinking iced water and had started chatting with the man seated at her right. The conversation was about an artist. Waiters cleared plates and served the entrée course. The meals had a country kitchen sensibility, in keeping with the theme established earlier with the finger food. Vienna sampled her red wine and parted a large puff pastry. She'd requested the duck pie. Mason bit into a wild mushroom ravioli and wished she was a better cook. Most of the time, at home, she made Chinese food, and there were only so many ways stir-fried vegetables could be dressed up.

As they ate, the conversation around them drifted from speculation on who had purchased the Wildenstein townhouse, probably Len Blavatnik, say no more. And whether Art Basel in Miami would be worth attending this year now that it had turned into such a spectacle. There was something grubby about all those clueless instant millionaires in their bug-eyed sunglasses chugging Red Bull and switching between iPhones while they hassled famous collectors for hints on what to buy.

"Have you ever been?" Vienna asked Mason.

"It's not my idea of a good time."

"I delegate," Vienna said. "One of my senior staff is an art junkie. I send him as a surrogate. He knows how to stay within budget."

"You don't want to see the works he's buying?"

"He e-mails pics with his BlackBerry." Vienna smiled. "I'm

only going to see them when I walk through the building. The Blake collection is strictly business."

"What do you do for your own enjoyment?"

Vienna's gaze lingered on Mason's mouth before flitting away. She took more than a sip of wine. "I don't get a lot of time for hobbies."

"You adopt those horses," Mason said. "That's a very decent thing to do. If you ever need any help, you can call me."

"Thank you." Vienna moved a piece of food around her plate, then lowered her fork. She looked like she'd just found a cockroach in her *vol au vent*. "I gather I'm already in your debt."

If you only knew. Mason shrugged. "It's nothing. Rick helps me out, too."

"I didn't realize you look after my animals when he needs time out. You really ought to send me a bill for those days."

"Charge you for my services?" Mason couldn't keep her mouth from twitching. "I wouldn't dream of it."

Vienna reached for her wine, and drank carelessly this time, clearly rattled by the double entendre. Attempting to reply in kind, she said, "I'd hate to take advantage of you."

"Really? That's not my impression." Mason sliced open the artichoke heart accompanying her ravioli and slowly parted the folds. "You enjoyed yourself quite noisily the last time you...*took advantage*, if I recall."

The soft gasp was unmistakable. Mason guessed Vienna was trying to look cool and serene, but the tension in her shoulders showed in the deepening shadows above her collarbones. The pulse at the base of her neck beat more heavily. Her fingers were restive, tapping the table and rearranging the silverware. She fended off her unease with a brittle laugh. "You don't play fair."

"If you mean I don't play by your rules, then yes." Mason shook her head. "God, doesn't it get suffocating inside that straitjacket?"

"What are you talking about?"

"You weren't always such a conformist."

"We all have to grow up sometime, Mason. Even you."

"Ouch." Mason clapped a hand over her chest. "A low blow, my lady."

Vienna snatched up her glass. "Okay, enough foreplay. Let's cut to the chase. How much do you want for Cavender?"

Mason concealed her astonishment. Was she being invited to name her price? Vienna must be desperate to stave off the mutiny by her relatives. "For starters, I want you to stop sending that Italian over to my house with extra offers."

"I was trying to make it easy for you to sell."

"You think a wiseguy with a bullshit cover story makes it easier? He scares my horses, and we both know five million is a crazy price."

"The offer's for real." In an urgent whisper, Vienna begged, "Please, just take it. I know you need the money."

Mason met Vienna's overbright eyes. "Your duck pie's getting cold."

Vienna hacked at the pastry. "Do you have to be so damned stubborn?"

"If you don't want to live next door to me, why don't you sell Penwraithe?" Mason suggested blandly. "You're not there most of the time."

"Oh, you'd love that, wouldn't you?" Vienna tackled the wine once more. After a few angry gulps, she lifted her napkin and smothered a hiccup. Her voice was becoming frayed around the edges. "If you think I'm going to back off just because we had sex you're dreaming."

Mason knew from past experience that if she kept up the pressure, Vienna would steady her nerves with alcohol. At this rate she would be drunk before the dessert course. Casually, she dangled her bait. "Actually, if your terms were different, I'd probably accept."

A flicker of triumph registered before Vienna's long lashes fanned downward to screen her reaction. "Everything is negotiable. I'm flexible on the timetable for the transfer of assets if that's a problem."

Mason produced the defeated sigh of a woman weary of the fight. "I'm leaving the fine print to the lawyers. To be honest, this madness has consumed far too much of my life, and for what?"

Vienna nodded. "I know what you mean."

"I just want to put it all behind me and move on." Mason sighed, in part because there was some truth in that admission. "I hate to say it, but you're probably doing me a favor."

Vienna's eyes were bright with concentration. She had her prey cornered and could see an end to the chase. Mason was counting on her wanting to make the kill in person. "You know, sometimes the principals can settle things more quickly themselves," she said, toxically sweet.

"Maybe." Mason allowed reluctance to enter her expression. Then annoyance, as though she knew she'd just given too much away. "But our families don't have a history of civility and cooperation."

As she'd expected, Vienna pounced. "You and I are adults and realists. I'm sure we can agree to put our differences aside in the interests of getting the deal done. Look at us now. Sitting together in public."

Mason smiled. "I guess we should stop meeting like this. People will talk."

Vienna's soft laugh sounded forced. She seemed to collect herself then, sitting up a little straighter and placing her utensils neatly together on her plate. "Mason I know this has been tough for you, and I'm not going to pressure you, but this process has taken over both our lives and you may not believe it, but I'm ready to call it quits, too. Enough is enough." She placed her small hand over Mason's, sending a shock of sensation up her arm. "That's why I'm making a good offer. Are you willing to accept?"

Keeping her voice low so that Vienna had to lean in to hear her, Mason said, "I guess it's inevitable."

Vienna studied her face, at first with a trace of suspicion, then with poorly smothered elation of an amateur poker player convinced she held the winning hand. Apparently she thought it was time to be generous. "What I said…about the livestock…" Her breath stirred the hair that fell over Mason's cheek. "I didn't mean any of it. I spoke in anger. I'm sorry."

Mason angled her head a little closer. Her lips brushed "accidentally" across Vienna's cheek. "It's I who should apologize. I had no right to storm into your office that day."

The hand on hers tensed, the fingers biting down. Mason drew back, but only slightly. They stared at each other as a waiter cleared their plates.

"You don't seriously believe I had anything to do with the plane crash, do you?" Evidently Vienna was working her way down a laundry list of possible deal-breakers.

Mason hesitated just long enough to seem unconvinced. "Associates like Mr. Pantano don't inspire confidence."

"Pantano's harmless," Vienna said. "My father rescued him from a bad situation, so he thinks he owes my family a debt. He gets a bit carried away at times, but he had nothing to do with the accident, I promise you that."

Mason could see her weighing the alternatives. Stop the discussion before it went sour, and leave the rest to her attorneys? Or reach an agreement now and have the staff write up the details? Predictably, her instincts took over. Vienna wanted more than a victory on paper; she wanted to force the surrender and prove to anyone who doubted it that she had the chops to run the Blake empire. She'd seen an opening and was circling Mason with predatory calm.

"Mason. You've been honest with me, so let me tell you something. I'm only doing this because my family won't let me get on with my life until I do. I don't want your business or your house, but you'll be better off if you sell to me before the banks force you to liquidate."

"That's probably true," Mason conceded.

Vienna picked up her wineglass, then set it down again, untouched. A note of impatience entered her voice. "So, let's talk plainly. What's it going to take?"

"Do you really need to ask, after our last conversation?"

Vienna took shelter in raised eyebrows and fake laughter. "I can see I sent the wrong signals that day. How ungentlemanly of you to tease me." She lowered both hands onto her lap, sandwiching them together. "I'm just thankful one of us had the good sense to leave the Berkshires before we did something we'd regret."

Mason knew she was supposed to pretend they were indulging in mere banter. But she wasn't going to let Vienna off so easily. "No, you're not. You're angry with me."

"Okay, I was a little annoyed. It would have been courteous for you to get in touch." Vienna shrugged. "But I'm sure you had more pressing matters to attend to."

"As did you." Mason paused. "How's that battle coming along, by the way? When Andy phoned us the other day, I thought he must have taken over."

She watched Vienna process this information and temper her response, staring unseeingly at the floral centerpiece on their table. The only sign of her anger was the fretful attention she suddenly paid to her napkin, jerking it tight before rearranging it on her lap.

"I know they say keep your enemies close," Mason continued. "But VP?"

"How I deal with my family is none of your business."

"If only they knew the lengths you've gone to already, to get me… exactly where you want me. I believe those were your words. And that you'd do whatever it takes."

Vienna sat very still.

"Forgive me," Mason continued. "I overheard you on your cell phone at Penwraithe that day, talking to your mother. It didn't seem like the right time to announce myself, so I went back home."

"And left before our…date," Vienna completed blankly. The dent in her sangfroid was evident. She moistened her lips and looked everywhere but at Mason, clearly trying to figure out how she could reclaim the advantage.

Mason saved her the trouble. "Yes, so getting back to whatever it takes, I've had some time to think about acceptable terms."

"And?" Vienna regarded her warily.

"You for a week. Complete possession. Anything I want."

"I'm sorry?"

"You want me to spell it out in more detail?"

"No," Vienna retorted, clearly convinced that Mason was messing with her. "Very funny." She adopted a smooth, unruffled tone. "Just give me the cold, hard numbers, Mason, and we can get this over with."

"I'm not interested in numbers, I'm interested in fucking you."

Vienna blanched. "Don't," she whispered. "Not here."

"You're right. This isn't the place." Mason dropped her napkin on the table. Normally, she wouldn't speak crudely to any woman outside of the bedroom, but she'd accomplished her goal. Vienna was thrown off balance and, from the looks of her nipples, turned on to boot.

The waiters were still clearing plates. After a civilized amount of time, they would serve dessert and coffee. It really wasn't done to leave a dinner party like this one until the cheese plates came out and people started escaping to smoke, but no one would be surprised by Mason's departure. Vienna, however, would be stuck here for the next hour, keeping up appearances. Brooding. Upset. Aroused.

Mason slid her chair back. "I think we're done. I'm going to skip dessert and drive back to Laudes Absalom. Are you coming?"

"Now?" Vienna cast a frantic look around the table.

"Need some time to think about it? Take twenty-four hours,"

Mason said with calm indifference. "I'll be at the apartment for a while before I leave. Now, if you'll excuse me."

Leaving Vienna blinking in disbelief, she moved around the table to murmur her apologies to their hostess. She explained that she'd become emotional thinking about Lynden and had probably overestimated her ability to be around others. She made a point of thanking Buffy for helping her and Vienna to move toward healing the rift between their families. Buffy seemed delighted and even dropped a kiss on her cheek. Out of the corner of her eye, Mason could see Vienna watching her every move with a pinched expression. Both hands were in her lap and she kept glancing down.

She was text-messaging, Mason concluded, no doubt telling her attorneys to await her further instructions and ignore anything Andy Rossiter told them to do. With a polite nod in her direction, Mason left the party. As she waited for the doorman to summon a taxi, she weighed the odds and decided Vienna would arrive on her doorstep in NoHo in roughly ninety minutes. If Mason had already left by then, she could expect a petulant visitor tomorrow at Laudes Absalom.

❖

Vienna banged on the door of the wrong apartment. The cool urbanite who answered had a perfumed pooch tucked under his arm and a Bluetooth attached to his head. When she described who she was looking for, he directed her to a corner loft on the top floor, adding, "She's not selling. I asked."

Lynden's condo was probably a light and gorgeous designer masterpiece, if the building was any indication, but Vienna didn't get to find out. Either Mason had already gone or she wasn't answering the door. Feeling light-headed, Vienna leaned against the wall and tried to decide if she was relieved or let down. The last thing she'd expected of this evening was to find herself outplayed. Mason was ready to sell, yet somehow she'd backed Vienna into a corner. She'd expected a fight to the bitter end, but not this. Did Mason seriously expect Vienna to trade sex for her signature?

Vienna thought about the plane crash. From all accounts, Lynden was a novice pilot. He'd attempted an emergency landing when he wasn't ready for prime time. No one was to blame for another spoiled white man with money thinking he was some kind of god and could live by different rules. The plane had engine failure in poor weather. An expert pilot could probably have landed it. Why was Lynden at the controls and not Mason?

Was that what this was really about? Was Mason making their fight personal because she felt guilty and had to shift the blame somewhere? Vienna tried to think rationally. Mason had to know she would never accept such an absurd, humiliating condition to get the deal done. Become a sexual plaything for a week? It was outrageous. Mason was dreaming if she thought Vienna would barter her body like some medieval virgin, sacrificing herself for the good of her family. She had far too much self-respect.

Infuriated, she gave up ringing the doorbell and took the elevator back down to the street. Her mind felt thick with the effects of three glasses of wine, but she was sobering up and coffee would help. She was irritated that'd she'd consumed so much more than her usual small glass. Normally she was more careful, but tonight wasn't a normal evening.

She got into a cab, lost in thought. The driver was mercifully silent as they drove uptown, recognizing a New Yorker and sparing her the inquisition reserved for tourists. New York taxi drivers went to charm school these days and hers had obviously been awake for the session on how to get better tips. He switched off the rap music and called, "I got Brahms on CD. You like to hear that, ma'am?"

She played along. "Sure. Nice idea."

When they reached her building, he behaved with the gallantry commanded by a twenty-dollar tip, and paused to shoot the breeze with the doorman. Vienna hoped Marjorie would be asleep by now. She'd begged off Buffy's party because of a clash of events. She and Buffy were old friends and understood the give and take necessary at such times. Besides, Vienna's presence was decent compensation, as she only had time to attend a few events during the charity season now that she ran Blake Industries.

She let herself into the apartment, dropped her cashmere evening coat over a chair in the downstairs foyer, and peeped into her mother's bedroom. Marjorie was snoring happily, her face shrouded in the elasticized mask she wore each night to enhance the effects of her costly skin products. Vienna didn't know if this hallowed ritual actually worked, but Marjorie took no chances. She also spent weeks of every year in LA, having her face embalmed with mysterious treatments she described as "European." Despite regular Botox, she could still move her eyebrows. Vienna supposed that was something. Several friends had to resort to intervention when their mothers started overusing the needle. It got ugly.

She made a plunger of strong coffee and retreated to her room. Opening the French doors onto the wraparound terrace, she looked across Fifth Avenue to the familiar Central Park tree line. The Blakes took pride in their beautiful outdoor living space, a garden oasis that offered a tranquil escape from the noise and dreariness of the concrete world around them. Vienna could remember birthday parties here with her cousins and various children of her parents' friends. In hindsight, she realized the parties weren't really for her. They were events where adults socialized and competed.

She'd always wished she had a sister or brother to escape with, but her three closest cousins were all boys and older than her. They stuck together with Andy their ringleader. He'd always resented her, Vienna reflected, and he had no loyalty. Her father had rewarded him very generously for his mediocre work in the company, and there was even a time when Norris had considered a revision to his will, to provide Andy with his own shareholding. Vienna wasn't sure what had changed his mind, but he never mentioned the idea again after her brush with death the night of the ball. He probably didn't want her to feel she'd lost his trust.

Once Vienna was well again, life had returned to normal and her father had continued to fashion her into the son he never had, grooming her to take his place alone. Perhaps the most important thing he'd taught her was that power and responsibility go hand in hand. Most of the people she knew paid lip service to the maxim, but the Blakes took duty seriously. Vienna's name was her destiny; she knew that. Walking away, or giving up in the middle of a fight, was inconceivable.

She sat down at a small table beneath a vine-covered pergola and poured her coffee, wondering what Norris would have advised her to do about Andy. He'd become even more obnoxious of late, egged on by his mother. Since her divorce, Aunt Cynthia had far too much time on her hands and spent it making trouble. She spoke openly about her precious son taking over as president in the near future and had managed to establish a faction of supporters inside the company who reported direct to Andy. Vienna couldn't sack all of them.

The issue was leadership. When her father was in charge, no one would have dared go around him. Vienna had always imaged a scenario where she gradually took over his role, having him there advising her and maintaining a presence before he retired completely. But she'd found herself in charge overnight, forced to pick up the reins while she was so weighed down with grief she could hardly function. She'd often felt out of her depth and isolated, but she couldn't risk showing a lack of confidence with her aunts and cousins sitting around her like vultures, just waiting for her to make a mistake.

The Cavender deal was her first big test and she knew she had Mason on the ropes, that crazy condition notwithstanding. Should she take for granted her inevitable surrender, or should she strike now by raising the stakes? If she withdrew her offer, the whole house of cards would come down. The bank would call in their loans and the Cavender Corporation would be bankrupt. Either way, Vienna couldn't lose.

Mason was just playing chicken with her. Like all Cavenders, she was unpredictable. They were governed by their emotions and therefore prone to impulsive behavior. Tonight was the perfect illustration. Mason knew the end was imminent; in her own words she'd admitted she wanted to get it over with. But instead of making a graceful exit, she'd decided Vienna should suffer a little, too. Sipping the hot coffee, Vienna turned her face toward the breeze and willed her senses to snap into alert mode. She needed to think lucidly but her mind felt spongy and sluggish. By contrast, her limbs were tense and her breathing was too rapid.

There was nothing about Mason that warranted girlish swoons or romantic illusions; she was Vienna's stark opposite, a shameless womanizer. But the mere thought of spending a week as her lover made Vienna's pulse hammer out of control. She needed a cold shower.

Mumbling, "Get a grip on yourself," she pushed off her Jimmy Choo pumps and allowed her feet to settle on the cool brick cobblestones.

By now Mason was probably halfway to the Berkshires. Vienna knew she should be close behind, making the three-hour drive in the middle of the night so she could reclaim the advantage. Her father would have been knocking on the door at Laudes Absalom in the middle of the

· 154 ·

night to get this deal signed. He always did whatever it took. That was the Blake way.

Vienna drained her coffee and got to her feet. She could go tomorrow, she decided, unzipping her dress with a moan of relief. She wasn't going to fall for Mason's ticking bomb ploy. After adding the gown to a stack of clothing to be cleaned, she took off the Cavender Diamonds, dropped the necklace distastefully on her night table, and marched into the bathroom. Her mother was expecting her to tag along for a terrifying brunch with some charity committee types at L'Absinthe the next morning. Then Vienna was supposed to help her choose between several Oscar de la Renta designs for the Whitney Gala. By the time they found shoes to match, it would be late afternoon, and then she had a meeting with Darryl Kent over her aunts' latest legal machinations. She wouldn't get to Penwraithe until the evening.

Twenty-four hours. What then? Was Mason planning to walk away from the deal and self-destruct? No, even a Cavender wasn't that crazy. Vienna had increased her bid a week ago, making an offer Mason couldn't refuse: an even more inflated price for the corporation and a flat-out crazy amount for Laudes Absalom. If the deal got any richer there would be howls of outrage once her aunts saw the figures. She *had* to get Mason to sign.

Bothered by the thought, Vienna pinned up her hair and removed her makeup. A day wouldn't make any difference. The time limit was a game. Vienna adjusted the shower temperature and stepped beneath the soothing jets of water, trying not to hear Aunt Cynthia's voice accusing her of procrastination. She soaped herself and watched white, fluffy suds roll down her legs and gather around her toes. *Was* she delaying the coup de grâce? If so, why?

Mason's face drifted before her, the eyes darkly glowing, that mouth too close for comfort. In those final moments at Buffy's, with Mason's breath on her cheek, Vienna had wanted to turn her head and take the kiss that always thickened the air between them. She could feel Mason's body summoning hers. Like a phantom in a dream, it reached for her, and Vienna felt she had no choice but to reach back.

Was that the real reason she was standing here making excuses for herself? Was she afraid of her own weakness? Vienna scrubbed her back and shoulders angrily. It wouldn't be the end of the world if she accepted Mason's terms. So what if she had to swallow her pride? She would spend a week enjoying herself sexually *and* get what she wanted. Why the hesitation? Did she doubt her ability to keep the necessary emotional distance?

Vienna's hands shook as she turned off the water and dried herself. She closed her eyes, trying to blot out the image branded inside her eyelids: Mason, tearing back her white shirt, exposing those breasts, taunting her to shoot. That wretched woman had always been able to destroy her peace of mind. If she had any sense she would hand the deal over to her cousins and tell them to wipe Cavender off the map. But instead she was going to drive to Penwraithe tomorrow knowing anything could happen.

Worse still, a traitorous part of her hoped that it would.

CHAPTER FIFTEEN

There was a corner in the walled garden where Mason liked to sit and read, just as her mother once did, in front of the small summerhouse that had held her prized exotic plants. Azaria had placed a bench there beneath a trellised archway. Mason could remember her with a book on her lap, her face shaded by a tidy straw hat. Back then creamy roses and jasmine had trailed over the archway, adding their fragrance to air sweet with lilac and boronia. Honeybees flew sluggishly from one blossom to the next, weighed down with nectar, and the ravens that nested in the south wing would congregate along the herbal border, awaiting the bread she scattered.

They still frequented the garden; in fact, Ulysses was a fledgling Mason had found six years ago with a broken leg. The summerhouse was overgrown now, smothered in ivy and clematis, the glass dropping from frames buckled by time and neglect. Lichen crawled up the stained walls and the few surviving plants within were pale and straggly for want of light. Mason couldn't get the door open to rescue them for fear of bringing down the whole fragile structure. She knew she should simply accept its demise; it hadn't been built to withstand the toll of time. But she didn't want to build a clean and tidy replacement while she could still feel her mother's presence in this secluded oasis. For the same reason her father had insisted the garden stay untouched exactly as she'd left it. Mason used to watch him from an upstairs window, wandering along the path toward the summerhouse, pausing over objects Azaria had positioned here and there. Statuettes. Planters. Gifts he'd contributed to her bower.

After her death, the parasites took over, imposing on her retreat the wilder nature she'd held at bay. Yet her stamp lingered in the patterns of the cobblestones along the herbal borders and the flowering shrubs she'd planted, now rangy and monstrous with neglect. A clement wind breathed their scent on Mason—dead leaves and decay. Summer had departed, and with her the last of the late blooms.

Mason planned to begin work on the garden when spring came. She and Lynden had sat here not long before the accident, talking about a future unbound by the edicts of their father. A new beginning. The walls could come down. The ruined south wing would be leveled and something useful built. An indoor swimming pool, perhaps. Lynden had pictured children playing here, a new generation of Cavenders who would never know the Laudes Absalom he and Mason grew up in. The curse would be lifted.

"Your visitor has arrived." Mrs. Danville's immaculately polished shoes halted just in front of Mason's boots. "I've served coffee in the yellow parlor."

Mason stubbed out her cigar and signaled Ulysses. He flew down from his vantage point on the summerhouse roof and caught hold of the leather shoulder perch she wore when she took him out.

"That bird of yours stole a coconut macaroon," Mrs. Danville said.

"He has good taste," Mason said as they set off toward the house. "Your cookies are superb."

Mrs. Danville gave a small sniff and glared at the unrepentant raven. "I have some news concerning our neighbor."

She'd spoken with Bridget Hardy, Mason surmised. She wondered if Vienna had arrived at Penwraithe yet. She'd resisted phoning the house to find out. The move would show weakness. Mason suspected Vienna would try holding out, expecting Mason to come crawling to her apologizing for her uncouth proposal. Grinning at the memory of her shocked face, Mason held the back door for Mrs. Danville. If Vienna couldn't bring herself to come to Laudes Absalom and try for better terms, let her return to the bosom of her family empty-handed. She'd be back.

Mrs. Danville adjusted the keys on her chatelaine. "It's about the Cavender Diamonds."

"Yes, I know she has them," Mason said.

A tiny, smug smile subverted her housekeeper's poker face. "Not all of them."

Mason passed a treat up to Ulysses, who bobbed restlessly, sensing the excitement in his goddess.

"The pear is a fake," Mrs. Danville confided with just enough dignity to mask a flash of glee. "Miss Blake has Mrs. Hardy tearing the house apart, looking for the real diamond."

"Le Fantôme is *lost*? How do you lose a three-million-dollar diamond?"

"Indeed." Mrs. Danville picked a speck of lint from her cashmere sweater. "Yet that's not the question weighing upon our neighbor. It seems poor Miss Blake has no clue if she was ever in possession of the real stone in the first place."

Mason spent a few seconds absorbing this information. "When did all of this come to light?"

"She found out last night last night when a man from De Beers looked at it. From what I hear she was flabbergasted."

Mason thought back to her discussion with Vienna about the necklace. She hadn't said a word about wearing a replica but her unease was palpable. Mason had imagined the tension was about *her*, but this new information shed a different light on Vienna's behavior. Mason should have known better than to think she would rush out here on her account. The Blakes had always been more interested in material possessions than people or principles. After all that attention during the diamond competition at the party, Vienna must have been mortified to learn that her multi-million-dollar bauble was just a piece of glass. She'd probably stayed in town to hunt for it in the family's apartment.

If only she knew that while she was gnashing her teeth over a fake last night, Mason had fifty carats of fine stones in her pocket and was doing a deal with Sergei Ivanov. And the Russian had brought an unexpected dividend to the table. He'd driven to the Azaria factory first thing in the morning and when he phoned Mason to confirm his investment he mentioned a pet banker who owed him a favor. On his recommendation Mason had a meeting arranged for the coming week. If she could refinance Cavender's debt and add some extra working capital, she was sure she could avoid bankruptcy. Vienna's offer was looking less appealing by the minute.

Mason wondered where the diamond was. She still couldn't

believe her father had willingly sold the necklace to his enemies. "Mrs. Danville, did you know the Blakes had the necklace?"

"No, I knew your father had sold it a long time ago. Your mother preferred simpler jewelry."

"I remember her wearing the necklace when her portrait was painted." Azaria had allowed Mason to try on the diamonds along with a fancy gown, confirming for both of them that she should stick to boy's clothes, her usual attire.

"She was so beautiful, God rest her soul." Mrs. Danville allowed herself a wistful sigh, then smoothed her skirt and adjusted the collar of her blouse. "I suppose we must be thankful."

"Yes, we have her in our memories."

"Quite so. And I was also thinking of the necklace. Now that it's around a Blake neck, perhaps the curse will go with it."

Mason stared at her. "Do you really believe that?"

"I know it. The necklace is cursed."

"Why, because Nancy Cavender was wearing it when the train hit her?"

"Heavens no. It was cursed long before then." Mrs. Danville cast a quick, apprehensive glance around the great hall, then hauled the front door back and pointed at the statue of Estelle and her Saluki. "She did it. She was a witch."

"A witch." Mason suppressed a chuckle. She had never taken Mrs. Danville for the superstitious type, although the housekeeper was a walking repository of Cavender family legend. There had always been dark rumblings about Estelle and her cowardly decision to drown herself and leave her poor husband to raise their son alone, but Mason had never heard her described as a witch.

"The Unhappy Bride," Mrs. Danville asserted with conviction, "that's her."

Mason was perfectly willing to accept that Laudes Absalom was haunted; she'd felt the strange presence herself too often to pretend otherwise. But she'd thought the Unhappy Bride was Mrs. Danville's invention, a scapegoat for vases inexplicably broken and windows banging in empty rooms. She stopped outside the yellow parlor and sent Ulysses up toward the vaulted ceiling.

Conscious of keeping Josh waiting, she said, "We should discuss this later, Mrs. Danville."

She had papers to sign. Sergei Ivanov was as good as his word and was so eager to invest that he'd insisted on signing a preliminary agreement to that effect, just in case she changed her mind or found an investor whose money smelled better. Josh had decided to drive to Laudes Absalom immediately so they could get the paperwork in order for their meeting with Sergei's pet banker. They would have two million in cash from Sergei next week, most of which would be spent on machinery made by Cavender. The arrangement was a huge win.

Mrs. Danville swept into the parlor ahead of her and imperiously announced, "Ms. Cavender will see you now."

Josh wasn't in the room.

A fresh-faced stranger in a suit jumped to his feet and stuck out his hand. "Detective Trent Sherman. I'm with the DA's office."

❖

"You've reopened the case?" Mason hoped she didn't sound as stunned as she felt.

"Ms. Blake approached us a couple of weeks ago and I was hoping to re-interview your father and your brother. But your housekeeper explained that both are deceased." He cleared his throat. "I'm sorry for your loss."

"Thank you," Mason said. It hadn't crossed her mind that Vienna would go to the police after she'd grilled Mrs. Danville. To buy herself time to assemble her thoughts, she picked up a cookie she didn't want to eat and casually bit into it.

"I thought perhaps you could fill in a few details." Detective Sherman flipped open his notepad.

Mason chewed mechanically, then said. "I'm not sure what I can tell you. It's a long time ago."

"Ms. Blake denies having a romantic relationship with your brother. In the statement you gave at the time, you claim to know nothing about such a relationship. Is that correct?"

"They weren't involved with each other."

"You sound very certain of that."

"My brother and I were close. He would have told me."

"Yet your father had the same opinion as Mr. and Mrs. Blake. That they had hidden their relationship to avoid disapproval."

"Detective Sherman, if my brother had been meeting Vienna Blake that night, she would not have been assaulted. He would never have allowed her to walk over here unescorted."

"Where was your brother?"

"Isn't it in your file?" Mason steadied her breathing. "He was the one who disturbed the attack. He was knocked unconscious."

"And where were you at the time?"

"At the barns. One of our horses was foaling. I was assisting our vet." That, at least, was the truth.

"Ah, yes." Sherman tapped his pen thoughtfully against the pad. "The vet left at ten p.m. and you then remained in the barns with a member of your staff."

"Yes, Mr. Pettibone."

"Is Mr. Pettibone still employed by your family?" At Mason's nod, he asked, "Where can I find him?"

"At this time of year, he'll be raking leaves if he's not in his apartment around the back of the house. I can give you his cell phone number."

"I'd appreciate that." Detective Sherman glanced out the wide bay window into the garden. "That's where she was found, isn't it?"

"Yes, over to left, near the cemetery."

"A note was found at the scene." He rummaged in his briefcase and produced a set of photographs. Handing one of these to Mason, he asked, "Have you ever seen this before?"

"Yes." The words danced in front of her.

It's time we talked. Would you do me the honor of joining me for dinner next Saturday? Please reply below.

"Is that your brother's handwriting?"

"No."

"Your father stated that it was."

Perspiration damped Mason's hairline. "Detective, I wrote the note myself."

Sherman studied her closely. "Why didn't you say so before?"

"No one asked me."

Mason's hands were cold despite the fire she'd lit when she knew

Josh was coming. She stared out into the garden and felt the past pressing down on her. If she hadn't sent that note, Vienna would not have been wandering through the grounds in the middle of the night. Mason had thought she was being wildly optimistic to hope for a reply; she'd never imagined Vienna would want to give her answer in person or she would have gone with Pettibone's grandson and waited outside. She'd drawn the obvious conclusion when the boy didn't return to the barn after an hour or so. It wasn't the first time she'd offered an olive branch, and her overtures were usually ignored. But this time Vienna had sent the Pettibone boy to the kitchen for a meal after telling him she would take the reply to Mason herself.

The change of heart had always plagued Mason. She didn't know if Vienna intended to express annoyance or accept the date. Either way, the consequences were the same. Whatever might have been was swept away.

"Why did you invite Ms. Blake to dinner?" Sherman asked.

"As you probably know, our families weren't on the best of terms," Mason said. "I thought things could be different for us. She hadn't been at Penwraithe for awhile, but I knew she would be at the ball, so I sent the note over with Mr. Pettibone's grandson."

"And Ms. Blake came over here in the dead of night to see *you*?" Sherman eyed her with sudden suspicion. "How well do you know each other, Ms. Cavender?"

"Are you asking if we were having a lesbian relationship?"

"Were you?"

Mason stretched her legs casually in front of her. "Unfortunately not."

The detective rifled through his notes, his cheeks slightly flushed, then handed her another photograph. "This necklace was also recovered. The Blakes confirmed their daughter was wearing it that night. There was speculation that the attack could have been a robbery attempt."

"It's a valuable necklace," Mason said.

"Ms. Blake telephoned this morning and informed me that this is the necklace known as the Cavender Diamonds." He finally seemed to be getting to the point. "Is it possible that your father saw Ms. Blake wearing this important heirloom and lost his temper? Could he have seized the opportunity to get the necklace back?"

"My father is the one who sold it to the Blakes," Mason said patiently. "Besides, he wasn't at Laudes Absalom when Vienna was attacked."

"But you and your brother were. How did you two feel about seeing your neighbor's daughter wearing that necklace? After all, it should have been yours."

"Detective Sherman, the first time I ever saw Vienna wearing that necklace was last night."

Undeterred, Sherman said, "Would you object to providing a DNA sample?"

"Are you suggesting that I had something to do with the attack?"

"DNA wasn't so widely used ten years ago," Sherman said. "But we now have the opportunity to re-examine the evidence. If we have a sample, we can rule you out."

"Then I have nothing to lose."

Sherman whipped out a kit and swabbed her mouth. "We appreciate your cooperation, Ms. Cavender."

"No problem." Mason stood.

As Detective Sherman walked with her to the door, he said, "I have one more question."

Mason had been waiting for the shoe to fall. "Yes?"

"Do you know who did it?"

"I'm not a detective," Mason said. "All I can tell you is that it won't matter what you find out. The Blakes have never wanted to know the truth."

Chapter Sixteen

I don't have the faintest idea what you're talking about," Marjorie said. Her tone was whiny. She had a fashion show to get to and Vienna's questions were holding her up. "Oh, damn. I've just applied the wrong fragrance. Bal à Versailles in the middle of the afternoon. No one will be expecting *that*."

"Think of it as a style statement," Vienna said unsympathetically.

She sorted through another set of letters from the 1840s, correspondence between the Famous Four, most of it pertaining to Sally Gibson, the younger sisters' governess. Stacks of papers were piled on her desk in bundles according to the decades in which they were written. Vienna had set herself the daunting task of inspecting absolutely everything in the study at each of their homes in case her father had misfiled some crucial paperwork that would lead her to the diamond.

"Dad must have told you it was the Cavender necklace," she said as she removed letters from protective plastic envelopes and opened those tied together with ribbons. "He told you everything."

"Not in this instance," her mother insisted. "I'm as shocked as you are. The first time I saw that necklace was the day you turned twenty-one."

"Great-aunt Rachel knew. Did she say anything to you?"

"Not a word."

"I heard her telling Dad it was cursed."

"That's absurd," Marjorie said, but her voice wavered with uncertainty.

"Really? Think about what happened the next time I wore it."

Vienna hadn't intended to raise the subject of the ball, but she'd been frustrated ever since she spoke with Mrs. Danville. It gnawed at her that there was some kind of bizarre conspiracy at work to prevent her from filling in her mental blanks. Even the police were less than forthcoming, fobbing her off with some lame excuse about a filing problem. A young detective had finally told her he would go to the building where the cold case files were stored and locate hers. That was two weeks ago and she'd only heard from him this morning.

As usual, her mother placed the topic firmly off-limits. "I don't think either of us has anything to gain by dredging up the past. Really, Vienna, it's not like you to be superstitious."

"I just want to know where the diamond is." She pushed a button she knew would make her mother sit up and take notice. "I was actually thinking it would make a stunning pendant for your black pearls. Cartier could create something quite superlative."

Marjorie fell silent for a few seconds, no doubt enchanting herself with the possibilities. "Your father ordered the replica when you were in the hospital. He decided it would be safer not to wear the real one." She paused. "The police never ruled out robbery, you know."

"So Dad replaced Le Fantôme, but didn't tell me?"

Marjorie delivered her stock answer to all questions about that night. "We didn't want to upset you."

"I'm not upset, Mom." Vienna had hit upon the perfect explanation for her quest. "I just need to update the insurance. So, where's the diamond?"

She could hear the sound of nails tapping. Finally Marjorie said, "I don't know."

"Is there a safe I don't know about?"

"No." Marjorie sounded mystified and resentful in equal measure. "I searched, you can be quite sure of that. Even the estate attorneys didn't know anything about it."

"Then Dad must have sold it," Vienna said. "And we've been paying a fortune to insure a stone we don't own anymore."

Even her mother could see the unlikelihood of that. Norris was the kind of man who calculated tips exactly and paid not a cent more. Marjorie had always been so embarrassed by his penny-pinching, she slipped cash to waiters when the family dined out. "It has to be somewhere. I'll speak to Wendell."

"Please don't," Vienna said firmly. "We have to keep this to ourselves for now in case we compromise our position. I'll have to explore all avenues if I can't find it. Theft. Fraud." She paused for dramatic effect. "Tax evasion."

Marjorie gasped. "What do you mean?"

"I'm starting to think Dad bought the necklace off the Cavenders for peanuts, then removed Le Fantôme and sold it at a huge profit. If so, he might owe money to the IRS. That could explain why we're still paying the insurance premiums."

"Are you suggesting Norris was covering up a taxation fraud?" Marjorie shrilled.

"Do you have a better explanation?"

While she waited for her mother to stop hyperventilating, Vienna unfolded a thick bundle of letters and spread several pages on the desk in front of her. She could almost read girlish giggles between the lines. The youngest of the Famous Four had witnessed something unusual between the governess and their brother Benedict. She shared her feverish speculation with an older sister, who wrote back demanding more information. There ensued regular communications, most of which reported with bated breath incidents remarkable only for their tedious formality: Benedict knocking on the schoolroom door to advise Miss Gibson that the carriage was now available should she wish to take her charges for a turn. The arrival of a new atlas, compliments of their brother. A letter of thanks penned to him by Miss Gibson that included the shameless words "you are the epitome of kindness." Hardly torrid stuff.

"Maybe it's in Bonnieux," Marjorie said weakly. "I didn't look there."

"Then perhaps you should make those travel arrangements for next year after all."

"Will you come if I'm there?" Marjorie switched to the little girl voice she used for emotional blackmail.

"Of course." Vienna loved spending spring at Bonnieux. The family had often done so when she was a child, returning to the Berkshires just before the goldenrod came into bloom in July. When she could, she still followed that familiar pattern, drawing comfort from the happy memories it evoked.

"By then you'll have taken care of the Cavender matter, thank God," Marjorie said. "And your aunt Cynthia will get off my back."

Vienna had been waiting for the prod. She sometimes wondered what her mother would do once the situation was resolved. The Cavender fixation had provided an outlet for her grief and anger, a link to her dead husband that had helped her through the aftermath of his death. While Norris was alive, Marjorie hadn't shown the same private zeal for their neighbors' destruction.

"Yes, one way or another, it will be over by then." Vienna flipped through several letters until she came to one written in a different hand. It was addressed to Benedict and signed by Sally Gibson.

"Well, I must be going," Marjorie said. "Keep me informed, won't you, darling?"

"If there's any news, you'll be the first to know."

"When are you coming back to town?"

"As soon as I have some answers."

"You know," Marjorie said as though trying to convince herself. "Your father must have had his reasons for not telling us about the diamond."

"I'm sure he did. Enjoy the show, Mom."

As the door closed with a sickly waft of perfume, Vienna read Sally Gibson's long letter with growing fascination.

> *Is it consistent with the character of a gentleman, first to triumph over the weakness of a woman by inducing her to believe in his affection and in consequence of that belief to obtain her consent; and to solicit convincing proof of her passion; yet afterward to deny his own solemn promises! In what light am I to consider your conduct? Had you no other reason to seek my submission than mere vanity?*
>
> *I admit the greatest fault was my own, for it was in consequence of my love for you that I discarded my conscience and consented to my own degradation. Alas, I am too well acquainted with these things and have too convincing evidence of your affability to remain ignorant of the condemnation I shall soon enough face from persons who*

upon learning of my plight will suppose the destitution of virtue to be mine.

It has been my constant study to merit the high regard of your honored parents since finding myself in their service, the good opinion of employers also being the indispensable necessity of all who find themselves in my situation. Too great is my regard to sacrifice your mother's peace of mind by burdening her with disclosure of the oath you have made light of.

I understand that a gentleman who makes a promise solely for the purposes of brutal gratification, and breaks it at his convenience, will be indifferent to the moral duty that would persuade a man of nobler character to consider his obligations. However, I am informed that you are soon to become engaged, so I hope you will be mindful of all that could mar your happiness. Whatever you may think, I do not seek from a spirit of resentment to do harm to your alliance by drawing the attention of vulgar minds to the impropriety of past actions. Yet, however odious, some impeachment of your character may be unavoidable. For although we do not occupy the same station in life, neither are we so separated by birth and the blessings of fortune that your merit as a gentleman entirely outweighs damage done to my reputation as the daughter of a gentleman, and my hopes of conjugal happiness should not weigh less heavily than your own.

Therefore, sir, I must beg on behalf of the child for which I shall soon be responsible, that you act with good sense if not humanity.

I await your answer with respect,
Sally Gibson

Vienna got to her feet and wandered into the kitchen, taken aback. Unless Sally Gibson was a compelling liar and a con woman, she must have been pregnant by Benedict Blake when she wrote that angry letter. He had obviously led her to believe he had honorable intentions, and then reneged on the promises he'd made as soon as he'd seduced her.

Vienna pondered the very different account of events she'd heard. The kindness of those early Blakes to their "fallen" governess was official family history. No one had ever hinted that all was not as it seemed. She supposed it was natural for a scandal of this kind to have been hushed up at the time, and the family wouldn't have wanted to tarnish Benedict's memory after he was murdered. So the half-truths surrounding Sally Gibson made sense, and the truth wouldn't have mattered if Sally had settled down happily with the head gardener and had a brood of children who vanished into the mists of time.

But Sally had given birth to Estelle, and Estelle's parentage mattered a great deal. In fact, it could change everything. Mulling over the ramifications, Vienna let herself out onto the terrace and sat down in a rattan chair. Estelle had married Hugo Cavender, and Hugo had murdered Benedict Blake, sparking the feud Vienna was still fighting a hundred and forty years later. The Blakes had always claimed the murder was a naked power grab, motivated by greed. And perhaps it was. But what if there was another explanation, one less black and white?

Vienna's stomach plunged as she thought about the famous rivalry for Estelle's hand between Hugo Cavender and Truman Blake. If the letter was believable, Truman was Estelle's *half-brother*. The name he'd chosen for the diamond jumped to mind. *The Ghost of Love.* All of a sudden, Truman sounded less like a romantic Victorian and more like a heartbroken suitor.

Vienna pieced together a theory. Truman had bought the diamonds for Estelle and then discovered the terrible truth from his father. The family must have told him when they realized how serious he was about marrying her. That was why he'd auctioned the diamonds. And Hugo Cavender was waiting in the wings to lay claim to Estelle as soon as his best friend backed off. But did Estelle love her husband, or had she loved Truman? It was impossible to tell from her genteel letters. A name leapt into Vienna's mind. *The Unhappy Bride.* The Laudes Absalom ghost. Intrigued, she went back inside and dialed Penwraithe.

"That ghost," she asked Bridget after the usual pleasantries. "The Unhappy Bride. Who is she?"

Bridget sounded amused by the unexpected question. "Mrs. Danville thinks it's Estelle Cavender."

"Why?"

"Well she was the first victim of the curse. It's a tragic story when you think about it…falling into the lake and drowning when she'd just had a brand-new baby."

"But did she fall or was she pushed?"

"Does it matter? She's just as dead either way."

Vienna thought about the marble statue of the angel, Estelle hurrying away from the house with her Saluki as her side. "I think it does matter," she said slowly. "I think it's at the heart of everything."

"Are we expecting you sometime today?" Bridget asked.

"Yes, quite late."

"You sound stressed. Is everything okay?"

"No, not really." Vienna let her thoughts spill out. "I've grown up inside a myth, and I don't know what I can believe anymore."

Bridget heaved a long sigh. "Everyone feels that way about the church sometimes. You need a few days at home. I'll take some venison out of the freezer and make a pie tomorrow. How does that sound?"

Depressing. Her father had loved game and Bridget took enormous pride in making glamorous meals out of pheasant, rabbit, and other creatures best admired in the wild. Vienna didn't have the heart to admit she felt bilious at the thought of eating Bambi, no matter how well disguised with fancy sauces and pastry.

"Perhaps something lighter," she suggested weakly.

"I have a nice capon in a marinade," Bridget announced. "Just the thing with some liver pâté on toast."

Covering her mouth, Vienna said, "Yes, wonderful."

"Oh, by the way, I heard the police were next door talking to your neighbor."

"What?"

Bridget laughed roundly. "Can you believe it? They asked Mason Cavender for a DNA sample."

"Oh, my God." Vienna felt the blood draining from her face. Detective Sherman didn't say anything about DNA when they spoke earlier. Mason was never going to sign the deal now.

"Don't worry," Bridget assured her. "Mrs. Danville says she's not angry, she's just sledgehammering those walls out front for the hell of it."

CHAPTER SEVENTEEN

"S he turned us down? Great." Vienna almost dropped her cell phone. She juggled with the steering wheel as she took her exit and merged with the northbound traffic on the Taconic State Parkway.

"She said something about a time limit." Darryl Kent sounded confused.

"Obviously there's a misunderstanding," Vienna said. What else could go wrong?

"So we're still negotiating?"

"Yes. It's just a stalling tactic. I'll sort it out."

"If she's for real, they'll be having a fire sale," Darryl noted dryly. "The only reason they haven't filed Chapter Eleven is because Lynden Cavender had their bankers on a leash."

"He was about to marry a billionaire's daughter. Now that she's out of the picture, the money has to come from somewhere." Vienna got impatient with the cars crawling along ahead of her and changed lanes. She'd left New York even later than she'd intended. It would be one in the morning by the time she made it to Penwraithe.

"Mason can grandstand all she likes, but the banks are on our side," Darryl said.

"Did you get anywhere with Josh Soifer?" Vienna asked, reading the bumper stickers on the back of the pickup truck ahead of her. I'M PRO-LIFE was sandwiched next to SHOOT FIRST, LET GOD DO THE REST.

"They'll cave," Darryl said with the certainty of a logical man. "Soifer thinks she's delaying the inevitable while she comes to terms with Lynden's accident."

Vienna snorted. She was done pandering to Mason's tender

feelings. That woman had threatened her with a gun, for crying out loud, and she thought she could blackmail her into a humiliating sexual arrangement. Now she was angry over the police visit. Vienna didn't know why she cared. It wasn't like her father was around to face charges if they finally proved he did it. Formally declining the Blake offer was a huge gamble, a winner-takes-all bet. Did Mason really imagine she could drive the price higher? She had to know that Vienna was holding all the cards. What on earth was she playing at?

"Call him, raise the bid by a million, and tell him they've had our best and final offer," Vienna said. "They know the score. If we withdraw and the banks step in, they'll get pennies on the dollar."

"I'll phone him at home."

"Remind him that I have a nice corner office with his name on it."

"Don't order the plaque," Darryl said dryly. "He's addicted to that family."

"Jesus, what's up with that?"

"Masochism?" Darryl suggested.

"I just don't get it." Vienna had been trying to lure Josh Soifer to Blake Industries ever since Lynden took over. Soifer was too talented and highly qualified to waste his time working for the Cavenders and Vienna didn't need the hassle of liquidating the Cavender Corporation assets herself. Soifer knew everything about the business, so she intended to give him the task of wiping it off the map. She'd just offered him a package no right-thinking executive would decline.

"I'm not going to repeat where he told me to shove the signing bonus," Darryl said. "And that was after we doubled it."

"What the hell does he want?" Everyone had their price, but it always surprised Vienna that some people weren't satisfied with hard cash and had to be won over with the equivalent of the "free gift." Soifer didn't seem like the type who would fall for a glossy sweetener like a high-end car or a luxury cruise, but Vienna wasn't averse to such perks if that's what it would take. "We're not buying a company jet just for him," she told Darryl. "But you could offer a Merc."

"I put a few feelers out last time we talked, but he says he has to look at himself in the mirror."

"Oh, God, he has a hero complex." As if Mason Cavender would let anyone rescue her. The woman was completely impossible. An image flashed across Vienna's mind. The two of them, clinging to each other, Mason buried in her, deep and hard. Blood rushed to her cheeks and her hands started sweating on the steering wheel. She lowered her window and gulped a sharp breath of mountain air.

"The guy isn't stupid," Darryl said. "There has to be something keeping him there."

"Well, we don't need him. The offer was just a courtesy." Vienna knew she sounded miffed. She'd expected Soifer to jump ship as soon as Lynden was buried, and without him there propping her up, Mason would be screwed. She was like her father, too hotheaded to run a business. If Soifer left maybe she would finally understand that it was all over. Time to throw in the towel.

"She's not going to sell that house to you," Darryl said. "I think that's the big stumbling block. Why don't we put it on ice till we have a deal on the corporation?"

"If we drag this out any longer Andy will make a move on Blake Aerospace."

Her cousin had been demanding the top job there ever since Vienna took over and he had almost enough support from senior staff to force the issue. But she knew how that scenario would play out. He would be running his own empire, nominally reporting to her but in reality cutting her out of the loop. Before long she would become irrelevant, a mere figurehead, and he would have the real power because Blake Aerospace was the fastest growing part of the parent corporation.

"I think we should go to the banks," Darryl said. "Tell them to pull the rug out and we'll deal directly with them."

"That's our last resort. We can play this out for a few more days."

"Why does it sound like you have a plan you're not discussing with me?"

Vienna smiled. "Think of it this way: plausible deniability is always a good thing."

"Don't break any laws." Darryl offered his customary warning. "And if you do, don't leave any bodies."

"Duly noted. Keep in touch."

Vienna dropped the cell phone onto the passenger seat and settled into her usual driving tempo, changing down as the road began to climb into the Hudson Highlands. The terrain was more rugged now, but the winding route was so familiar she didn't have to pay attention to landmarks or signage. When she drove to Penwraithe she always took the time to think through work challenges and come up with fresh ideas. Lately, all she'd been able to focus on was the Cavender problem. She should never have let it come to this.

As the miles vanished and the traffic thinned, she contemplated her next move. What if she went to Mason and agreed to the one-week affair? If Mason honored her end of the seedy bargain and handed over both the corporation and Laudes Absalom, did it really matter how the victory came about? Vienna could survive a dose of wounded pride and it wouldn't be the only sexual fling she'd ever had. There'd been a few since college. Short-lived, mutually satisfying liaisons. No one got hurt.

She thought about her rat-fink cousins. Her father had dealt with the same problems when he first took over the company. There were cousins who'd formed factions and issued ultimatums. Vienna wondered how he had neutralized them. It crossed her mind that her father had a strong motivation to fight off threats and safeguard his legacy. He had *her*. Maybe she would be equally ruthless if she had a child's future to think about.

An image of a baby sprang to mind, cradled to her breast, looking up at her with Mason's dark eyes. Disconcerted, Vienna almost missed making the turn onto Route 7. She slowed down and started the wipers as plops of rain bounced erratically off her windshield. The weather was changing as it often seemed to when she crossed the state line. Clouds suddenly obscured the sickle moon and wind rushed in through her open window, making her face feel tight and damp.

Snow wouldn't come to the Berkshires until Thanksgiving but she could feel its promise weighing on the night air. Before long, a dense white frosting would smother the sylvan beauty of these hills, draping the trees in petticoats of ice and silencing the earth. The birds would stop singing. The green, honeyed scent of sunlight and grass would succumb to a metallic wet pine aroma, and the tracks of small animals would carve winding patterns across the white expanses. Vienna loved the sparkle and crunch of new snow. She loved getting up early on winter mornings and watching the sun wipe clean the leaden monochrome of night.

A huge moth crashed into the glass right in front of her, making her start. She turned her wipers on high for a few seconds and slowed down until the smeared remains no longer obscured her vision. Her eyes were heavy and her mind kept floating. It was crazy, of course, to have set off so late, but she'd found her way to Stockbridge and would soon be home. The streets were deserted, the windows dark in all the familiar stores and buildings. She started up Pine Street, drove past Naumkeag, and wove a path alongside the thin luminous white ribbon that divided the asphalt. Gnarled tree trunks reared up as she braked and made the turn toward for home. She would be there soon, passing the black iron gates of Laudes Absalom, then the long belt of trees before Penwraithe appeared, lit up on the rise ahead.

Vienna heaved a sigh of relief as the road narrowed and undulated, twisting through the valley. She swerved in tiny increments to avoid imaginary objects and shadows, but the black trees on either side seemed to encroach, creating a sense that she was driving blindly into a tunnel, going too fast, the countryside a blur. The rain was heavier. She turned the wipers up again. Their slow, regular pulse was hypnotic.

"Concentrate," she ordered herself sharply.

It was the last thing she said before a pair of eyes glowed in front of her and she hit the brakes and swung hard on the wheel to avoid a pale figure. There was no way she could stop the car before it smashed into the shape. She braced herself but the impact never came. Her tires hit gravel, her cheekbone crunched against the window, and her headlights bounced off trees. A latticework of branches filled the windshield. She wrenched on the wheel and felt the back of the car spin out. Dragging on the wheel, she hit the gas and careened alongside a row of squat tree trunks, then fishtailed back onto the road.

She drove a few yards, her heart deafening her, then braked and pulled over, immediately killing the engine. For a few seconds, she stared into nothing, then she let her head fall forward, crying in shock and relief.

❖

"Vienna?"

Vienna jerked up off the steering wheel. Her neck felt stiff and her head ached.

A face filled the window, pale and wild-eyed. "Unlock the door," Mason demanded.

Dazed, Vienna groped for the handle.

She barely had time to release the catch when the door was yanked open and Mason reached in, grabbing her shoulders. "Are you all right?"

"I must have fallen asleep."

"Why are you parked out here?" Mason shone a flashlight into the car. "Your face. What happened?"

Vienna lifted her fingers to her cheek and winced. "I saw something. I swerved to avoid it and…"

"A person?"

"Maybe a deer. Or a dog. I don't know. I was tired. It's a three-hour drive."

Mason studied her quizzically. "I thought you weren't coming."

Vienna had no answer. She looked away, trying to unscramble her muddled emotions. The shallow breathing wasn't helping. She felt light-headed. "You were wrong."

Mason helped her out of the car. "Come on, I'll drive."

"I'm perfectly capable of driving myself."

"So I see."

Irritated, Vienna said, "This could have happened to anyone."

"And it could have been a lot worse." Mason steered her firmly around to the passenger side. She sounded angry. "You should have waited until tomorrow. You could have been seriously hurt. What then? What if I hadn't found you?"

Vienna could feel herself flagging, close to bursting into tears. "Mason, I don't want to quarrel with you. Just go, okay? I can get home by myself."

"What makes you think I'd allow that?" Mason opened the door, ordered her Doberman to get in the backseat, and pushed Vienna into the car. As she fastened the seat belt, she said, "After I've taken a look at your face we'll decide whether you need to go to the hospital."

"It's just a bruise." Vienna probed the tender area and winced again. The lump on the side of her face was huge. She would probably have a black eye tomorrow. Very sexy. She licked a smear of blood off her fingers. "I'm perfectly fine."

Mason settled behind the wheel and started the car. As she pulled out onto the road, she muttered, "I wish you'd phoned me before you came out here in the middle of the night. I could have saved you the trip."

"Don't worry, I still got your message. Darryl called as I was leaving the city."

"And you came anyway?" Mason's face was in shadow and her tone was flat.

Unable to interpret her expression, Vienna said, "I wanted to see you."

"Why?" The black gates creaked open as they approached Laudes Absalom and Mason tucked a remote control back into her coat pocket. "Were you hoping the police would find some reason to arrest me?"

Vienna stared out at the motionless woods, knowing she was too weary to win a fight. "Let's not have that discussion now. Truce?"

"Sure. It'll keep."

"Anyway." Vienna forced a lighter note. "While we're on the subject of late-night excursions, what are *you* doing wandering around at three in the morning?"

"Ralph woke me." Mason reached back to pat the watchful Doberman. "He must have heard the car."

Vienna doubted it. Laudes Absalom was set back too far from the road. She stared up at the building taking melancholy shape in the headlights. Except for the lamps on either side of the front entrance, the house was entirely in darkness, its ruined wing a grim outcrop, the windows as vacant as the eyes of a corpse. The sight was so bleak, Vienna wouldn't have been surprised to hear a wolf howl, perhaps one of the taxidermied creatures from the great hall. In a grim fancy she imagined it quickening suddenly on its wooden stand and leaping down, thirsting for revenge on its killers.

Mason parked the car in a long garage behind the north wing and they followed the Doberman though a series of passages and up a narrow staircase that had probably been built for servants. A door at the top opened onto the broad gallery that ran the length of the great hall. Feeble moonlight struggled in through the high leaded panes along the front of the house but failed to defeat the gloom. Only the ponderous tick of a clock and the sound of their footsteps carved life into the uncompromising silence.

Mason hit a switch on the wall and a chandelier flickered into life, casting a yellowish luster over all that lay beneath. Vienna's gaze fell on a portrait. A stunning, willowy blonde in an elaborate gilt frame. She wore a ball gown and carried a few drooping lilies. Her expression was one of wayward frankness, her pose a dare. From the uneven look of the canvas, she'd tempted some disorderly brushstrokes from the artist who thought he could paint her. Vienna recognized the diamonds around her neck. A brass plaque beneath the painting read: NANCY CAVENDER.

A few feet ahead, Mason pushed open a door that probably weighed more than her and said, "Please come in."

The lofty room they entered had probably been a formal drawing room at one time but its purpose was unclear now. The oaken floors softly protested with every step on the wide, dark boards. The furniture was uniformly comfortless, some of it shrouded in dust covers. Between faded green draperies and blackish wood paneling, more portraits lined the walls, many of them depicting horses. Several huge diagrams were displayed and Vienna realized she was looking at equine genealogy charts. Bookshelves contained tall leather-bound volumes with dates gold-lettered on the spines. On a table nearby, one of these books lay open next to an inkwell, blotter, and several nib pens.

Vienna glanced down at a page as she passed by. She knew the beautiful handwriting immediately and remembered the note the raven had dropped into her lap two weeks earlier. The same dark bird probably frequented this room, if the perches positioned next to the windows were any indication. Vienna glanced up, half expecting to see a dark shape lurking in a remote recess of the carved plaster ceiling. She felt like she was being watched.

"Sit down." Mason waved toward the main fireplace a few yards away.

Two armchairs and a deep sofa were arranged around this. Like every other piece of furniture in the room they bordered on tattered disrepair. But no cloud of dust rose as Vienna moved a cushion to perch on the sofa. Whatever Mrs. Danville's flaws, and however thankless the task, she kept Laudes Absalom clean. It couldn't be easy, with so many musty old rooms and an accumulation of furniture and feudal trappings that would daunt the staff of any castle.

Mason set a crystal rocks glass down on an ornate occasional table next to Vienna and said, "Drink this."

"Really…there's no need. It's a superficial cut, that's all."

Ignoring her, Mason discarded her pea coat, poked at the stack of paper and kindling arranged on the grate, and lit the fire. As the blaze started to take, Ralph settled himself in front of it, stretched long, his head down on his paws.

"Warm up," Mason said, adding some small logs. "I'll be a back in a minute."

She left without a second glance at Vienna. Watching the door close behind her, Vienna sipped the brandy, then stretched her hands out toward the flames. When she'd absorbed the toasty heat for several minutes, languor crept up on her and she knew if she lay down, she would fall asleep. The idea was tempting but she resisted. Determined to stay awake, she got to her feet and scanned her surroundings, listening for the sound of returning footsteps. If this house wasn't such a mausoleum, she would track Mason down and excuse herself. All she wanted right now was to take a hot bath and fall into bed. Whatever they had to discuss could wait until tomorrow. She needed to have her wits about her so she could make the right decisions.

She wandered over to a display easel and lifted the sheet that covered a painting. The smell of linseed oil greeted her. The work was fresh, the paint still soft. The artist had captured Mason and her brother to perfection, revealing both the harmony of close siblings and the contrast of two very different adults. Each was physically striking and sensuously self-aware. But where Lynden's body language was open and engaging, Mason's wary reserve was apparent. Her expression was cool, no softness in the contours of chin and jaw. Her dark eyes bored into the observer with a mix of unease and defiance, yet there was also eloquence in their depths. And the artist had seen what Vienna saw in her. That unsettling vulnerability. He revealed it in the tender curve of her wrist and the expressive line of her mouth.

Feeling like a voyeur, Vienna dropped the sheet and stepped back.

From behind her, Mason asked, "What do you think?" She crossed the room with an indolent swagger that made Vienna's throat close.

"It's a fine likeness."

Mason patted her dog, then deposited a large nylon medical bag on the table and unzipped a couple of gusseted pouches. She'd changed out of her damp clothes and now wore a plaid shirt tucked into a pair of loose, faded jeans. Rolling up her sleeves, she said, "It's too soon to hang it."

Vienna didn't know what to say. From the looks of the supplies, the first aid kit was normally used for horses.

Mason pulled out a chair, inviting, "Sit down. This won't hurt a bit."

"I can take care of this myself." Vienna reached for the alcohol wipes.

"Indulge me." Mason gently lifted her hair aside and cleaned her cheek. "I always wanted to play doctor and nurse with you."

"You're incorrigible." Vienna tried to keep her breathing even by concentrating on her surroundings. She indicated a portrait of two soldiers, almost identical in looks. Each wore the khaki uniform and overcoat of World War One doughboys. "Who are they?"

"Harland and Hope. They were twins." Mason applied a Band-Aid. "It's only a minor cut, but you should put ice on your cheek for the bruising." She pulled an icepack from her bag. "You can borrow this."

"Thank you." Vienna held the compress to the side of her face, knowing she should be thankful that she could finally take her leave. But she delayed the moment. "Hope? That's an unusual name for a guy."

"She passed as a man so she could go to war with Harland."

"Your family allowed that?" Vienna was astonished. No Blake would ever have allowed one of their offspring to be served up as cannon fodder for warmongering politicians. A couple of scions had glittering military careers, retiring as generals. The family held them up as examples of Blake patriotism if the necessity arose. And of course, there was Patience Blake's daughter, Colette, who'd made the ultimate sacrifice. But Vienna's father was at Harvard during Vietnam, and the family made sure that he received the necessary deferments to avoid the draft.

"The family only found out later. As the story goes, Harland was socializing in London while Hope was at art school in Paris. When the first U.S. troops arrived to join the Allies, they enlisted."

The decision sounded typically Cavender, two young people throwing caution to the wind, imagining an adventure.

"What happened to them?" Vienna asked.

"Harland was killed in action on the Western Front. Hope was wounded at the same time. That's when they discovered she was a woman."

"I don't think she was the only one. A predecessor of mine also died in Europe during the First World War. I have some letters of hers. She was a nurse and talks about a soldier who I think was a woman. They were in love."

Mason discarded the wipes and wrappers and fastened her medical bag. "She was a lesbian?"

"I'm only guessing, but yes." Vienna allowed herself a wry smile. "Statistically, we're probably not the only gay people on our family trees."

"What became of the soldier?" Mason asked.

"I don't know. All I have is a photograph. No name."

"Maybe it was Hope."

"That would be quite a coincidence."

"Maybe not. You and I aren't the only Blakes and Cavenders who've been hot for each other," Mason reminded her softly. "Fanny married Nathaniel, and your grandfather had an affair with my grandmother. I guess that love/hate thing has been going on awhile."

Vienna didn't want to continue down that track. She needed more information before she could discuss Estelle and Benedict. She set the ice pack on the table and got to her feet. "You must be tired."

Ignoring the cue, and their temporary truce, Mason said, "You should have stayed in New York."

"You didn't." Vienna tried to sound offhand, but her voice wasn't cooperating. The Doberman sprawled in front of the fire stared up at her with a looked of pained sympathy. "Apparently you didn't think I was worth waiting for."

"And you didn't think I was worth leaving the party for," Mason retorted. "Are we even?"

"So this is all about ego? Don't tell me you rejected the offer because you have hurt feelings."

"I thought we weren't having this discussion now."

"You started it." Perfect. Now they were bickering like six-year-olds. Calming herself with thoughts of a bath and soft pillows, Vienna said, "I'm going home."

"Good idea."

"For the record, I came by your apartment after the party and you'd already gone." Vienna marched toward the door.

"Aren't you're forgetting something?" Mason dangled a set of car keys. She stayed where she was, leaning against the back of a chair.

"I'll walk," Vienna threw at her. "I'll send someone over for the car later."

Mason's eyes glittered. "You're not walking home by yourself."

"Just watch me." Vienna slammed the door behind her as she exited the room.

With a quick glance at Nancy's portrait, she hurried along the gallery to the broad staircase. Below her the grand hall looked sinister, its shadows only deepened by the weak pool of light from the chandelier on the level above. Suppressing her nerves, Vienna descended. The house could be beautiful, she thought, as she clung to the banister. If she owned it, the first thing she would do was improve the lighting. Then she would bring in a demolition crew to get rid of that eyesore south wing. Who let half their home fall into ruin after a fire and not rebuild, or at least cart away the rubble?

She turned the front door handle. The door didn't budge. Cursing beneath her breath, she inspected various bolts and chains. No one had secured them. She dragged at the handle again.

"It's deadlocked," Mason said.

Vienna spun around. Her nemesis was standing at the bottom of the staircase, her hands loosely at her sides. There was a stillness to her, a watchful expectancy. She was imposing her will, making Vienna come to her.

Indignantly, Vienna said, "What happened to good manners?"

"If you insist on walking, I said I'd escort you," Mason replied with an edge of sarcasm. "What happened to gracious consent?"

Vienna stole a quick, frantic glance to one side. Her body twitched with the urge to make a run for it. Apparently she didn't hide her intentions very well.

Mason surveyed her with amusement. "There's nowhere you can go. The house is locked up."

"Just open the door," Vienna snapped.

"Tell me something," Mason said. "Were you planning to accept my proposal?"

Vienna bit back the first reply that jumped to mind, and considered the question carefully. "What if I were?"

Mason reached past her and slid a key into the lock. "Yes or no?"

"Whatever the answer, it's no longer relevant."

"You don't know the answer," Mason taunted softly.

Her proximity was disabling. Fast losing ground to the weakening of her limbs and resolve, Vienna sought refuge in counterattack. "Oh, please. Like the math is that complicated. Of course I was going to say yes."

She paused to let her glib declaration sink in. She could tell Mason was upset. In the ghostly half-light, a tiny pulse stirred the hairline at her temple. Its throb transfixed Vienna. She pushed away a desperate yearning to stroke the translucent skin stretched over it.

"Bullshit," Mason said.

"Believe what you like. It's academic now. That ship has sailed."

"And yet, here you are."

"Not anymore." Vienna stepped back, pointedly waiting for the door to be opened. She put her hand out for her car keys. "Thank you for your hospitality. I'll tell Darryl that you've made your final decision and it's time for us to walk away and give our *gracious consent* for you to self-destruct." She smiled sweetly. "Good luck with the liquidation, Mason. You'll need it."

She was halfway down the front steps before she heard Mason. "Vienna!"

Vienna turned around and caught her breath, disconcerted by the sight of Mason, standing tall and dark just behind the pale shape of Estelle. The statue almost seemed alive in that instant and Vienna had a flash of the beautiful woman she'd dreamed about, those hypnotic blue eyes pleading with her, the outstretched hand held open. Vienna glimpsed a flash of light, then realized an upstairs window had just lit up.

"Come back inside," Mason asked.

"Why, so you can play with me some more?"

"No." Mason's voice was a shredded undertone. "Vienna, I have to talk to you."

"I'm too tired for this," Vienna said dispiritedly. "You win, okay? I'm going back to Boston tomorrow and getting on with my life."

"What about Le Fantôme?"

"What about it?"

"That's why you're here isn't it?" Mason descended the steps to stand just above her. "I know you can't find the real stone."

"You think that's what dragged me out here in the middle of the night? A goddamned piece of overpriced carbon with a jinx on it? You think that *matters* to me?" Vienna's eyes stung with tears. "Go fuck yourself."

Even as the words tumbled out she realized how little she cared about the necklace. She would have driven here whether she'd found the diamond or not, and whether Mason accepted the latest offer or threw it back at her. The knowledge filled her with misery. Mason thought she was so shallow she would trade her body for a business deal and make a crazy trip out here for the sake of an expensive rock. It didn't matter what she said, Mason would never trust her, and Vienna only had herself to blame for that.

"What else would I think?" Mason demanded. "You sent the police out here."

Vienna yelled a curse and stomped down the rest of the steps. Pausing at the bottom she turned and faced Mason angrily. "I went to the police because no one will tell me what happened that night. It's not my fault if they noticed the case was fishy. I'm not the one who's been covering up the truth for ten years."

"No, that was your parents' idea."

"They were protecting me."

"They were protecting themselves. God forbid the Blake family name gets dragged through the mud." Mason stopped short, her chest heaving. "Has it ever occurred to you that I'm not the enemy?"

There was a savagery in her stare that drove Vienna back. Wrapping her arms around herself, she demanded, "What are you talking about?"

"Ask your mother to tell you about the deal. The one your father did with mine that night."

"What *deal*?"

Mason was silent at first, then gave an ironic laugh. "You know something funny? The first time I saw you with those people, I wanted to rescue you. I knew you didn't belong there. You were so...perfect." Her steady regard slid away and she seemed to retreat into her thoughts.

Almost absently, she said, "I'm as guilty the rest of them. I fed you to the wolves."

Vienna couldn't lower her arms. She was afraid if she did, she would humiliate herself by keeling over. "What are you talking about?"

Mason jerked her head around as bright light spilled down the steps. A thin, straight figure stood in the doorway.

"I heard voices," Mrs. Danville said. Her hair was tucked inside a white scarf but for a row of small spiral curls that lay across her forehead, each flattened between two pins. "Is there a problem?"

Vienna started to speak but Mason cut her off. "Nothing's wrong. I was just walking Miss Blake to her car."

Vienna held her ground, determined not to leave without some answers. "I can find my car," she muttered, trying to form a question for Mrs. Danville that would not sound accusatory.

Mason touched her on the shoulder, gently warning her off. "This is between you and me."

Infuriated, Vienna said, "Then tell me what's going on. Don't you get it? This secrecy isn't protecting me, it's making me crazy."

"Go home and get some sleep." With a polite hand gesture, Mason guided her toward the archway that led to the back of the house. "We can talk tomorrow."

"I'll want the truth," Vienna said, opening the car door.

"So will I," Mason replied softly.

Chapter Eighteen

S he was here when I came down," Mrs. Danville whispered as Mason locked the door. "I saw her."

"Who, the Unhappy Bride?"

Mrs. Danville nodded. "She was standing outside your father's study."

Mason glanced along the hallway. She'd never liked passing that room and Ralph always growled when they approached the study door. Over the past week Mrs. Danville claimed to have seen the resident ghost more than once, the first time she'd had such encounters. Mason wasn't sure whether to attribute the sightings to stress or the supernatural. Mrs. Danville said the presence must be a sign.

"Did she say anything to you?" Mason asked.

Mrs. Danville flicked a cagey glance at her, as though suspecting she was being laughed at. "Ghosts don't generally converse, so I'm told."

"What do you think she wants?"

"She can't rest peacefully in her grave," Mrs. Danville said dolefully. "There can only be one reason for that. Mortal sin."

"Murder?"

"Or suicide, God save her soul."

They stood in silence, waiting and staring. When the ghost failed to appear, Mason said, "Maybe we should try the Ouija board sometime."

Lynden had insisted on performing this parlor trick whenever he brought an impressionable guest to the house. Sometimes he dragged Mason in to make up numbers. The Unhappy Bride had never appeared on any of those occasions, although there were episodes with flickering lights, and predictably the name "Estelle" had been spelled out a few times.

"Then there's the dog," Mrs. Danville said.

Mason looked around automatically, wondering where Ralph had got to. She'd left the door open when she followed Vienna downstairs. Normally he came after her. She gave a low whistle and a dark head poked out from between the banisters directly above. Mason signaled for him to come down, but he whined and retreated back into the gallery.

Mrs. Danville glanced up. "I was talking about the pale dog. You've seen it and so has Mr. Pettibone. It's *her* dog."

"You think the stray Saluki is also a ghost?" Mason suppressed a grin. "The Hound of Laudes Absalom...very catchy."

Mrs. Danville didn't seem to appreciate the humor. "Your mother saw the two of them, you know. She had a clairvoyant come out here once."

"Really?" Mason turned out the lights and started up the stairs. "To do an exorcism?"

"I don't think so. He was a peculiar individual. Fond of my roast goose with Armagnac. He walked around your father's study for a while, touching things and communing with the...other side."

"Did he discover anything?"

"Only the wine cellar."

Ralph greeted them at the landing with panting relief. Stroking him around his chin, Mason said, "I suppose we could try a psychic, since the Bride seems to be hanging around at the moment. Maybe a medium like the one on TV."

"She's just an actress." Mrs. Danville smoothed the white chiffon scarf firmly over her hair. "I hope you don't mind, but I took the liberty of finding a suitable person. I believe she'll be here later in the morning."

"You have a ghost hunter coming to the house today?"

"She won't bother you at all. I'll give her clear instructions." Mrs. Danville's tone was one of martyred distaste, as if they were discussing a cockroach exterminator she would be obliged to serve with refreshments. "She comes highly recommended."

Mason wondered how performance evaluation worked in the psychic business. "Where did you find her?"

"That private investigator of yours was very helpful," Mrs. Danville said. "When he was here going through Lynden's papers, I asked him if he knew of anyone. He used to be a police officer in New Hampshire and he said there was a psychic who had something to do with a serial killer case."

"I thought the police didn't use psychics."

"This one appears to be an exception. Your PI got in touch with his colleagues and I received a phone call from her on Friday. The odd thing is, she said she was expecting to hear from us."

Mason rolled her eyes. "I bet that's what they all say."

"Perhaps, but Miss Temple asked if the name Benedict meant anything to me."

"She probably did some homework on the Internet. There's been a lot written about the Cavender Curse and the shooting."

"Perhaps," Mrs. Danville agreed diplomatically. "Although I don't know what would make her believe Benedict was Estelle's father. I asked her, naturally."

"What?" Mason's head felt fuzzy. "Did you say Benedict was—"

"Yes. Estelle told her."

Mason felt like she had just stepped into quicksand. There had to be a logical explanation. Mrs. Danville stepped in to provide it.

"Miss Temple sees dead people."

Something rattled a windowpane below them and they both stood very still, their eyes trained on the shadowed recess near Henry's study. Beyond the tall windows, the sky was no longer black. It would be dawn soon.

"Well, thank you for handling this." As she moved toward the north stairs, Mason asked, "Do you think it's possible, Mrs. Danville?"

The housekeeper took her time answering. "My mother thought so." She paused. "That was servants' gossip, mind you."

"Which probably makes it reliable."

Mason didn't ask why she'd never heard the story before. None of the staff at Laudes Absalom or Penwraithe would openly contradict the official history of the two families. They had their jobs to think about. Mason went up to her room, stripped, and fell into bed. Sleep rushed up to her almost immediately and with it the half-formed thought that the truth could solve everything, if only she and Vienna could uncover it.

❖

Mason was aware of Vienna before she spoke. She charged the afternoon air somehow, lifting the hair on Mason's neck and stirring the dark garden of her desires. Turning slowly, she hid the painful thrill that surged through her.

"What can I do for you, Vienna?"

Mason wasn't used to hesitance in her adversary, but Vienna seemed to be fighting emotions she did not want witnessed. An uncertain smile fled her face and she stood with her hands clasped before her. A sunbeam burnished the fine, loose hairs that floated out around her head. She looked frail and easily bruised, hemmed in by the tortured trees and shrubs, their long predatory fingers plucking at her thin skirt.

"Mrs. Danville let me in," she said, moving farther along the path toward Mason. Her steps were gingerly taken, avoiding broken bricks, encroaching plants, and a finely wrought bird's nest still that still held the fragments of a blue egg. "Could we talk?"

Another step and Mason would be able to touch her. The thought made her hands tingle. "Please, go ahead."

As if she knew she was about to ask a strange question, Vienna covered her mouth for a split second before letting the words rush out. "Do you know why Hugo shot Benedict?"

Mason raised her eyebrows. She'd expected a different line of attack. A conversation about DNA samples from the night of the ball and what they would reveal. "You want us to compare notes a hundred and forty years after the fact."

Vienna's dreamy blue-green eyes met hers. "It's long overdue."

"Okay, so…why did he shoot him?"

"I can't say for sure, but Benedict was Estelle's father and I have the correspondence to prove it." Vienna seemed to be waiting for an explosive reaction, swaying forward a little on the balls of her feet.

Mason said calmly, "Strange, isn't it, how that changes things."

Vienna held her gaze. "You knew?"

"I've been doing my own research, and I had an expert in the house all morning. We went through my father's papers."

"What do you think happened back then?" Vienna asked.

"I think Estelle didn't know whose baby she was carrying." Mason heard a swift intake of breath.

"The baby…are you sure?"

Mason decided not to embark on the psychic angle immediately. She was still trying to absorb all she'd heard from Phoebe Temple and the discoveries she'd made in her father's office.

"Estelle drowned herself after her son was born because she couldn't live with her guilt," Mason said. "I found her suicide note."

Vienna cupped her hands to her face in horror. "She was having an affair with Truman? Even after they found out they were half-siblings?"

"No. Truman was her first love, but Hugo was her husband and it seems as though they were happy."

Vienna frowned. "Then what went wrong? What did her note say?"

"It was a letter to Hugo. She said that after their marriage she was raped by Benedict. He was in a rage over the diamonds. Truman had bought them without his permission, then they were sold at a loss when the engagement couldn't proceed. The old man thought he was entitled to recompense in kind and extracted it from Estelle."

"His own daughter?" Vienna gasped in disgust. "Oh, my God."

The story was hard to tell. Mason kept herself in check by pausing to take slow breaths. "When Estelle found she was pregnant she was terrified that she might be carrying Benedict's child. She was very depressed after he was born."

"And she took her own life," Vienna whispered.

"She blamed herself for the rape," Mason said. "In the letter she told Hugo what Benedict had done. A few days later Hugo went to Beacon Hill and shot him."

"What else could he do?" Vienna murmured. Her face was very pale. "Did Hugo tell Truman why he did it?"

"He must have, and I guess Truman didn't believe him."

Vienna seemed to be taking Mason's measure. Strange that for all her scheming, she could keep her regard so steady, drawing her close, exactly the way Mason drew a nervous horse. Holding open a door, but making no demand.

With quiet resignation, she said, "I wish I knew the truth about the night of the ball." She hugged herself and rocked slightly on her heels. "I'm not an idiot. They think they're protecting me by not talking about it."

"You've also been protecting them," Mason said with an edge of cynicism.

Vienna lowered her arms and turned her head away. Her tone hardened. "I'm not the only one. Mrs. Danville's been lying to protect the Cavender name all these years. Can you look me in the face and deny it?"

When Mason was silent, Vienna closed the few paces between them. Anger seemed to jolt her hands up to Mason's face, setting off a defensive tremor that made her muscles knot. Every nerve quickened. Mason heard a dry swallow and thought it was her own until she saw Vienna part her lips.

"Well?"

Somehow, despite the paralysis of throat and body, Mason's heart continued to beat and her lungs to inflate. "No, I can't deny it."

They stood very still. Vienna slid her hands from Mason's face to her shoulders, using her for balance. Her full, beautiful mouth was trembling. With every short, shallow breath, her breasts rose and fell sharply. She didn't shrink back when Mason put a steadying arm around her waist.

"Tell me, Mason." The plea was raw.

There was no going back. Mason had the sense that she was balanced on the edge of a precipice between two worlds. The leap from past to future was impossibly far and she was filled with dread at the risk she would have to take, yet she was weary of her lonely exile. Even that banishment she could have endured indefinitely, if it meant sparing Vienna sorrow. But she could see her silence had produced the opposite effect.

"It's not my father she's been protecting," she said finally. "It's me."

"You?"

She heard the wounded sigh a split second before she felt the air leave Vienna's body. Her red hair swung forward and she seemed to fold at the waist. Mason caught her as her legs gave way, and then held her tightly, outlasting her ineffectual struggles. Vienna threw her head back and the wild green of the garden seemed to wash into her eyes, enlarging them before coursing into her lashes and down her cheeks. One of her fists flew free, landing a glancing blow to Mason's jaw.

Mason caught the wrist and locked it behind Vienna, forcing her in, trapping her. Their bodies were crushed so tightly, she could feel Vienna's heart slamming against her own.

"Stop fighting me and listen," she said next to Vienna's ear. "It's not what you think."

Vienna turned her head away and twisted helplessly. "Let me go."

"Not a chance. We should have had this conversation a long time ago."

Vienna kept up her struggles for a few more seconds, then drooped against her. "I don't believe it." She almost seemed to be talking to herself. "You would never do that."

Mason let her lips brush the gossamer skin where Vienna's cheekbone protruded. "No. You're right. I would never hurt you."

"I was raped." Vienna's voice caught on a sob. "Everyone thinks they can hide it from me, but I know."

Mason shook her head. "Do you really think I'd allow that to happen?"

Vienna's eyes narrowed. "What are you saying?"

"I was too late to stop him from knocking you unconscious, but I stopped him before he could do anything else."

"You were there?" Vienna's mouth trembled. "You saw *him*?"

"I dragged him off you and we slugged it out."

Why didn't you say so?" Vienna halted, a hand at her throat. "Oh, no...no. You were protecting your father."

"No," Mason said starkly, breaking the promise she'd made to hold up the Cavender end of the bargain. "Your family was protecting Andy Rossiter." She paused, trying to fight off her self-disgust. "I should have turned that disgusting creep over to the cops the night it happened."

"Andy?" Vienna whispered, her eyes wide and dark with disbelief.

Mason tightened her embrace. "I beat him up pretty badly. Your family could have had me charged with attempted murder."

From the dawning realization on Vienna's face, it was clear that she could see where this was going. "The meeting…"

"Yes, your father and mine came up with a deal. My silence in exchange for theirs."

Tears rolled down Vienna's cheeks. "My parents let him get away with attacking me…they blackmailed you to be silent. They blamed your father…"

"There was something else, too." Mason took a small pouch from her pocket and emptied the contents into Vienna's hand.

"Le Fantôme?" Vienna asked in bewilderment.

"It must have come off your necklace during the struggle. Your father gave it to mine. His payment for allowing himself to be blamed. I found it in Dad's desk with the agreement they signed."

"And my father made up that story about the replica stone having to be replaced. God, I've been so…gullible."

Mason lowered her head. "Vienna, please forgive me. Letting your aunt drive off with Andy was the worst mistake of my life."

"No." Vienna shrugged helplessly. "You're not the criminal. He is. I can't believe they covered this up."

The garden seemed to ebb, leaving them stranded alone on an island. The air was so heavy they could almost swim in it. Mason eased her grip and they floated out, each still anchored by the other.

"I love you," she said. "I've always loved you, Vienna."

She heard Vienna whisper her name, then say it again more slowly, as if its syllables dripped a mysterious flavor on her tongue. Her fingers fluttered in Mason's hand. She moved closer until their faces met, then begged, "Kiss me."

Mason's body leapt. Blood rushed like butterfly wings in her ears. Her nipples were so painful she held back a gasp as her shirt scraped across them. She let her cheek rest against Vienna's while she subdued the part of her that hungered and craved. She kissed Vienna carefully, her body burning for more. A hand caressed her neck. Vienna drew her deeper. Buried in the moist bliss of her mouth, Mason closed her eyes and let herself fall.

Vienna's voice summoned her back. "I love you."

Unsure if she'd really heard the words or just wished them into being, Mason gazed at the face upturned to hers. Was this really happening? Or had she conjured this moment, as she often did? She'd kept her heart intact for this day, for those three words, and she wanted to hear them again. As if Vienna knew, she lifted Mason's hand to her lips, tenderly kissing the fingers. Then she cradled it to her cheek.

"I love you, Mason. Please let me stay."

Chapter Nineteen

The door slammed shut behind Vienna and they were in a spacious bedroom with high windows and a Doberman standing guard at the end of a huge bed. He inspected them in bemusement.

"Don't worry about him," Mason said, dropping her boots next to an old armoire. "I've never brought anyone up here before."

Anticipation stirred in the pit of Vienna's stomach. She wasn't sure when her childhood crush became love, but she knew now that even if she hadn't read Sally Gibson's letter, she would still be here. Sometime during the past several days, she'd stopped fighting the feelings Mason aroused. And now, standing in front of her, she wanted to hold nothing back.

Blushing, she looked down at herself. Her skin was pink and her nipples were tightly bunched against her flimsy lace bra. She touched herself between her legs. Her thighs were wet and her panties clung to her fingers. She wanted Mason so much she couldn't think.

"I have something to tell you," she said shyly.

"It's okay." Mason unbuckled her belt and unzipped her jeans. Her eyes glinted with intent. Her nipples showed beneath her tight khaki T-shirt. "I know you didn't save yourself for me."

"Actually, in a way I did." Feeling light-headed, Vienna unfastened her dress and let it slide to the floor. "I've never been in love with anyone else I've slept with. You're a first."

Tenderness softened Mason's predatory smile, but only briefly. "And I'll be the last."

She discarded her jeans and briefs and advanced on Vienna,

backing her toward the bed. She took complete control of her, cradling her breasts and sliding her tongue sensuously past Vienna's, wreaking havoc with her breathing. With exquisite pressure, she flattened both hands over the nipples, working them against her palms. At the same time, she kissed a downward path from Vienna's lips to her throat, and then sank her teeth into the muscle of her shoulder, sending a shock of anticipation from her neck to the small of her back. Her limbs felt heavy with arousal. Her hands shook as she explored the hard, unfamiliar contours of Mason's body. The flesh beneath her fingertips flinched and goose-bumped with each relentless caress.

Mason yelped softly when Vienna found her nipples and slowly squeezed them. Urgently, she murmured, "Touch me."

Wanting to see the body she was pleasuring, Vienna drew Mason's T-shirt up over her head and dropped it on the floor. There was no bra. Smiling, she dragged a single fingertip from Mason's bottom lip to the bony channel between her breasts. She could sense a boiling urgency in Mason, something deep down and dangerous. A knee pushed roughly between her thighs and applied pressure until Vienna responded in kind, bearing down hard. Wetness spread where Mason's thigh crushed the swollen flesh. Vienna could hardly stay upright. She could feel herself opening, her clit throbbing in appeal.

Their eyes met. Mason's were black with desire, the pupils huge within a ring of slate gray. There was a subtle alteration in her expression, a darkening. With a groan, she hooked her thumb into the thin silk of Vienna's panties and pulled them down, then pushed her back onto the bed. Caressing the inside of her thighs, she nudged them apart, exposing the pale copper swirl of hair.

She stared down, resting on her heels. "Oh. God. You're perfect."

Instinctively, Vienna brought her knees together. A rush of awe stifled her breathing as Mason slid her hands between them and lifted the knees, then spread her wide again.

"I want to look at you."

She lifted Vienna a little higher on the bed, so she was propped against the pillows, compelled to watch as Mason's fingers gently parted her. She dragged them back and forth with avid concentration, gathering then tasting Vienna's fluids. Needing more, Vienna lifted her hips toward the hand that kept skimming past her wet, craving flesh. A thumb worked her clit. Mason circled and teased.

"Please," Vienna whispered. The impression Mason left in her flesh had faded after their first lovemaking and she'd felt unbearably hollow ever since.

Just when she thought she couldn't stand another tantalizing caress, Mason moved over her, gazing down at her with fierce hunger. Then she was inside, so fast and so hard, Vienna cried out in shock and pleasure. A hand pushed one of her knees up and back, and Mason drove deeper, awaiting no cue and barely pausing with each delving thrust.

"You're mine," she choked out and Vienna hardly recognized the face inches from hers. The expression was glazed, the jaw taut. "Say it."

"I'm yours." Vienna gripped Mason's shoulders, needing something to hold on to. Her skin was hot and damp. The muscles surged beneath her fingers.

A spiraling tension compressed Vienna's core and she clamped down, almost expelling the fingers buried inside. Mason's response was visceral and immediate. She shifted her weight, pushing Vienna's legs wider, filling her, kissing her, pounding into her.

"Is that good?" Her voice was low and rough in Vienna's ear. "Is that what you need?"

"Yes." Holding her gaze, Vienna met each stroke with a whimper of pleasure. "I love you," she gasped, only seconds from letting go.

"Then give yourself to me," Mason said.

And Vienna had the strangest sensation of her flesh caving in. She was flooding, suddenly empty, aware only of an unraveling within as her body clamored to be filled again.

"Mason," she sobbed, stranded on the brink.

Frantically, she opened her eyes and found Mason staring down at her with such naked emotion she couldn't look away. Tears blinded her and she cupped Mason's cheek and drew her into a kiss so profound her body convulsed. Mason stroked her hair and kissed her forehead with deep tenderness, then moved down her body, and everything seemed to zero in at her core.

Sweet tension rose in steadily building waves as Mason's thumb inched delicately around her clit. Every tiny slithering stroke, every feather-light caress, made Vienna whimper for more. She tilted her hips as she felt the warm, slow glide of a tongue. Mason lapped and sucked far too gently, making her nerves scream and carrying her close to orgasm, only to ease off just as she felt herself nearing the crest.

Vienna moaned in frustration, and this time Mason drifted away, breaking contact entirely, before returning to the slippery gateway of flesh and slowly pushing several fingers inside, stretching Vienna and then easing back until she was invited deeper. Carefully, by degrees, she rotated her hand until Vienna gave herself completely. In return Mason stayed perfectly still, allowing her to control depth and rhythm.

Time slowed and they watched each other as Vienna's responses gathered intensity. Her face was wet with sweat and tears. She could feel a deep pulse at her center, but couldn't tell if it was entirely her own. All she knew was that the pulse was getting more powerful, opening and consuming her, spasming out like a living thing until it bloomed through her entire body. Vienna could only give herself in complete sensuous abandon; shuddering and heaving, she was taken over.

When the reverberations finally subsided, peace stole over her and she drifted in a daze of bliss. She didn't have the strength to move and barely protested when she felt Mason slowly withdraw. They lay sprawled in wordless aftermath, Vienna on her back, Mason on her side, her arm over Vienna's waist. For a long while, they were silent, then Mason's lips found hers, bestowing a kiss of such sweetness and delicacy, Vienna felt something squeeze her heart.

"I love you, Mason," she whispered. "And I want your body… very soon."

Mason laughed. "We have all night."

Vienna rolled over to face her. "Mason, I'm sorry for—"

"Don't." Mason's arms enfolded her. "Everything I have is yours."

Vienna curled in close. "I have all I want. You, my love."

They kissed again and Mason said, "We can take down the fence. Blakes and Cavenders on one estate. More room for horses."

"Is it okay if I live here, at Laudes Absalom?"

"I'd like that. And I have a feeling our ghost will, too."

"What about Mrs. Danville."

"Er…let's break it to her gently."

"Speaking of gently," Vienna teased, "where do you want my mouth?"

Mason grinned. "Temptress."

Vienna tilted her head back and stared into Mason's eyes. "You belong to me."

"Yes," Mason said. "Always."

About the Author

New Zealand born, Jennifer Fulton lives in the West with her partner and daughter and their animal companions. She started writing stories almost as soon as she could read them, and never stopped. Under pen names Jennifer Fulton, Rose Beecham, and Grace Lennox she has received a 2006 Alice B. Award for her body of work and has been a Lambda Literary Award finalist in both romance and mystery.

Jennifer can be contacted at: jennifer@jenniferfulton.com.

Books Available From Bold Strokes Books

The High Priest and the Idol by Jane Fletcher. Jemeryl and Tevi's relationship is put to the test when the Guardian sends Jemeryl on a mission that puts not only her in harm's way, but back into the sights of a previous lover. (978-1-60282-085-2)

Point of Ignition by Erin Dutton. Amid a blaze that threatens to consume them both, firefighter Kate Chambers and property owner Alexi Clark redefine love and trust. (978-1-60282-084-5)

Secrets in the Stone by Radclyffe. Reclusive sculptor Rooke Tyler suddenly finds herself the object of two very different women's affections, and choosing between them will change her life forever. (978-1-60282-083-8)

Dark Garden by Jennifer Fulton. Vienna Blake and Mason Cavender are sworn enemies—who can't resist each other. Something has to give. (978-1-60282-036-4)

Late in the Season by Felice Picano. Set on Fire Island, this is the story of an unlikely pair of friends—a gay composer in his late thirties and an eighteen-year-old schoolgirl. (978-1-60282-082-1)

Punishment with Kisses by Diane Anderson-Minshall. Will Megan find the answers she seeks about her sister Ashley's murder or will her growing relationship with one of Ash's exes blind her to the real truth? (978-1-60282-081-4)

September Canvas by Gun Brooke. When Deanna Moore meets TV personality Faythe she is reluctantly attracted to her, but will Faythe side with the people spreading rumors about Deanna? (978-1-60282-080-7)

No Leavin' Love by Larkin Rose. Beautiful, successful Mercedes Miller thinks she can resume her affair with ranch foreman Sydney Campbell, but the rules have changed. (978-1-60282-079-1)

Between the Lines by Bobbi Marolt. When romance writer Gail Prescott meets actress Tannen Albright, she develops feelings that she usually only experiences through her characters. (978-1-60282-078-4)

Blue Skies by Ali Vali. Commander Berkley Levine leads an elite group of pilots on missions ordered by her ex-lover Captain Aidan Sullivan and everything is on the line—including love. (978-1-60282-077-7)

The Lure by Felice Picano. When Noel Cummings is recruited by the police to go undercover to find a killer, his life will never be the same. (978-1-60282-076-0)

Death of a Dying Man by J.M. Redmann. Mickey Knight, Private Eye and partner of Dr. Cordelia James, doesn't need a drop-dead gorgeous assistant—not until nature steps in. (978-1-60282-075-3)

Justice for All by Radclyffe. Dell Mitchell goes undercover to expose a human traffic ring and ends up in the middle of an even deadlier conspiracy. (978-1-60282-074-6)

Sanctuary by I. Beacham. Cate Canton faces one major obstacle to her goal of crushing her business rival, Dita Newton—her uncontrollable attraction to Dita. (978-1-60282-055-5)

The Sublime and Spirited Voyage of Original Sin by Colette Moody. Pirate Gayle Malvern finds the presence of an abducted seamstress, Celia Pierce, a welcome distraction until the captive comes to mean more to her than is wise. (978-1-60282-054-8)

Suspect Passions by VK Powell. Can two women, a city attorney and a beat cop, put aside their differences long enough to see that they're perfect for each other? (978-1-60282-053-1)

Just Business by Julie Cannon. Two women who come together—each for her own selfish needs—discover that love can never be as simple as a business transaction. (978-1-60282-052-4)

Sistine Heresy by Justine Saracen. Adrianna Borgia, survivor of the Borgia court, presents Michelangelo with the greatest temptations of his life while struggling with soul-threatening desires for the painter Raphaela. (978-1-60282-051-7)

Radical Encounters by Radclyffe. An out-of-bounds, outside-the-lines collection of provocative, superheated erotica by award-winning romance and erotica author Radclyffe. (978-1-60282-050-0)

Thief of Always by Kim Baldwin & Xenia Alexiou. Stealing a diamond to save the world should be easy for Elite Operative Mishael Taylor, but she didn't figure on love getting in the way. (978-1-60282-049-4)

X by JD Glass. When X-hacker Charlie Riven is framed for a crime she didn't commit, she accepts help from an unlikely source—sexy Treasury Agent Elaine Harper. (978-1-60282-048-7)

The Middle of Somewhere by Clifford Henderson. Eadie T. Pratt sets out on a road trip in search of a new life and ends up in the middle of somewhere she never expected. (978-1-60282-047-0)

Paybacks by Gabrielle Goldsby. Cameron Howard wants to avoid her old nemesis Mackenzie Brandt but their high school reunion brings up more than just memories. (978-1-60282-046-3)

Uncross My Heart by Andrews & Austin. When a radio talk show diva sets out to interview a female priest, the two women end up at odds and neither heaven nor earth is safe from their feelings. (978-1-60282-045-6)

Fireside by Cate Culpepper. Mac, a therapist, and Abby, a nurse, fall in love against the backdrop of friendship, healing, and defending one's own within the Fireside shelter. (978-1-60282-044-9)

A Pirate's Heart by Catherine Friend. When rare book librarian Emma Boyd searches for a long-lost treasure map, she learns the hard way that pirates still exist in today's world—some modern pirates steal maps, others steal hearts. (978-1-60282-040-1)

Trails Merge by Rachel Spangler. Parker Riley escapes the high-powered world of politics to Campbell Carson's ski resort—and their mutual attraction produces anything but smooth running. (978-1-60282-039-5)

Dreams of Bali by C.J. Harte. Madison Barnes worships work, power, and success, and she's never allowed anyone to interfere—that is, until she runs into Karlie Henderson Stockard. Aeros EBook (978-1-60282-070-8)